The Grandmother

THE GRANDMOTHER

JANE E. JAMES

JOFFE
BOOKS

Joffe Books, London
www.joffebooks.com

First published in Great Britain in 2024

Cover art by Nick Castle

ISBN: 978-1-83526-736-3

For Rikki

THE CHILDREN

Seated at the kitchen table, which is strewn with textbooks, notepads and pencil cases, Daisy and Alice Spencer appear to be working hard on their school homework, but in reality, they are just watching their mother. Daisy, the eldest sister, is especially aware of their mum's battles with depression and poor mental health. When she was admitted to hospital last year and placed on suicide watch, they were forced to stay with their father and his new partner. It was clear they weren't wanted there. When their dad dropped them off after school today, their parents got into another loud dispute over child maintenance. Their mum is drinking more than usual as a result, sipping wine from her favourite mug which reads "Best Mum in the World". It was a gift from the girls two Christmases ago. They're surprised it's survived this long and hasn't been flung at Dad's head before now.

Their mum despises their dad's new girlfriend, Leah, even more than they do. Since the arrival of their half-sister, their dad has been struggling to support two families and hasn't been around as much. Their mum is still finding it difficult to come to terms with the divorce *and* his betrayal. Being diagnosed with agoraphobia means she can no longer do fun things with her daughters and is confined to their concrete matchbox, situated in one of the worst housing developments in the city. There are moments when it seems like the girls lost their mum at the same time they did their dad.

They can hear shouting next door and the wail of a police siren in the distance. Their neighbours have broken-down cars in their driveway and call the girls names they dare not repeat, especially to their mother. Should she become aware of this, it would trigger her fierce maternal instinct, causing her to go on a rampage. The *pigs*, as they are known around here, would be called then. When their dad lived with them, they were here often.

Though she rarely eats anything herself, their mum would ordinarily be in the middle of preparing their tea by now — chicken nuggets and chips — but she is hunched over her phone, staring at it, with a torn piece of paper in her hand. When she lifts the handset and taps in a number tentatively, the girls exchange worried looks. They can't remember when their mother last made a phone call. She has no friends or family and only ever talks to their dad. The last time her phone was used was when Daisy had to call 999 when their mother was unable to get out of bed for three days running.

Nervously running the phone's curly cord through her fingers, their mum murmurs into the mouthpiece, 'Hello, is that you?'

After a lull in the conversation—

'It's me, Scarlet,' she says in a sad whisper.

Then, gasping, she lets out a panicky, 'Wait, you don't sound . . .'

Another pause, longer this time.

'No,' she replies, frowning. 'You can't be. You're not . . .'

A gulp of wine, and then, 'Something's not right. What's going on?'

Face tightening in fear, she insists, 'That's not true. You're lying.'

CHAPTER 1: THE GRANDMOTHER

In the background, Radio 2 is playing at an appropriate volume so as not to disturb the neighbours. On a Saturday afternoon, I enjoy listening to Rylan. I think it's because of his strong bond with his mother, Linda. What a good son he seems to be. With the kitchen windows open, I can see trailing blooms of violet wisteria outside and roses with colours reminiscent of Spanish dresses. Oh, how I wish I were in the garden, breathing in their alluring scent. Still, there are plenty of mouthwatering aromas emanating from my kitchen. I'm baking bread and potting home-made jam today. I picked the raspberries myself at my allotment, and munch on a handful while I work, their juicy, slightly gritty texture bursting on my tongue.

When I take the loaves of bread out of the range oven, they smell like malt and have a honey-coloured crust. My stomach churns with hunger. One is for Mr Burgess who lives next door. At seventy-two, he's even more ancient than I am. The other is for our village allotment association chairman, *I'm-just-Ken* Church. Allotment plots are like gold dust around here, so it's best to stay on his good side. I'll also be dropping them both a jar of ruby-red jam along with the bread when I pop by later.

I'm tempted to cut a slice of bread, slather it with butter, and eat it right now while gazing out of my window, but I'm already on the plump side, so I decide against it. At sixty-five, I'm well past menopause, but the weight continues to pile on even though I exercise. It's disheartening, especially when I walk for an hour every day. Working an allotment is also really physically demanding. There's a certain amount of freedom and comfort in slipping into old age though. Being invisible has its advantages. Old, grey-haired, tweedy ladies go unnoticed and that suits me just fine. I'm in awe of women my age who appear twenty years younger and wear trendy ripped jeans and have butter-blonde waves cascading down their backs, but I don't envy them. I like things just the way they are. A severe bob, spectacles and elasticated trousers will do me.

Everyone knows I relocated to the village of Ryhall in Rutland after the death of my beloved husband Charles three years ago. The five-bedroom 1960s detached house on Thorpe Road in Peterborough, where we lived for the duration of our thirty-one-year marriage, proved too much for me to manage alone, so I downsized to Wisteria Cottage a year after his death. It was the best choice I could have made, since I adore the rural lifestyle and the community here embraced me, making me feel very welcome. Volunteering has enabled me to make a lot of new friends. Or, more accurately acquaintances, as I prefer to keep to myself and don't tend to form intimate bonds with people. I am now a member of all the important social groups in the community, including the WI, the village hall association, the Neighbourhood Watch, and the village fete committee. I also regularly attend morning prayers at St John the Evangelist.

With its picturesque setting of limestone cottages, stone bridges, and the River Gwash meandering through it, the parish of Ryhall and Belmesthorpe is home to around 2,000 people. It's so idyllic that I sometimes feel as though I'm living in one of those *Midsomer Murder* mystery dramas that I occasionally watch on TV. I'm fortunate enough to live in the centre of the village, on the square, where I can observe people coming and going. My house faces the village store across the road and the pub, The Green Dragon, is just a few steps away. My big-bellied, squashy-faced cat, Hero, and I spend hours watching the world go by while sitting on the living room sofa. The saying that people resemble their pets is true, since like my grey tabby friend, I have a crushed nose and a primordial belly. As my sole companion these days, he is overindulged. Who else do I have to spoil?

When I hear the ding-dong of the Ring video doorbell the village handyman kindly installed for me, I don't answer it. Not because I don't want to, but rather because I'm unsure how to. Usually, by the time I've managed to open the app on my phone and then try to speak into it, the caller has given up and gone away. I'm not averse to technology but it moves too quickly for someone like me to keep up.

As I walk into the living room, intent on finding out who is at the door, I check that the gold-fringed sofa cushions are plumped and the landscape paintings are absolutely straight. I make it a point to look for dust everywhere I go. I've even been known to secretly swipe my finger across the counter in the village store. I can't stand untidiness. I come from a generation that was raised to think that cleanliness is next to Godliness. As the saying goes, the closer you are to God, the devil has less power over you. When I first moved into Wisteria Cottage my neighbours were shocked when I removed the frothy net curtains from its windows, warning me that passersby would always be looking inside. Little did they know that it was I who wanted to watch over them, not the other way around.

And right now, I'm doing just that — hiding behind a heavy, floor-to-ceiling floral curtain and peering out of the casement window at the square. As is typical for this time of day, it is jam-packed with vehicles. People park here to visit the store and the pub. Local walking groups also use it as a meeting place. But what I'm not expecting to see is the police car parked outside my window. Fear strikes me then, like a spade in hallowed ground, and my heart begins to pound in my chest. When I hear a second ding-dong and the sound of a voice crackling on a police radio, I know for certain they are here to see me.

I scurry out of the living room into the hall, fearing that my heart will explode in my chest, pausing to cringe when I see the two black-uniformed silhouettes through the front door glass. When I say "scurry" it's more of a fast hop because since I had a hip replacement three months ago, I'm not as lively on my feet as I once was, and now have to rely on a walking stick of all things. I'm not yet a pensioner but I think it's a good idea to be cautious, which is why I put a sign on my door that reads "No canvassers or cold callers". Even though I know it's only the police at my door, and not a thief or a conman, my fingers are shaking as I release the security chain. When I eventually open the door, I can't help but notice their serious expressions. I deduce from this, in a Miss Marple kind of way, that they aren't knocking on doors to solve rural crimes like illegal metal detecting or the worrying of livestock.

'Mrs Castle?' The young female police officer gives me one of those don't-underestimate-me-because-I'm-a-female-cop looks.

Plastering a sweet-old-lady smile on my face, I cheerfully reply, 'Yes.'

CHAPTER 2: THE FATHER

When I was picked up and brought to the station under caution, the police appeared more interested in my facial injuries than my girlfriend, Leah, had been when I'd got them two days prior. When I found out her ex, Wayne, was messaging her on WhatsApp and liking her social media posts, I raced around to his house to confront him. As for Leah, I'm pissed off with her too for lying and for posting bikini pictures on TikTok. *She's the mother of my child,* for fuck's sake. I even accused her of cheating on me, but she laughed it off and said, "You'd know all about that, wouldn't you, Vince?" She's right. I do. But Scarlet — the woman I'd left for Leah — the mother of two of my daughters and my former wife, would never have lowered herself by sharing sexy pictures of her body online.

I was a fucking idiot for starting a fight with a much younger guy who is also a lot bigger and more physically fit than I am. I was the one left with a black eye and a burst lip. I'm also convinced that Leah is silently punishing me for coming off worse in the scrap, as if I have somehow become diminished in her eyes. Shit, I'm not in my twenties anymore, unlike Leah's ex. I'm thirty-two, and a father of three. *How the fuck did that happen?* The trouble is I've never been able to control my temper.

I used to get into some vicious fights with Scarlet when we were together — *she knew how to push my buttons* — and we would both lash out at each other, mostly verbally, but occasionally physically. Especially if we'd been drinking or were high on drugs. Our relationship had been a toxic one, but I stupidly believed those days were over. And yet here I am again, this time with Leah. I'm starting to think that leaving my wife for a twenty-two-year-old was a mistake. Maybe I am the reason why my relationships fail. The common denominator if you like.

The interview room is dirty and grim. Like my life. It stinks of sweat and piss and reminds me of my heroin days — the best and worst times of my life. These days I'm clean. All I need to kick now is the booze, fags, and occasional joint. I've been read my rights but have been waiting for more than twenty minutes for the interview to commence so they can begin formally questioning me. The arresting officers only asked routine questions such as my whereabouts the previous evening, the source of my injuries and the last time I saw Scarlet. I insisted repeatedly that the fight I had with Wayne happened two nights prior, not last night, and that it takes two to start a bust-up, so I don't understand the reason for my being here. Or why they are so interested in my ex when she had fuck all to do with it.

When I hear footsteps approaching, followed by the painfully slow turning of the key in the door, I take several deep breaths. I may not have done anything illegal, *this time*, but I'm shitting myself anyway. For years, the pigs have been wanting to send me down so I wouldn't put it past them to try and pin something on me.

I bury my face in my hands and let out a groan when the door bursts open and a loud, smug, voice sniggers, 'Well, well, well, if it isn't my old pal, Vincent Spencer.' This isn't the first time I've encountered Detective Sergeant Alan Mills. It won't be the last.

8

DS Mills is accompanied by a tall, willowy female detective with competent eyes who he introduces as DC Fox. She unwraps and loads new media into the recording device, and then takes a seat beside Mills.

'Long time no see,' Mills snorts.

'What is this about?' I watch with jealousy as Mills, a big, bearded man with a mop of black wiry hair, slurps loudly from his steaming Starbucks coffee. No one has thought to offer me a drink.

'All in good time,' advises Mills.

Crossing my arms defensively, I mutter belligerently, 'I haven't even been asked if I want a solicitor.'

'Do you?'

I hesitate before saying, 'No, but that's not the point.'

When Mills's invasive jade-green stare comes to rest on me, as if to say, "What *is* the point?" I'm unable to maintain eye contact with the giant. He always looks like he wants to beat me up and I've had enough of having the shit kicked out of me, ta very much.

'Am I under arrest?' I ask, bunching my shoulders.

'Not at this time,' complains a disgruntled Mills.

I straighten up, ready to make a bolt for it. 'Then I'm free to go?'

'Not so fast,' cautions Mills. 'This might be a voluntary police interview for now but we can soon change that if we have to.'

Letting my shoulders fall, I raise my hands in surrender, saying, 'It was a fight between two adults, nothing more.'

Mills puffs out his cheeks in indignation. 'A fight that led to a young woman's death.'

Fear is building inside me, the sense of danger making it hard for me to breathe. I'm shivering with dread and adrenalin as I ask, with a catch in my voice, 'What are you talking about? What woman?'

As the detectives shake heads and exchange glances, I stare down at my scuffed, ripped-off Adidas trainers and fight back

9

the feeling of grey prison walls closing in on me. Squeezing and suffocating me.

'Where were you last night?' Mills wants to know.

'I already told the other police officers. I was at home, with my girlfriend Leah.'

'But before that, you were at your former wife, Scarlet Spencer's house?' Mills continues. 'Is that correct?'

'Sure. I dropped the kids off after school, like I do every day. Why?'

The detectives look at each other again, convincing me that they know something I don't. I become even more nervous then. Sweat breaks out on my palms and forehead. I feel physically sick.

'Neighbours claim to have heard raised voices at the victim's address on the day of the murder. Can you verify that this was you and Scarlet?'

My eyes dart erratically between the male and female detectives as I try to understand what they're implying. As it dawns on me that this has nothing to do with the fight with Wayne, and everything to do with my ex-wife, I lurch to my feet, crying, 'Murder? What murder? What are you trying to say? Is Scarlet dead?!'

Ignoring my outburst, Mills demands, 'What was the row about?'

'She was demanding money I didn't have,' I exclaim, panic-stricken and wide-eyed in disbelief. My mind is racing. I can't think straight. 'I would never hurt Scarlet. I just wouldn't. Ask anyone,' I beg.

'Vincent, that's not strictly true, is it?' Mills narrows his eyes triumphantly. 'During the time you lived at 7 The Green, your former wife reported you on seven separate occasions for domestic abuse.'

CHAPTER 3: THE GRANDMOTHER

'There you are my dears,' I chirp, placing two bone china mugs of tea on the coffee table that doubles as a bridge table at night. They both politely declined my offer of a drink when I asked, but I insisted in a way that only older ladies can. 'Help yourselves to biscuits,' I add, clasping my hands together and perching on the edge of the dusky rose floral armchair opposite. Realising that I still have my frilly apron on, I slip it off and fold it neatly before resting it on the arm of the chair. My pink-tinted glasses are still fogged up from removing the warm bread from the oven, so I give them a cursory wipe before popping them back on again. The female officer scowls the entire time as if I had deliberately put her at a disadvantage.

The male police officer does not have the same problem. He smiles warmly at me as if I were his mother. I watch him curl one hand appreciatively around his mug while picking up a biscuit with the other. However, the female now seems to be more interested in glancing about the room than in me. She's very young, probably only in her mid-twenties so my old-fashioned living room with its deep pile carpet, royal-rose rug, patterned sofas, dark wood polished furniture, fringed lamps, and ornate gilt-framed paintings must seem antiquated and last century to her.

With a twitch of a smile, I say, 'Now what was it you wanted to talk to me about on this beautiful summer afternoon?'

'I feel like we should be standing for this,' the female officer complains, getting to her feet. The male police officer seems awkward and uneasy as he sets down his cup, swallows his biscuit, and follows suit.

I blush and say, 'Goodness me, it can't be that bad, can it?' My hand flutters to my heart as I ask, 'I'm not under arrest, am I?'

'No, Mrs Castle, of course not.' The male police officer steps in to rescue me. PC Carter, I think he said his name was.

The female officer flips open her notebook and slides her questioning eyes over it. 'We have reason to believe that you may know someone called Scarlet Spencer.'

With a nervous gulp, I grab the apron off the arm of the chair and begin folding it all over again. 'Yes,' I admit with a dejected nod. 'She's my daughter.'

'Your daughter?' PC Carter gasps, looking shocked. I try not to look annoyed when I see the biscuit crumbs on his bottom lip because I don't want them falling onto my carpet. I hoovered it only this morning.

'You seem surprised. Don't I look old enough to be some-one's mother?' I chuckle flirtatiously, but in reality threads of anxiety are pulling at my insides. Just hearing Scarlet's name said aloud has thrown me into a panic. But then again, haven't I always known in my heart that the police would one day track me down and bring me news of her?

'We spoke with Mrs Spencer's neighbours and immediate family, but they were under the impression that you were a distant relative, not her mother,' the female police officer stammers by way of an explanation.

I begin huffily, 'That sounds very like Scarlet to describe me as such. We had a fallout, you see, although that was over ten years ago now. Her father, God rest his soul, wasn't very approving of her lifestyle . . . but hold on, you mentioned that you spoke to Scarlet's neighbours and family, rather than to her directly. Is she okay?'

When I see the anxious stares exchanged between the police officers, I realise they're here to inform me that something terrible has happened and I feel my breath catch in my throat. The female takes the lead, standing up taller, as though about to salute, and saying in a professional tone, 'I'm very sorry, Mrs Castle, but I'm afraid your daughter is dead.'

'Dead!' I cry, stumbling to my feet only to discover that fear has loosened my knees and I collapse back onto the armchair, where I choose to remain.

PC Carter is immediately by my side, patting my hand and asking, 'Are you okay? Can I get you something? A glass of water?'

I shake my head, relishing the feeling of being touched by another human being. He is a kind boy, I can tell, and I expect he treats his mother well, in contrast to . . . but I can't go there right now, not when they're attempting to convince me that Scarlet is—

'How?' With tears in my eyes, I turn to face the female police officer. Only then do I realise her surname is printed on a black Velcro tab on her white shirt.

Mouth drawn into a thin line, PC Anderson explains, 'At this moment, we are unsure. She may or may not have passed away in her sleep.'

My eyes stretch in disbelief on hearing this. 'She was only thirty-two. That's much too young surely to die in such a way. And what do you mean by may or may not?'

PC Anderson's gaze dips uncomfortably before returning to rest on me. 'Her body has been taken away for a post-mortem. We can't be positive until then, but—'

'But,' PC Carter softly interrupts, 'the fibres found in and around her mouth indicate she might have been smothered with a pillow.'

'Oh, good Lord, no,' I moan, a spark of terror in my voice. Feeling like I might faint, I rest my elbows on my knees and get my head down.

'You've had a shock, that's understandable,' PC Carter acknowledges.

13

Incredulous, I ask, 'Who would do such a thing to Scarlet?' I take a moment to remove my glasses so I can dab my tears on the cotton handkerchief I keep in my pocket. Then, as I direct my grief-stricken gaze on PC Anderson, who I already know is more likely than her male colleague to tell me the truth, I ask, 'Do you know who did this to her?'

'We have a suspect in custody who we believe was the last person to see Scarlet alive, aside from her young daughters, that is.'

'Who?'

'I regret that we are unable to say at this time.' PC Anderson chews on her bottom lip. 'He hasn't been charged with anything as yet.'

'So, it's a *he* then.' I observe cynically, and then, with a prickle of alarm at the back of my neck, I exclaim, 'It's Vincent Spencer, isn't it? Scarlet's husband. That's who you're talking about.'

Their cautious glances and mutual silence seem to confirm this, leaving me to agitatedly run a hand through my neatly blow-dried hair, ruffling it. 'I warned Scarlet about him being a bad influence on her but she refused to listen! He was a complete waste of space and was always in trouble with the police even back then, ten years ago. I see nothing has changed.'

Ignoring my explosive comments, PC Anderson takes another quick look at her notepad, before saying, 'Her daughters, Daisy and Alice, are currently with social services, while their dad is . . . otherwise engaged. As their grandmother you are the closest living relative to them and they have nowhere else to go.'

When I remain stubbornly silent, I sense a shift in her tone, as though she's about to wrap up our conversation because she has more important things to attend to. She is ambitious, I'll give her that. Just as I used to be. However, she is barking up the wrong tree if she is implying, as I think she is, that my grandchildren should come to live with me. That would be sheer madness.

'But I've never met them and they've never met me,' I object, twisting around to stare at PC Carter, who I'm certain

14

will be more understanding of my situation, only to find him looking sheepishly at me, much in the way I imagine my son would if I had one.

'Now, you will have the opportunity to.' He speaks to me as though I had just agreed to the proposal. After that, I can hardly refuse, can I? Because what would they think of me? A grandmother refusing to provide her own grandchildren with a home when they most need it.

Without intending to, I mumble aloud, 'I don't know if I'm up to the challenge. I mean, I'm a bit stuck in my ways and, at my age, I'm not used to being around very young children. I'm also incredibly houseproud. Always have been. And children are messy, aren't they?'

'Very.' PC Carter chortles in agreement.

'What if they don't want to come and stay?' I ask hopefully.

'They will. It's either that or a foster or care home,' PC Anderson warns darkly and I suspect her of judging me then. However, I soon come to the realisation that there are two other people's opinions that are far more important to me than hers. My grandchildren's.

Eyes widening in apprehension, I ask, 'But what if they don't like me?'

'Impossible, Mrs Castle. Impossible,' PC Carter states with authority.

On hearing this, I gaze into my lap, ominously silent as I think, *Hmm, but you don't know the real me. Nobody does.*

15

CHAPTER 4: THE FATHER

I've had the shittiest couple of days, banged up in a police cell for thirty-six fucking hours while being questioned about the murder of my ex-wife. What pissed me off most was the fact that I'd been told I was there voluntarily and was free to leave at any time. Fucking lying pigs. They're more corrupt than any of the robbing bastards on the Nene Fields estate, which is where I'm now headed. It's home, a hellhole from which you can never escape once born there. Scarlet is the only person I know who wasn't brought up there, having come from quite a well-to-do background whereas I was dragged up as a latchkey kid, and these are my streets. When I left Scarlet for Leah, I ended up moving only two streets away.

Deciding that I need a drink tonight after the day I've had, I've stopped by the Spar to grab a pack of beer. There are no overpriced Waitrose or M&S stores on our estate. They're not for people like us. But poverty, unemployment and crime are. Shit, I still can't get over the fact that the police suspected me of killing Scarlet. Thank God Leah gave me the alibi I needed because if she'd been in the mood to play games, I would have been fucked. Yet she screwed me over in another equally ball-breaking way by telling the police, when they asked if she could have the girls while I was being questioned, "No fucking way am I having them here. I've got a baby of my own to look after." My blood boiled when I found out the cops were arranging to send them to their bitch of a grandmother who wouldn't recognise her grandchildren if she saw them in the street. But it seems there isn't a single fucking thing I can do about it.

Leah. What a bitch. She got me in the gonads good and proper by doing that. But am I that surprised? What Leah wants, Leah gets. Don't ask me why, but she wanted me and she got me, even if I'm not sure that's still the case. She wanted a child. I didn't. I already have two that I'm unable to support. But she got pregnant anyway while lying to me about using contraception, and when I found out, she just shrugged her shoulders.

'If you were that adamant about not wanting a baby then you should have worn a condom. I'm not responsible for your failures,' she'd argued.

So, I now have three kids, one just a few months old. I love all of my girls, but unless I move out of Leah's and find someplace else to live — *zero chance of that happening given how brassic I am* — I have no hope of getting Daisy and Alice back. They must be feeling abandoned, especially since they've just lost their mum, and that makes me feel sick to my stomach. But if I walk out on Leah, it'll mean abandoning little Saffy.

I head towards the counter after grabbing the cheapest six-pack I could find. The girl behind it is new. I've not seen her in here before. She's young, fresh-faced, and pretty. I can't help but feel she won't last long in this place where she'll be sworn at, yelled at, or even physically attacked. With all the hormonal teenage hoodies prowling outside the shop, I wouldn't want to be in her shoes for any amount of money.

'A thirty-gram packet of Amber Leaf, please,' I say, pushing the cans in her direction for scanning. But instead of turning and opening the cigarette display stand, she wrinkles her nose in disgust and covers her mouth like she's about to puke.

Ah, I get it. My breath stinks like an ashtray. I haven't been able to brush my teeth in nearly two days. But I'm still a human being and have feelings the same as anyone else. She eventually stops cringing and proceeds to put my items through the till, but her reaction when she has to take the two soiled, crumpled twenty-pound notes from my hand is so over the top she might as well be wiping my arsehole.

I don't thank the stuck-up little cow as I storm out of the shop to hop into my beat-up old Renault Megane parked on double yellow lines outside. There's no ticket slapped to the windscreen as the council stopped sending traffic wardens to the estate years ago due to them receiving persistent verbal abuse and death threats, not to mention being spat at in the street.

Tossing the beers onto the front passenger seat, I make myself a roll-up from the tobacco and light it. Inhaling deeply, I lean back in my seat and rotate my shoulders to release some tension. The rush of nicotine helps, but I can't shake off the way that girl stared at me, as if I was a fucking down-and-out with serial killer eyes. I may not be much of a catch, being just under five feet eight tall and nowhere near the six foot two girls seem to demand these days, but I'm not bad-looking.

I have been underweight, to the point of appearing emaciated, all my life and no matter how much I eat, I never gain weight. Leah tells me to grow out my crew cut and hide my wolf neck tattoo as it makes me look wasted all of the time — as if I were still using. She has a point. I don't have a job right now, not many people do around here, but I make extra cash selling ripped-off gear to top up our benefit payments. I sound like a loser, but when it comes to the opposite sex, I always seem to punch above my weight. Take Scarlet. Take Leah. Both women are attractive but in very different ways.

Unlike most of the blokes I know, who secretly hate women and use them for one thing only, I enjoy their company. Put it this way, I prefer hanging out with them to men. Women are surprised by how much I like to talk, and not just about football and cars. This, according to Scarlet, is what made her want to get to know me. Fucking hell. She can't be dead. She was my first love, we met each other when we were both twenty. How will my kids cope without their mum? And what will I do without my best friend? The extent of how much I hurt her by having the affair with Leah, and then leaving her with two small children to bring up when she was depressed, has been on my mind a lot lately. I stupidly assumed I would be happier with Leah, but things haven't worked out that way.

But I'm not the only one to have broken Scarlet's heart. Her hard-nosed bitch of a mother has to take some of the blame. When we were behind with the rent a few years ago and were in danger of being evicted, Scarlet broke her promise to herself to never talk to her mother again, by reaching out for help. But, although she was loaded, Mrs Castle coldly refused to give it, and hung up on her daughter, declaring, 'You will never receive so much as a penny from me while you are still with that man.'

That man was *me*.

So, for Scarlet's sake, I'm going to make the old woman eat her words. See if I don't. But in the meantime, she has my kids. And I have no doubt that she'll try her hardest to turn them against me.

CHAPTER 5: THE GRANDMOTHER

In my living room, two similar-looking children — I'm told they're my granddaughters but it's impossible to think of them in this way as I've never met them before — stand with their heads bowed but their eyes peer up at me from under their eyelashes. With her flame-red hair, freckled nose and pale white complexion, Daisy is the spitting image of her mother. From what I can tell, she appears to be determined to save her younger sister Alice from their evil grandmother, acting like a mother to her and wrapping one protective arm across her thin, pointy shoulders. Daisy is nine and Alice is seven. Daisy clings onto a scary-looking and eerily realistic doll with wide-awake eyes that gives me the creeps. I get the impression it never leaves her side, even though she's probably too old to be this attached to a toy. Both sisters are tall, with waist-length hair that drapes about their faces like curtains. It doesn't appear to have been washed in a while.

When PC Carter and the social worker, a nondescript mouse of a woman with a blunt fringe and bored eyes, brought the girls to Wisteria Cottage, each held onto a plastic bag full of clothes and toiletries and stumbled into the house as if being pushed. They scowled at the kitchen table, which was set for tea with dainty sandwiches, a pot of tea, cakes and jelly, as if it were poison.

'Perhaps later,' the social worker suggested, ushering us into the living room instead, which I took offence at since it was my house. I had gone to a lot of trouble to make the girls feel welcome: baking scones, and making a pink, wobbly rabbit blancmange especially for them. But when we followed each other in a grim little procession into the living room, where the sun greeted us through the windows, they hardly acknowledged me. But I remind myself that everything has moved along so fast and it's been such a shock for everyone. Thirty-six hours ago, these children had a mother and had no idea I existed.

Alice eyes me boldly before asking, 'Are you our granny?', earning herself a jab in the ribs from her sister.

'Yes,' I reply with a forced cheery smile as I glance back and forth between the two of them.

Daisy appears quiet and reserved, but definitely in charge, whereas Alice is more impulsive and says what's on her mind with no filter. I like that about her. At least I'm going to know where I stand with her. Daisy is not so easy to read.

'So how come we never met you before?' Alice demands with a frown.

'It's a long story,' I mutter apologetically. 'Won't you sit down? Can I get you a drink of anything, some home-made elderflower cordial perhaps?'

I gesture to the big floral sofa with the lace embroidered doilies on top, and both girls shuffle uncomfortably towards it, perching on the end, as if fearful of leaving behind an imprint. They are still clinging on to their bags of possessions as though afraid someone might steal them.

Daisy blurts out, 'Coke,' as if she were somehow defying me. It's the first time I've heard her speak and the intensity of her gaze is meant to be intimidating.

'You mean Coca-Cola? I'm afraid I don't have any.'

I feel sorry for Daisy when I see her lower lip tremble, so I then offer, 'If you'd like, we can grab some from the shop later. It's just over the road.'

'Do they sell sweets?' Alice wants to know.

'They do indeed,' I chuckle.

I see PC Carter trying to get my attention out of the corner of my eye, and when my gaze comes to rest on him, he gestures covertly in the direction of the door.

'If you'll excuse me for a moment,' I glance from the social worker to the girls before gulping nervously, 'I just need to have a word with the nice policeman.'

'Nice?' Daisy scowls and wrinkles her nose as if she couldn't imagine a copper ever being nice. Alice snorts mischievously, mimicking her.

When we go to the kitchen, PC Carter pats his pockets as though he's searching for something, and I feel as disappointed in him as if I *were* his mother when I see the lighter wedged in his hand and catch a whiff of tobacco on his breath.

'You smoke,' I say with a grimace.

'I'm afraid so. You need something for the stress in this job,' he admits disarmingly, before adding conspiratorially, 'Anyway, I just wanted to give you the heads-up.'

'About Scarlet?' I gasp. 'Is there any news?'

'They've let him go.'

My eyes swing from the wilting sandwiches and the cooling pot of tea back to him. 'Vincent Spencer?' I enquire, raising my eyebrows.

PC Carter squirms, clearly wishing he had better news. 'He has a solid alibi.'

'Hmm, from his girlfriend no doubt,' I respond cynically. In a previous phone call with the social worker, I had been updated on all that had been happening in Scarlet and the children's lives up until her death. The affair. The separation. The divorce. The new baby. The agoraphobia.

PC Carter shrugs his shoulders, and when his eyes dart towards the inner door that leads into the hallway, I can tell

22

he's eager to escape and that the allure of nicotine is too strong to hold him any longer. 'We have no reason not to believe her.'

'But wouldn't the girls have seen or heard something that night if Scarlet had got up to let the killer in?' I lower my voice to a soft murmur, 'If Vincent *is* lying about the alibi and he *did* kill Scarlet, then they could be covering for him. After all, he is their dad.'

He gives me a pitying look, as if I've just had a stroke, and confides, 'Your daughter didn't let anyone in. They let themselves in.'

'What do you mean?' I cry out, astonished.

'We couldn't be sure until we had the lab reports back, but it looks like somebody punched a hole in the back door glass and then crept up the stairs while Scarlet and the children were sleeping. Because broken glass isn't uncommon in that part of the world we had to be certain the damage happened around the time of her death and not before to determine whether it was suspicious or not.'

'Oh, my goodness, what if the girls had woken up? They might have seen who it was . . . they might have ended up—' My hand flies to my mouth in horror. I'm unable to conjure up a scene so terrible.

'How Scarlet was found suggests that it would have been quick,' murmurs PC Carter in an attempt to sound consoling. 'The sleeping tablets she was taking meant she never woke up and there was no struggle.'

'Thank heaven for small mercies,' I echo bitterly.

He coughs into his hand and adds, 'I'm sorry about your daughter, Mrs Castle,' before approaching the inner door, where he pauses to thoughtfully add, 'But at least now you have your granddaughters and they need you.'

Desperate to keep him for a while longer in my kitchen, I call out, 'Wait.' Anything to buy me some time before I have to return to the living room and face the accusing stares of my grandchildren — who have lost their mother and now find themselves living with a stranger. The poor darlings deserve someone much better than me, because I have no idea how I will cope. 'Who found Scarlet's body? Please don't tell me it was the children?'

'I'm afraid so,' he sighs. 'Your eldest granddaughter is much older than her years. Brave too. After discovering that her mother was dead, she made sure not to let her little sister into the bedroom. She even got her some breakfast and sat her down at the table before ringing 999.'

I nod sadly, mouthing, 'Thank you for telling me this,' with tears in my eyes. I then say, 'Goodbye,' and let him go, understanding that I will never see the nice young man again, but I'm used to having people come and go from my life. Just as I am about to pour the cold tea down the kitchen sink, I hear a piercing scream coming from the living room.

CHAPTER 6: THE FATHER

As usual, the place is a shithole and stinks of soiled nappies, cigarette smoke and cheap perfume. Leah's house is identical to the one I shared with Scarlet and the children at 7 The Green. Except Scarlet always kept our place tidy. Not so, Leah, who points out, "If you want it tidy, you clean it. It's not like you've got anything else to do," which is another dig at me for not having a job. She has a point. I could and should do more. Just like my old house, this one has two bedrooms, an upstairs bathroom, a kitchen-diner, and a living room. The only difference is our door is painted post-box red and Scarlet's is battlefield green. Both are surrounded by overgrown patchy grass and steel railings. Social housing has a prison feel.

I crack open a can of beer, take a thirsty gulp, turn on the TV, sprawl out on the ripped black leather corner sofa, ditch the trainers, and spread out my legs. I'm hoping Leah isn't in one of her foul moods because it's been a tough few days and I could use some company right now, a cuddle even. Above me, I can hear the faint sound of Saffy crying. When I first got in, I shouted out to Leah upstairs to let her know I was home, but even after a thirty-six-hour absence, all I got in return was an unenthusiastic grunt.

I'm only pretending to flip through the TV channels when Leah clip-clops downstairs in high heels, the baby slotted on one hip. The picture I carry of her in my head whenever I'm apart from her doesn't match the real-life Leah. Even though she has long, wavy, bleached blonde hair and is tall and slim, beneath all the heavy make-up and fake brows and eyelashes, she's just average-looking. When she first started flirting with me, I thought she was gorgeous, like a model, and I couldn't believe my luck. But, as I've come to know her, I've realised that she's ugly on the inside.

She may not struggle with mental illness like Scarlet did, which over time drained me — until her depression became my own — but she is cruel, selfish, and doesn't give a shit about anyone except Saffy and maybe her mother. I've learned too late that she can't hold a candle to Scarlet who is, *was*, kind, empathetic and would have done anything for me and our girls. But, because of her long-drawn-out illness, I changed from a devoted, caring partner into somebody I no longer recognised. A cruel, vicious bastard, much like Leah, who just wanted to escape the craziness and fighting. You could argue that Leah and I deserve each other.

She pouts with glossy lips, 'You're back then,' and immediately hands me the baby, who I take and snuggle into my shoulder. She smells of cigarette smoke, like the rest of the house, and it makes me wince with shame. *Fuck, surely, we can do better for her than this.*

'You look nice,' I lie because my girlfriend looks like a cheap tart in her skimpy black mini dress that leaves nothing to the imagination.

'Thanks.' She gives me one of her rare smiles, but it ends too soon.

'You off out?' I ask, scowling.

'Got to get my kicks while I'm still young, and having an unemployed boyfriend who has fuck all else to do but babysit has to have some perks.'

At that, my back stiffens, but I rein in my annoyance. 'I thought we could spend the night together in front of the telly with a takeaway.'

Her painted-on eyebrows shoot upwards. I wish she knew how ridiculous they appear. 'What? And give up a night out on the town with the girls?'

In amazement, I demand, 'You're not going to ask how it went, down at the station?'

But she has already turned her back on me and is rummaging in her fake designer handbag, looking for something. 'How did it go down at the station?' she parrots when she finally glances up to see me glaring at her.

'Scarlet's dead.'

Leah pauses rummaging and lets her jaw drop. 'Dead? What the fuck? Are you serious?' She laughs uneasily as if she cannot believe it.

I nod, gazing down at my worn socks and fighting back the urge to put my head in my hands and sob. 'They think she was murdered.'

'Fucking hell,' Leah exclaims, gobsmacked for once.

She comes over then to settle down on the sofa beside me and puts her hand on my leg. 'How?'

'I don't know. They wouldn't say. Only that they thought—' I stall, unable to continue.

'That you did it,' she finishes for me, scowling.

I grumble, still not over it, 'Thirty-six hours they kept me in that shithole.'

Leah narrows her eyes. 'And did you?'

I'm confused. 'Did I what?'

'Do it?'

'No. Fuck, Leah. Why would you say something like that?' I stand up abruptly, wanting to be away from her, jiggling a sleeping Saffy up and down.

'You two used to fight a lot, that's all.' She purses her lips at me as if I were a school kid, looking at me like I were some kind of monster. A killer.

I yell at her the same words I'd flung at the police, 'I would never hurt Scarlet.' *But I had hurt her, hadn't I?* Multiple times over the years. There had been bruising and broken bones. I'm not proud of myself but sometimes she got hurt because I was defending myself from her. Half of those calls made to the police that Mills brought up were made by me in an attempt to stop Scarlet from attacking me.

Leah shakes her head dismissively, bored all of a sudden. 'All right, Vince, don't have a go at me.' She climbs to her feet, snappily chewing on gum. 'If it weren't for me giving you an alibi, you'd still be banged up.'

'Yeah,' I growl. 'And I also have you to thank for the cops sending my kids to live with their grandmother who they've never even met.'

'I told you when we first got together that they're your kids, not mine. I never signed up to be a step-mum to that bitch's kids.'

My eyes well up with furious tears. 'Fuck, Leah, what did Scarlet ever do to you?'

'Had two kids with you for one thing.'

'They're my kids too. You'd better remember that,' I bellow.

'Yes, but you're not spending time with Saffy and me when you're with them,' she sneers petulantly.

'You don't give a shit about spending time with me. Let's be honest.'

'With Saffy then,' she admits.

'Scarlet's dead. Show some respect,' I warn her, lowering my tone when Saffy's arms begin to flail about in response to my raised voice.

Leah's eyes light up nastily as she muses, 'At least the crazy bitch is out of our hair now.' But when she sees my angry expression she bursts into a contagious giggle. 'I'm just kidding. Besides, didn't you once tell me the grandmother is loaded?'

I screw up my face in surprise. 'Scarlet's mum?'

Her hard eyes find me. 'You know if you play your cards right you could do well out of this.'

'How do you mean?'

'She'll be desperate to keep hold of the girls now that her daughter is no longer in the picture.'

I stare at her. 'Where are you going with this?'

'I bet she'd be willing to pay a lot of money to keep custody of them. Enough for you to buy me that pedigree chihuahua I've always wanted.'

'You're talking about blackmail . . . That's not something I could do to my kids' grandmother.'

Leah shrugs. 'I don't see why not. She stole your kids from you.'

'Leah, that was *your* fault,' I remind her.

Leah erupts, 'The least you can do is give me something in return! Because I earned it.'

'How exactly?' I scoff sarcastically.

The chewing gum pops in her mouth once more as she warns dangerously, 'You know I lied to the police by giving you an alibi when the truth is I have no fucking idea where you were that night, which means you could have killed your ex-wife for all I know.'

CHAPTER 7: THE GRANDMOTHER

'Whatever is it?' I cry, hobbling into the living room, only to have my cat Hero fly out of the door and nearly trip me over. His ears are flat, his eyes frantic, almost like he's pleading for help. Alice stops screaming when she sees me but remains in floods of tears. She extends one arm bearing a bright red scratch. Daisy is comforting her in a motherly fashion. Meanwhile, the social worker looks on, doing nothing except sighing.

Fearing the worst, I blurt, 'What happened?'

'The cat attacked her.' Daisy fastens her accusing gaze on me, as though I were the one responsible for this.

'Oh dear, I'm sorry about that, Alice. Let me see.' I approach the children, keen to help, only for Daisy to give me an even sterner look as she warns, 'You'll only make it worse.'

'Well . . . Can I do anything to help?' I hover by the sofa but keep my distance. The social worker, who is going through a mountain of papers that I will need to sign, shrugs and gives me a faint grin as if to imply that she is no longer in charge of the children. I am now responsible for them.

'He's never done anything like that before,' I worry, biting my lip, hoping Hero is okay. Alice would have scared him with her screams. He is not used to children. I'm careful not to come across as overly critical, as I hesitantly suggest, 'You must have touched the cat. He wouldn't have scratched you for no reason.'

Daisy narrows her eyes and scoffs, 'Dad says only witches have cats.'

I would like to respond, but I don't. Rather, I go into the kitchen and retrieve the first aid kit. When I return to the room, I offer it to Daisy. 'Just wipe the scratch before you put a plaster on it.'

'No,' Alice whimpers, as she pulls her arm away. 'It'll sting.'

Daisy firmly scolds, 'No it won't. Don't be such a baby,' but Alice squeals and jerks her arm away as soon as the wipe touches her skin.

'I want Granny to do it,' she pouts, defiantly jutting out her chin.

At that, Daisy's eyes find mine and I can tell she believes I'm the enemy by the look she gives me.

She hisses angrily in her sister's ear, loud enough for me to hear, 'Don't call her that,' and then she stomps across the room and throws herself onto a different chair, where she comforts herself by rocking the evil doll in her arms, which I've secretly named "Chucky" in my head.

Wanting to whip it away from her, I sigh deeply, realising that this is not the start I had hoped for. But I hunch over Alice anyway, who extends her arm for me to inspect. This time, when I clean the scratch before applying the plaster, there is no reaction. I dare not turn around to witness Daisy's affronted response.

'What's the cat's name?' Alice is curious.

'Hero,' I tell her, smiling.

'Why is he called that?'

'Because he saved me at a time when I most needed it.'

Alice cocks her head to the side, frowning. 'Same as us?'

'What do you mean?' I mumble, aware that I am clinging onto Alice's arm for longer than is necessary.

'You're saving us as well,' she speaks softly to keep her sister from hearing.

Tears well in my eyes as I murmur, 'Perhaps we are all saving each other.'

Then Alice smiles, and for a split second, I think everything will be okay. 'How about a slice of cake?' I ask her.

The mere mention of cake makes Alice's vivid blue eyes sparkle.

'Is it okay if I take the children into the kitchen for something to eat and then come back in to do the paperwork?' I ask, glancing at the social worker.

'Yes, that's fine, Mrs Castle.'

When Alice stands up and puts her hand in mine, I feel my heart swell. My youngest granddaughter has a great capacity to trust, I observe, whereas the eldest is much more cautious and suspicious of adults. Together, Alice and I approach the door.

'Are you coming, Daisy?' As I say this, I don't look the oldest sister in the eye, intuitively sensing she would see it as a challenge on top of her sister's betrayal. She surprises me by putting the doll down and following but wears a sour expression and drags her feet as though to indicate that she hasn't been won over yet.

Back in the kitchen, I motion for them to sit at the table while I fetch them glasses of milk. Daisy gives her drink a questioning glance as if she has never had milk before, and then she raises an eyebrow at me.

'We'll get you some Coke later, I promise,' I tell her.

I turn to face Alice and see that she has a milky moustache already.

'Do you like jelly?' I ask, gesturing to the wobbly bowl of orange jelly. Both girls give me a strange look and shake their heads, as though I'm crazy for even suggesting it. I watch them out of the corner of my eye as I cut two slices of Victoria sponge cake and place them on side plates.

'Daisy, look — a rabbit.' Alice excitedly points to the pink blancmange.

Daisy reaches out and gives the plate a small jolt, causing the rabbit to wobble and come to life. This makes the girls chuckle. I join in on hearing their laughter, but it doesn't last long. Daisy starts to scowl.

She growls at her sister, 'We're not supposed to laugh when Mum has just died.'

Alice begins to cry again, and I go over and put my arm around her when Daisy doesn't move to comfort her. She surprises me by pressing her wet face against my waist, and I mutter the unavoidable, 'There, there.'

Glaring at her sister as if she were the biggest traitor in the world, Daisy grabs her slice of cake and shoves almost all of it into her mouth. She then proceeds to eat it with her mouth gaping open, letting bits of it fall out. I'm too smart to tell her to "mind her manners". I know when I'm being tested.

Instead, I say casually to no one in particular, 'Your mum had a rabbit when she was little.'

Daisy stops chewing and Alice stops crying. Both of them are staring at me, urging me to continue.

'She called him Snowy.'

'Is that because the rabbit was white?' Alice speculates.

'Indeed, he was. I have a picture of him somewhere. I'll have to find it so I can show you.'

'Do you have photos of Mum too?' asks Daisy.

'Of course. Lots of them.'

The girls exchange glances and I can see right away that this is important to them. They will feel more connected to their mother when they look at photos of her.

'If you'd like, we can get them out when the social worker leaves.'

Both girls nod at me, entranced. Sensing a small win, I don't know what comes over me, but I can't help but add, 'Your mum had a cat too, Daisy.'

CHAPTER 8: THE FATHER

It's gone 2 a.m. and Leah still isn't home. She's not answering her phone either, even though she's been posting drunken pictures of her and her mates on Instagram. I had to stop scrolling through my phone when I saw a group photo taken outside Wetherspoon's with a body builder type hovering in the background who looked a lot like Wayne.

Saffy's been restless all night from teething but she's finally fallen asleep in the bed next to me. She looks so tiny and helpless lying there, it makes me feel like a prize wanker. What good is a dad who can't protect his kids? I feel like I've let Daisy and Alice down big time. Will I be letting Saffy down as well if I end up breaking up with Leah? Would Leah cope any better at being a single mum than Scarlet? She's much tougher, that's true. And she doesn't need me the way Scarlet did, so maybe she would be all right. A part of me doesn't want to face up to the fact that I would be replaced the second I walked out of the door. The thought of another bloke bringing up my baby girl gets to me every time.

The window is open and the remains of the cat fight I heard earlier, which first awoke me, has died away. All I can hear now is the muffled thud of a neighbour playing loud music two doors down. Because I used to have terrible nightmares as a kid, I've been left with a real fear of the dark so the hall light has been left on to illuminate the room. "Whoever heard of a so-called killer being afraid of the dark?" is what I should have told the police when they accused me of attacking Scarlet in what they called "a horrible row-that-went-wrong moment and then making it look as if somebody had broken in".

I glance around at the shadowy corners of the room. Flimsy bits of Leah's lace underwear spill out of the drawers and her make-up is scattered all over the dressing table as usual. An assortment of high-heeled shoes has been abandoned on the threadbare carpet, creating a war zone. I swear Leah does it on purpose to trip me up. I'm dying for a fag but dare not get up from the bed in case Saffy wakes up, so I stare at the ceiling instead counting the number of poisonous aertex swirls on it. It's a hot and sticky night and I'm wearing just my underpants. The bedsheets smell of Leah. Fake tan. Perfume. Spearmint chewing gum. Sweat.

Leah never once mentioned being sorry about Scarlet or even showing any concern, horror, or surprise, unlike the rest of the Nene Fields estate who are out in their droves spending money they don't have on bunches of flowers so they can leave them on the front doorstep of 7 The Green, even though no one lives there anymore.

Just a minute. I sit up. That means if things get really tough with Leah I could always go and stay there. I still have a key. And the girls could join me. But because I had already moved out, would the council allow me to remain there indefinitely?

Everyone's talking about what happened to Scarlet. When I spoke to one of our neighbours earlier tonight, I found out rumours were going around that Scarlet had been strangled in her bed. Bad news travels fast around here, but nobody is able to tell me where Daisy and Alice are.

The last I heard, Scarlet's mum sold the family home on Thorpe Road and moved to the countryside. But where? Scarlet pointed out her old house to me once in a drive by and it looked like a mansion to me. Her dad was a head teacher at some fancy school and not short of a bob or two. Nor was his wife, who Scarlet said had been left a shit load of money after her husband died. When I asked Scarlet if she was likely to inherit any of it, she'd pulled a face and told me she had been written out of the will. Because of me, no doubt.

Leah has a point in that Yvonne Castle owes me in some way. Or if not me, then Scarlet. Fuck knows, the woman probably hates me enough to give me a wad of cash just to disappear, but I could never do something like that, could I? Even though it would set me, Leah, and Saffy up for life . . . But I'm forgetting at what cost. I would be giving up my girls. Forever. Besides, even if I did know where she lived, the police have warned me to stay away for now. I'll have to wait until the funeral to meet with Scarlet's mother to ask for visiting rights. No matter how much she may loathe me she can't deny me that. I'm the girls' father. But as their mother found out, being a single parent is fucking hard and I'm not sure if I'm cut out for it.

I wonder if Leah has any idea what life as a single mum would be like if I were to leave. I don't think she's learned anything at all from Scarlet's suffering. Leah has always been jealous of Scarlet and seemed to hate her even though the woman had never done anything to hurt her. As a result, she never took to my kids either. They were an unwanted reminder of my past. She hates the fact that I was married to Scarlet and haven't yet proposed to her. I know she's angling after a ring but, as things stand, she'll have a bloody long wait on her hands. At the moment I don't trust Leah at all. First there was Wayne, and now she's trying to get me to blackmail the girls' grandmother for money just so I can buy her a dog. As if!

And let's not forget her veiled threat about giving me a dodgy alibi, which somehow implied it could be reversed at any time. "You could have killed your ex-wife for all I know," she'd screamed at me. But what she's forgetting is that an alibi works two ways. Because I also have no fucking idea where Leah was the night Scarlet was murdered. All I know is that Leah left Saffy with her mum for the night and didn't return any of my calls.

CHAPTER 9: THE GRANDMOTHER

Hero is curled up on Alice's lap, purring contentedly across the room. Alice is asleep on the sofa, her mouth hanging open. Daisy is still poring over the stack of photographs I brought down from my converted attic office. The doll is lying discarded on the floor, and I keep expecting it to sit up and scare the life out of me by giving me the evil eye. Now and then Daisy takes a sip of ice-cold Coke, bought from the village store earlier this evening. Fidgeting in my seat, because my hip is killing me this evening, it takes all of my willpower not to go over and pick up Alice's sticky sweet wrappers that have been discarded on the sofa arm.

Even though it's past the girls' bedtime, I decided to let them stay up a little longer on their first night here. The heavy curtains have been drawn. The fringed, velvety lamps are lit and the living room has taken on a cosy feel. Daisy sits on the opposite end of the sofa from her sister, her legs tucked up beneath her. Her eyes widen in alarm whenever the cat moves or even looks at her.

'How old was Mum in this one?' Daisy holds up a picture of Scarlet in her school uniform. She's already asked me this same question a dozen times with a dozen different photos.

Squinting through my glasses, I say, 'She would have been about nine, the same age as you. You look very much like her, Daisy.'

'What was she like, when she was younger, I mean?' she asks, as tears well up in her eyes.

'Funny. Clever. Playful. Stubborn. And very chatty, like Alice.' I can't help but smile as I reminisce.

'That doesn't sound like her at all,' Daisy replies dejectedly, adding, 'How come we never got to meet you when she was alive?'

I sigh. 'We hadn't spoken in over ten years.'

'Why not?' Daisy frowns.

'It's complicated.' I stall for time, but when I see the determined look on my granddaughter's thin pointy face, I give up and accept that I will have to offer an explanation. 'Scarlet was exceptionally bright and did well at school. Her father, your grandfather, my late husband, Charles was very proud of her academic achievements. But when she began drinking and smoking at the age of sixteen, she started hanging out with what he termed "the wrong crowd". As a result, he became overly strict with her and she rebelled.'

'How?' Daisy tilts her head curiously.

'She used to bunk off school and disappear for days at a time. The last straw for Charles, who was a head teacher, was when she got herself expelled from school for showing up to class drunk.'

At this, Daisy arches her eyebrows in what can only be described as a cynical adult gesture, as if to suggest that her mother hadn't changed all that much over the years. I realise at this point that I am talking to her as an equal, an adult in fact, when she is still a child, but there's something so worldly about her, despite the doll, that I decide not to adapt my approach.

'Scarlet moved out as soon as she turned eighteen, and after that we only heard from her when she needed something from us.'

'You mean money?' Daisy observes intuitively.

I nod. 'Yes, but when we found out she was taking drugs, her father and I, well we decided that we could no longer help her financially. We did offer to pay for her to go into rehab but she laughed at that, claiming that all young people experimented with drugs and that it was just a phase.'

'Did you ever get to meet my dad?' Daisy wants to know. By now she's given up any pretence of still being intrigued by the photographs and is listening intently to everything I say.

'Not in person, no. Although we heard all about him, of course, from Scarlet . . . when she was speaking to us, that is.'

'Didn't you even go to their wedding?' Daisy exclaims, shocked.

'We weren't invited. Charles didn't approve of the match, you see.'

'Because they were always fighting?'

'Exactly, and they were both drug users at the time. I understand from the social worker that this was no longer the case for your mum and dad.'

Daisy nods mutely as if she would rather not talk about it. However, she surprises me by suddenly announcing, 'Mum told me about you being her mum.'

'She did? But according to the police Scarlet hadn't told anyone I was her mother, except for your dad of course, claiming instead that I was some distant relative.'

'Well, she told me and made me promise to keep it a secret,' Daisy argues.

'It sounds like she wanted you to know about me after all,' I marvel. 'What exactly did she tell you?'

'That you didn't think Dad was good enough for her and that you hated him.'

'Nobody is ever good enough for their daughter, are they?' I attempt to make my granddaughter smile but she's having none of it.

'I love my dad and he loves me,' Daisy suddenly cries angrily, as she hugs her skinny, badly bruised knees. 'And I know

39

that you think he killed Mum, just like the police do, but I know for a fact he didn't.'

'How do you know that for sure?' I ask, puzzled, thinking it's a strange topic for her to bring up. I'm not certain where she's getting her information from but I'm beginning to suspect that this is a child who listens in at doors.

'It doesn't matter,' she shrugs, withdrawing into herself. 'But Mum said you were horrible to her and Dad, and that she hated you for it.'

I nod in agreement as I pause to take off my glasses and wipe my wet eyes. 'I suppose I deserve that. Scarlet must have thought I was cold and heartless but Charles and I felt we were doing the right thing. I now regret not helping her more, particularly after he passed away. I was unaware that she had separated from your father and was all by herself.'

'She wasn't all by herself.' Daisy is scathing. 'She had me. I helped her.'

'I'm sure you did, Daisy, but you are still just a child.'

'I've never been just a child,' Daisy murmurs in a too-mature manner. 'And if I tell you something, will you promise not to say anything?'

'Of course.' I nod, secretly thinking that Daisy is far more traumatised by her mother's death than I have been led to believe. Understandably, she has a mountain of anger and guilt inside her.

'Not even to the police?' she cautions, wild-eyed.

'What is it, Daisy?' I ask suspiciously, unwilling to commit to a promise I can't keep. 'You're starting to make me feel nervous, because if you know anything at all about your mum's death then you must—'

'You have to promise first,' Daisy interjects fiercely.

'Okay.' I nod, wondering if I will live to regret this.

Daisy's eyes swirl with horror as she mumbles softly, 'I know Dad didn't do it because I'm the one who killed Mum.'

CHAPTER 10: THE FATHER

Smoke from my roll-up wafts over to the piled-high wheelie bins outside the back door, enveloping the trash in a cloud of toxic mist. The rough patch of grass that we call a garden stinks of leftovers from cheap ready meals, burnt oven chips, empty beer bottles and cans of baked beans. It's still dark outside, but the surrounding poverty and the night sky are illuminated by the full moon. After somehow managing to return Saffy to her cot without her waking, I've nipped downstairs for a smoke. I'm standing in my pants by the back door, which is where I do my best thinking. I can still hear my neighbours talking and the thrum of music two doors down. It's a hot, muggy night. Too warm to be inside. It's almost 4 a.m., and I wonder for the umpteenth time where Leah is. Saffy will be screaming for her breakfast any minute. I might as well stay up now.

I've finally found the image I was looking for on my phone. The one Leah would have a hissing fit over if she knew it existed — me, Scarlet, Daisy, and Alice — on a rare day out at Big Sky soft play in the city centre. The four of us are on a huge rainbow-coloured slide with big grins plastered over our faces. It hurts to remember that by the time this picture was taken, about a year-and-a-half ago, I had already begun seeing Leah behind Scarlet's back. What a cheating scumbag I was! Just as I'm thinking this, I see a small dark form vanishing into one of the bins. The rat is easily identified by its long, stiff tail, but it ignores me as if it recognises that I too am vermin, *a love rat no less*, as it continues its search for food.

I've never had high expectations of myself, impossible when you've been brought up on the Nene Fields estate, but I'm self-aware enough to know I'm not the man I want to be. Or could be. But for people like us, *council-house-and-proud*, as the saying goes, the odds of being given a second chance are about as good as winning the lotto. Once a benefit scrounger always a benefit scrounger. Isn't that what's said of those unlucky enough to have been "dragged up" on one of the most deprived council estates in the UK? One day, the whole of Nene Fields will be demolished. It can't happen soon enough. Still, for me, it's home. I was born into this life and I know it like the back of my hand.

When I was a kid, my playground was made up of underground walkways where the homeless used to sleep and occasionally die. And where kids as young as ten dealt in drugs, and sometimes guns. I was first exposed to knife crime at the age of twelve when an older boy, Gary Pearce, stuck a blade in the back of my hand, *for fun*, he said. Being a smaller-than-normal, scrawny kid meant I was bullied severely, but my dad insisted I fight back "or else", so I would usually come home from school black and blue. If I didn't stick up for myself, Dad would hit me with his belt buckle. I still carry inside me the anger and hatred from those beatings. But the same goes for everybody else around here. Being poor has pushed us all into a corner, as if we were bait dogs. The government has failed every single one of us. We live in our concrete boxes with metal railings around them to keep us hidden from view of nice, well-educated, middle-class folks. We're out of sight, out of mind.

I worry about Daisy and Alice's future. They're both clever girls. Into books and homework in a way I never was.

They have their mum to thank for that. Until Scarlet met me, she had something of a privileged upbringing and went to a posh private school where her dad was the headmaster. All my girls can look forward to is a shitty, poor Ofsted-rated education in a massive concrete academy where the teachers are more afraid of their students than the guards are of their inmates at Peterborough Prison.

Even though I'm gutted about Scarlet, especially since I secretly hoped we might get back together at some point, I'm also kind of relieved that Daisy, my oldest, can finally enjoy her childhood. She had taken on the role of a carer for her mum since I left, looking after Alice among other things. She cooked, cleaned, shopped, put her mum to bed when she had been drinking, and cleared up her vomit. A carer at nine years old. It was an absolute shame. And I am a fucking disgrace for allowing it to happen. Hadn't I always known that Scarlet was incapable of coping on her own? I still walked out on her and the kids though. I'd somehow let Leah convince me that Scarlet was using me as a meal ticket. The truth was, Scarlet would get the same benefits without me as she did with me.

Back then I'd let my dick do the thinking for me. I had a new toy. A hot, young body. Even hotter sex. It was more of a fix than an H-bomb of heroin. There were no threats of physical violence, self-harm, or suicide with Leah, just a chilled-out vibe, at first anyway. She showed her true colours later. I had to have her though — she was all I could think about, day and night. But now, in the cold light of day, I can see her for what she really is. Cruel. Cold. Selfish. A liar. A user. Everything she'd accused Scarlet of being. I'd been made a mug of.

The phone call I received from Scarlet the night she died is a secret I won't be sharing with Leah or the police any time soon in case it puts me back on the police's radar. She was sobbing uncontrollably and ranting about some "bitch" threatening her over the phone. *Could that have been Leah?* Scarlet was in a terrible state and had obviously been drinking more than usual because of the way she was slurring her words. She begged me to come over straight away, saying she didn't feel safe, and I agreed I would, but I got there much later than planned . . .

Leah was mostly to blame for this since I had to convince her to come home first because I was, as usual, home alone with the baby, nursing a bruised body and a burst lip after being beaten up by Wayne the night before. I didn't tell her where I was going and she didn't ask, which in and of itself was strange, as if she'd already guessed my destination. She simply took off with the baby, saying she was going to stay at her mum's. Except she didn't, because when I rang there, I was told that she'd abandoned the baby and gone out on her own. I didn't buy that for one second, though. Leah couldn't stand to be by herself and needed to be surrounded by friends and family at all times. When all of my calls to her mobile went straight to voicemail, it seemed as though my suspicions that she was seeing Wayne behind my back were confirmed. *Where else could she be?*

I arrived at 7 The Green over two hours late, torn between wanting to go out and find out what Leah was really up to and helping my ex-wife and my kids, who might also be in danger. I called up the stairs and got no response, so I went up and knocked on Scarlet's bedroom door before opening it. I knew she was dead the moment I saw her lying on the bed, her glazed-over eyes fixed on the ceiling. I assumed Scarlet had taken an overdose. This wouldn't have been a surprise. I half expected it for years.

How I managed to convince the police that I knew nothing of my ex-wife's death I'll never know. I must be a fucking good actor, that's all I can say. So much so, I think I managed to convince myself of my ignorance.

What I most recall about that night though, which brings me out in a cold sweat even now, was not the horror of seeing Scarlet's lifeless body . . . it was the faint creak on the landing that made me turn to see what was making the noise. My heart twisted in my chest when I saw my daughter standing there in her pyjamas, cradling a pillow against her waist.

CHAPTER 11: THE GRANDMOTHER

Fortunately, this room was already girl friendly before Daisy and Alice moved in. It features a pretty meadow-print wallpaper, a blush-pink carpet and a white French-style armoire and dressing table. With everything happening so rapidly, I didn't have much time to prepare before they arrived, so all I could do was put some new light pink flowery bedding on the twin beds. Since the girls are accustomed to sharing a bedroom, I decided to leave it that way for the time being. However, they might want to think again once they realise there is another bedroom available.

I managed to rouse Alice long enough to get her to brush her teeth and change into her pyjamas before she fell into bed. She was asleep again within minutes. Not so Daisy, who is now chewing on her fingernails nervously while sitting on the bed and cradling the doll in her arms like an anxious mother. I'd warned her that we needed to talk more about what happened the night her mother died once Alice was asleep, I didn't want her sister to overhear us.

'Daisy,' I whisper, summoning her with a beckoning finger. 'Come here.'

Rolling her eyes and shrugging impatiently, she does however get up from the bed and follow me onto the landing.

'In here,' I say as I move to open my bedroom door, my walking stick tapping on the floor in front of me.

Daisy takes everything in with wide eyes. The antique Georgian dollhouse that has never been touched by a child's hands. The striking wisteria wallpaper, along with matching swagged curtains, a gleaming mahogany sleigh bed with a variety of cushions piled on top and a heavy satin bedspread in a grape hue. A myriad of photographs in pearly ornate frames fill a mirrored antique dressing table. There are pictures of the younger Castles, looking quite attractive and considerably slimmer. Some of Charles in various poses — graduating from university wearing a black cap and gown, fishing by a river, playing golf in a diamond-patterned jumper.

The focal point of this display is a black-and-white wedding photo. The newly wed Mr and Mrs Castle have confetti in their hair and are drinking champagne. Every time my gaze comes to rest on it, I touch the wedding ring on my left hand to serve as a reminder that I am still a married woman.

'Is that my granddad?' Daisy asks, curious.

'Yes.' I smile warmly at her, wanting her to know that she isn't in any trouble. 'But I'll tell you about him another time.'

'And is that you, when you were young?' Daisy asks, approaching the dressing table so she can physically touch the picture frames.

'It is indeed. I was quite a doll, wasn't I?' I chuckle and take a seat on the bed. Wrapping the belt of my long, velour dressing gown around me, I pat the bed invitingly. I can't completely ignore the voice in my head cautioning Daisy not to get sticky fingerprints on the photographs.

Instead, I say, 'Now, Daisy, tell me why you believe you had anything to do with your mother's passing.'

Daisy's eyes instantly sparkle with tears and I watch her wring her hands, much in the way an anxious old woman might, before she walks over to the bed and lowers herself onto it, not quite next to me.

She stoops her head in shame and looks away from me while insisting, 'Because it *is* my fault.'

'How exactly?' I shuffle closer but refrain from putting an arm around her shoulders since I don't think she's ready for that kind of closeness yet.

'Mum was crying a lot that night. She always did when she had too much to drink so I helped her upstairs, undressed her, and put her to bed,' she manages in between sobs.

I prompt gently, 'And then what?'

'I knew she wouldn't go to sleep without her sleeping tablet and I wanted to finish reading my book in peace. I only had forty pages to go.' Daisy stops and closes her eyes tightly, as if unwilling to recall the memory.

'And?' I give her another gentle nudge. I suspect she is experiencing some form of survivor syndrome and is riddled with guilt as a result. I happen to think talking about it will be cathartic for her.

Daisy gulps. 'So I gave her the pill and made her take it with some water.'

'Which she presumably did every night,' I suggest helpfully.

'Yes, but that also explains why, when the bad person broke in, she was unable to wake up.' Daisy's voice rises in panic and her shoulders go up a notch as she continues, 'If I hadn't made her take the pill, she would have woken up and been able to fight them off. Don't you see?'

Sighing deeply, as though the weight of the world is resting on this child's shoulders, I step in with, 'I can tell that you were an extremely good daughter to your mother and that you helped her a lot.' Once more, I stifle my inner critic's need to dramatically add that Scarlet ought to have been the one helping her daughter instead of the other way around.

I carefully add, 'But I don't think it was the sleeping pill that prevented your mother from waking up.'

'You don't?' Daisy looks up at me, mouth agape.

'When Scarlet first started drinking at the age of sixteen, she occasionally drank to the point that she would pass out and not wake up for hours. Despite our best efforts, your grandfather and I were unable to rouse her. I used to worry that she might choke on her own vomit.'

Daisy pulls a face, but she appears, in my opinion, much happier. Less serious. Her eyes have hope in them again. 'So, you see, the pill wouldn't have made any difference at all,' I reassure her, before continuing in the same vein. 'Sadly, it was the drink that caused her to black out.'

Daisy scowls before announcing crossly, 'I'm never going to drink alcohol. Even when I grow up.'

I nod my approval. 'Good for you. I hardly ever touch it myself, save for the occasional Christmas glass of port.'

Daisy smiles at me then, a gesture that warms my heart. Beneath the crinkled brow and hardened eyes, she's strikingly pretty. Just like her mother. Alice may appear to be the softer of the two sisters, but this child harbours deep emotions that she keeps locked inside her.

Daisy hesitantly asks, 'So, it wasn't my fault that Mum died?'

I place my wrinkly, age-spotted hand on top of hers, and feel grateful that she doesn't yank it away, when I reply, 'The person who put that pillow over your mother's face that night is the only one to blame for her death.'

48

CHAPTER 12: THE FATHER

Paint curls away from the woodwork on the front door to 7 The Green where bunches of flowers have been left. The petals are wilting and the cellophane is frying in the sun. Our neighbours have put cards with outrageous, misspelt lies on the doorstep, such as "One of our own taken in tragic circumstances" and "Scarlet, you're forever missed". The reason I say "lies" is because Scarlet was never truly accepted on the Nene Fields estate. She stood out as different and people around here don't take to that. It was the way she spoke. Something in her manner. Add to that her mental health struggles and volatile temper and it's easy to see why she never fitted in.

There is black-and-yellow "police crime scene" tape everywhere and, to keep nosy parkers from gawping in the front windows, the curtains have been drawn. Out of curiosity, I wander around to the rear of the property and see that the broken glass in the back door has been boarded up. Then I get the shock of my life when I see a tall, slim woman with long blonde hair letting herself out of it. She doesn't see me standing there as she's facing away from me and is having trouble inserting the key in the lock.

'Leah!' I exclaim sharply because I recognised the waves in her hair, fake designer crossover handbag and ripped skinny jeans straight away.

My mind screeches at me to stay calm as she spins around in fright, dropping the key onto the concrete slabs with a noisy clang. She stares at me with barely concealed loathing as she scrabbles around on the ground for the key. 'What the fuck!' she shrieks as though she was in the right.

'Exactly what I was thinking.' I glare at her while digging my hands into my cargo short pockets. She finally staggered in this morning at around 5 a.m. and I have no idea what she has done with Saffy but assume she has once again been left at her mother's. Clearing my throat, I demand, 'What the fuck *are* you doing here and where did you get that key?'

'I didn't steal it if that's what you're thinking. You always keep the spare on the key hook in the kitchen. I simply borrowed it that's all,' she says, tucking a strand of hair behind her ear in what is meant to be a seductive fashion, except it's wasted on me.

'Nobody is supposed to be in there,' I warn darkly.

'I left something . . .' she finishes lamely, her face pinched with awkwardness.

'What? When?' I'm flabbergasted. 'You never come here.'

'I was worried in case the police realised it wasn't Scarlet's,' she insists fiercely, gesturing to her clenched palm. 'It's mine.'

I take a step forward, wanting to see what she's holding. When she doesn't offer to show me, I reach for her hand but she snatches it away.

'What could you have left at Scarlet's that was so important you'd risk coming back to the crime scene for?' I demand, not having the courage to wrestle whatever she's holding from her. Knowing Leah and her sharp nails, I'd come off worse.

'I lost a ring.' Her face is unnaturally flushed as she opens her palm to reveal a gleaming gold band with a small glittery stone. Her eyes then flicker up to mine guiltily for a second before dropping away again. 'It's real gold, not fake,' she offers by way of an explanation.

'And you used my key to get in,' I observe, frowning. 'But why would your ring be in there? It doesn't make sense.'

She shrugs. 'It just was and I had to find it in case the police thought I had something to do with—'

'Scarlet's death? Like they did me?'

Leah's voice cracks as she whines, 'I gave you an alibi.'

'You gave yourself one you mean.' And the accusation lands just how I would have expected it to: she squints and sticks out her chin in defiance. My mind is blown to a million pieces when I figure out what she's keeping from me. 'You were here, weren't you? The night Scarlet died?'

There's a split second of hesitation from her before she cries, 'I was sick to death of her calling you all the time and trying to get you to go around to hers! I knew that's where you were heading that night. You spent more time with her than you did me. She was your ex, for fuck's sake.'

'Yes, but she was also the mother of my children.'

'Some mother,' she snips, before adding, 'She was a piss-head and a mental case. Face it.'

Her coldness makes me shrink into myself. My God, what was I thinking to leave Scarlet for her? I must have been mad.

'What were you doing here that night? What did you do?' I demand.

'Keep your voice down,' she hisses, glancing around and nervously running a tongue over her cherry-coloured lips. 'If you must know, I called around to warn Scarlet off that's all. But as it turns out I never got to see her. The door was unlocked when I got here and still intact then, but when I knocked, nobody answered, so I let myself in. When I called upstairs there was no reply so I left. I didn't realise until much later that my ring was missing and that I must have lost it here because I remembered taking it off my finger and putting it in my pocket before I got here.'

As I try to work out what time Leah must have visited Scarlet that night, I realise it was a close call and that I was lucky our paths hadn't crossed. The fact that the glass in the door wasn't broken indicates that Leah went to 7 The Green before I did. If the police ever found out we were both at the scene of the crime that night . . .

'Fucking hell, Leah, you could get us both arrested for going in there.' I drag a hand across my stubbled face, feeling empty inside. Just the thought of being locked up inside prison walls scares the shit out of me.

'They'll never know,' Leah scowls dismissively and hands me the key, which I slip into my pocket. 'It's not like you or I are going to tell them, is it?' She flashes me a brazen grin.

'Are you sure the glass wasn't broken when you arrived?' I stare at her, willing her to go on digging a hole for herself.

Sounding bored, Leah pops gum in the corner of her mouth. 'Yeah, why?'

'Because it means you got here before Scarlet died.'

'So?' She arches a pencilled eyebrow and crosses her arms over her braless chest. I notice that her nipples are visible beneath her vest top.

'Which means you were this close,' I press my thumb and forefinger together for emphasis, wanting to scare her, 'to running into the killer.' The smile freezes satisfyingly on her face as I go on. 'It could easily have been you that ended up in the morgue and not Scarlet.'

CHAPTER 13: THE GRANDMOTHER

A military line of solid green trees surrounds the allotment, offering shade from the scorching sun. I have a large plot, guarded at the entrance by a rickety old potting shack and a small rusting greenhouse. There's a gate with a hand-painted sign that reads "Welcome to Yvonne's allotment". It's a lie because I don't usually welcome anybody into what I think of as my private retreat where I come to switch off from the outside world. I'm at home with nature here, and it's beneficial for my well-being and my soul to get my hands dirty in God's own soil. That being said, Daisy and Alice have joined me today. They can hardly be left at home alone.

Alice is helping me harvest a crop of strawberries, but more of them end up in her mouth than in the bucket. She's thrown herself enthusiastically into the task and is on her knees in the aromatic sweet-smelling matted tangle of plants, her fingers stained a rich red. She has a creamy sheen of sunscreen across her nose and is wearing a frayed denim bucket hat. Daisy stays inside the potting shed, keeping the door open to watch over us while pretending to read, perhaps ironically, *The Secret Garden*. Daisy dislikes the sun and the outdoors and insists on dressing in gloomy, winter attire. The sisters

53

couldn't be more different if they tried, although I've noticed that Daisy often imposes her will on Alice.

I've gleaned a lot from listening to Alice. As I've said before, she has no filter and doesn't require any encouragement or coercion to gossip. I get the feeling that if I weren't here, there would be pinches to the skin and jabs of the elbows — anything to stop Alice from talking too much — as Daisy watches with a disapproving, occasionally scowling expression. However, I'm keen to learn more about the girls' lives with Scarlet so I allow Alice to prattle on unchecked.

'Dad left Mum for his new girlfriend, Leah, when he found out she was pregnant. Even though she was meant to be on the pill.' Alice shrugs casually, as though unaffected by any of this.

I'm shocked. 'But how could you know that?'

Daisy's indignant voice stabs at us from the potting shed. 'Dad tells us everything. And if he doesn't, Mum does . . . or did.' She sniffs.

I stammer, 'But you're still so young to hear such personal details of your father's relationship.'

'Is Dad still at the police station?' Alice asks, worriedly nibbling at her bottom lip.

'Of course he isn't. He never did anything wrong in the first place,' Daisy scoffs. 'The coppers have always had it in for him.'

Ignoring Daisy, who has a habit of interrupting me, I gaze sadly at Alice's bowed head and say gently, 'No, he was released without charge.'

Alice raises her head and blinks three times before asking hopefully, 'Have they arrested someone else then?'

Both children are staring at me now. They seem desperate to know more but at the same time, they must be filled with dread.

'I'm afraid not. But I have every confidence in the police that somebody will be brought to justice for what happened to your mother.'

Daisy, who is not a fan of the police, gives me a sarcastic harumph for this little speech, and I blame her father for this. And not just that.

'But we don't know for sure yet that she *was* killed,' Alice insists. 'It still might have been an accident. Mum could have died in her sleep like a princess who refuses to wake up.' The sweet girl.

'You could be right, Alice,' I concede, giving her a warm hug.

Alice frowns and shoves another big, ripe strawberry into her mouth, musing, 'Mum and Dad fought just as much when they were apart as they did when they were together so it was probably best that they split up.'

Furious, Daisy stomps her foot, throws her book to the ground, and cries, 'That's not true. Mum and Dad would have got back together if it weren't for Leah. They were in love.'

'Now, now, girls, let's not fight among ourselves,' I reassure them.

That's when it occurs to me that they have normalised fighting. Their upbringing in a home where their parents frequently quarrelled, were intoxicated, violent, and threatening to one another must have left its mark. I have faith that Alice, who is trusting and has been shielded from her parents' toxicity to some extent by her sister, can overcome her neglected upbringing though I wonder if it's too late for Daisy. Being the oldest and seemingly taking on all responsibility for her family, is she already too scarred by her past to ever have a happy, balanced, and healthy life?

Unlike the girls, I cannot pretend to be anything other than shocked by the way other people live their lives, especially Scarlet who wasn't raised that way. She had the ideal childhood in contrast with nurturing parents and a safe and secure home. Imagine, though, having the man you loved, even if he was a "wrong one" leave you for someone else after getting the new woman pregnant. I can see why she was in the state she was in at the time of her death. In my opinion *that man has a lot to answer for*.

When my mobile phone goes off in my pocket, I put a finger to my lips, shush the girls, and mouth the words, 'It's the police,' when I see the Leicestershire Police number, given to me by PC Carter — *such a nice young man* — flash up on my screen.

I chirp anxiously into the phone, 'Yvonne Castle,' and deliberately turn my back on the children, who are staring at each other with wide eyes.

'Mrs Castle, it's PC Anderson. We met at your house a few days ago.'

'Yes of course, hello, my dear,' I reply in the manner that is expected of a sweet, harmless older lady with a bad hip.

'The post-mortem is in,' PC Anderson announces bluntly, an edge to her voice as if she's expecting me to give her a hard time.

'And?' I lift my eyebrows and shoot a glance at the girls, trying not to reveal too much. They will need to know any outcome of course. I don't intend to keep anything from them. But I must first find the right words, to avoid traumatising them any further.

She gives it to me straight. 'It's as we expected. Death by asphyxiation.'

'So, it was murder then?' I find myself brushing away a stray tear as I mumble this.

As I listen to the police officer fill me in on all the gruesome details, my gaze drifts over to Daisy and I catch the fear in her eyes. With a guilty look, she turns away from me and retreats into the dark interior of the shed. This leads me to suspect that she hasn't told me *everything* about the night her mother died.

CHAPTER 14: THE FATHER

I'm on the bog, trying to take my mind off Scarlet and the girls by scrolling through my phone for daft TikTok videos when I hear the loud, insistent knocking on the front door. I shout for Leah to answer it, but she's sleeping off her hangover in the bedroom, so she can't hear me. Doesn't want to, more like. We haven't spoken since I found her letting herself out of Scarlet's back door this morning. I'm torn, not knowing what to think. What was Leah really doing at Scarlet's that night? Was it to warn her off as she claimed or did my lying, manipulative girlfriend have a more disturbing motive? Either way, I don't believe a word she said. Who in their right mind would go back to a crime scene and risk leaving their DNA behind for the sake of a piece of cheap, trashy jewellery?

Grunting in annoyance, I pull up my shorts and head downstairs, my footsteps creaking heavily on the stairs in the otherwise silent house. When I see the large shadow filling the glass in the front door, I pause. My first thought is that it's Wayne and that he's here to give me another kicking. Did Leah spend most of last night with him before crawling home in the early hours? If so, what the fuck am I going to do about it? Do I even care? The jury's out on that one. After refusing to take in my girls, I'm struggling to feel anything for her. It's Saffy I care about. I don't want to lose another of my daughters.

There's a twinge of unease in my stomach as I open the door since I'm not sure if I should brace myself for a fist rammed in my face but I'm shocked to see DS Mills framed in the doorway, blocking out the summer sky with his grizzly-bear bulk.

'Vince.' He nods grim-faced, a deep frown of concentration on his face.

'What are you doing here?' I blurt out, scanning the pavement rather than looking him in the eye. The sheer size of him is enough to make me want to piss my pants. I wouldn't put it past a bully like him to bulldoze his way in, so I pull the door closed behind me to block his view.

'What? You're not going to ask me in? And there I was thinking we were old friends.' Mills sniggers like a paid assassin. That's when I notice the black Mercedes parked outside with DC Fox behind the wheel. The street is otherwise deserted. Everyone's doing what they do best around here when they get a whiff of a plainclothes policeman . . . minding their own business. I fucking hate the pigs. They've never done me any favours. Leah at least shares this view. It's about the only thing we agree on these days.

I stare at him, blinking fast with my tattooed arms stiff by my sides as I ask nervously, 'Is this about Scarlet?'

Mills loses the phoney grin and gets down to business. 'We've had the results of Mrs Spencer's post-mortem back and it's as we suspected. Her death was caused through suffocation.' He looks away from me then, jaw tight, as if he still thinks I'm guilty.

My head snaps up at that. 'You mean Scarlet *was* murdered? Her death wasn't caused by an accident or a drug overdose?' A voice in the back of my head, wiser than my own, knows that a "death by accident" verdict is what I had been secretly praying for all along, even though I knew deep down that my ex-wife had not died peacefully in her sleep.

'We'll want to interview everyone again now that this is definitely a murder investigation.'

I baulk at that, feeling a hint of terror building in my voice as I bluster, 'I've told you everything already.'

'Then telling it a second time won't be difficult, will it?' Mills sneers, before adding, 'You have no trips to Bali or the Maldives planned, I take it?'

'As if!' I say sceptically.

'Just as well. We'll be asking you to surrender your passport for the time being.'

'What passport?'

'Figures.' Mills nods, a hand cupped under his chin.

Fighting off a sense of dread, I ask, 'What about the body?'

'What about the body?' Mills parrots as if this were a game. As if I weren't terribly affected by this news. *Scarlet is dead. She's never coming back.*

'She'll need burying. Scarlet deserves a decent send-off if nothing else.' I blow out my cheeks in exasperation.

'As her ex-husband, that's no concern of yours,' Mills tells me coldly. 'Her body will be released to her nearest living relative.'

'You mean her mother, Yvonne Castle? The same woman who refused to have anything to do with Scarlet for a whole decade,' I seethe.

'The one and the same.' Mills smirks, making me want to lash out and wipe the smugness from his face. I would an' all but I'd only get arrested for it. Is it any wonder people like me hate the police so much when they leave us powerless?

'I'm sure she'll be in touch about the funeral arrangements,' Mills adds unconvincingly, before setting off abruptly and striding down the path.

My voice is barely above a whisper as I mutter, 'Fucking pig,' after him. And then I'm slamming the door shut, making the glass tremble inside its frame, and storming back up the stairs, taking the steps two at a time, into the bathroom, where I slump onto the toilet. As I sit there taking a shit, with my shorts and pants around my puny ankles, fear washes over me, until I'm covering my sweating face with both hands.

The police have nothing on me. Whether I have a genuine alibi or not, I've done nothing wrong and they can't pin shit on me. But what about Leah, the mother of my child, who is clearly lying about something? Even more concerning, what about Daisy, my daughter?

When I turned around that night, after finding Scarlet's body on the bed, Daisy was standing there on the landing, looking pale and clutching a pillow in her hands. She appeared to be in some sort of trance as if she'd been sleepwalking, like she used to do when she was younger. At the time, I'd put this down to the shock of discovering her mother dead, but my gut feeling tells me there's more to it than that. Daisy was completely out of it, which was so unlike my oldest daughter, who had it together in ways I didn't. After taking her downstairs, I tried to console her while she sobbed uncontrollably and blamed herself for her mum's death. I can't shake off the awful words she'd screamed into my shoulder, "I killed Mum." And she wouldn't let go of the pillow — the now alleged murder weapon — that she'd taken from Scarlet's bed, even though it was drenched from her tears.

Thinking on my feet for once, as if I were a proper gangster, I'd told her what to do then, in great detail, explaining why I couldn't stay with her or call for help myself because doing so would have made me a potential suspect and I couldn't protect her from a prison cell. I made her repeat the plan back to me until I was convinced that she knew what to do. That is, when to bring Alice down for her breakfast and what to say when she dialled 999. But I worry that I won't be able to protect my daughter for very long. Not from afar. My concern is that she will eventually tell someone else about what happened that night. Her nerves won't be able to handle it. Daisy suffers from anxiety, just like her mother. Poor kid.

But if she confides in her grandmother, I'm convinced the bitch will go straight to the cops and tell them everything out of a sense of duty. Then, what will become of my daughter? She'll either be locked up or placed in care, that's what. Her life will be over. I can't allow that to happen. I would go to prison first. Although I've always maintained that I wouldn't let the police put me away for a crime I didn't commit, Daisy is a different story. But what if I don't have to? The answer is staring me in the face, like a mean-eyed heavy-weight boxer. I have to somehow find a way to get Daisy and Alice back from their grandmother. It's the only way I can save my oldest daughter. And me, from being banged up in jail.

I would stop at nothing to protect my daughter, so before I left number 7 The Green that night, I shattered the glass in the back door with a hammer, afterwards punching out the broken pieces, to make it look like someone had broken in.

CHAPTER 15: THE GRANDMOTHER

Sitting upright in bed, I'm sipping the last of a glass of cognac-coloured brandy, which warms my throat and my insides. It also helps take some of the pain away from my post-operative, sore-as-hell hip. Hero, a cloud of grey fur with large green eyes, is curled up next to me and is purring meditatively. I'm not exactly sure why I told Daisy I don't drink but I think it's because I saw it as an opportunity to win her approval. It's not like I'm a heavy drinker, far from it, but I do like a tipple of brandy every now and again as it helps me fall asleep. When you've lived the kind of life I have, sleep, like the truth, can be very elusive. But in the grand scheme of things, what's one more white lie? And what of Scarlet's lies?

Was it necessary for her to pretend she didn't have a mother? She should have known how painful that would have been to hear. Knowing Scarlet, this would have been deliberate on her part as she was never one to forgive easily. The one bright spot in this whole ordeal is that she finally revealed her secret to Daisy, therefore she must have wanted Daisy to know that she had someone to turn to if the family got into difficulty. Did Scarlet sense something bad was going to happen to her? Is that the reason she chose to tell her eldest child that she had a grandmother? Scarlet must have known that the girls' father couldn't be relied on to help them in a crisis. He's next to useless and always has been. It's just a shame she refused to listen to her parents all those years ago. Otherwise, she could have come home and would have received help raising the girls.

I can't lie. I'm feeling overwhelmed by all that has happened and the difficult path ahead. To the outside world, I'm a doting grandmother who has taken on her two precious grandchildren but I can't say any of this comes naturally to me. My formerly peaceful, orderly, and meticulously planned life has exploded, leaving me in charge of two demanding children, with a murder investigation to worry about and a funeral to plan. In addition, I have to silently cope with my own sorrow and regret. Never mind coming face to face with the man who is to blame for all this — Vincent Spencer. If it weren't for him, I'm convinced Scarlet would still be alive. I don't know how I will be able to bring myself to look at him at her funeral. His abandonment and emotional abuse of her obviously contributed to her depression and alcoholism. The police may have eliminated him from their murder enquiry, but that doesn't mean he isn't responsible for her death. People have been known to die of a broken heart before. I should know.

I believe the social worker who suggested that the girls and I would benefit from counselling could be right. I will look into it first thing tomorrow before any decisions are made about whether the girls should see their mother in the chapel of rest or if it would be wise for them to attend the funeral. I hadn't anticipated having to make so many difficult decisions at this stage of my life, but I have to be strong for Daisy and Alice's sakes. As PC Carter pointed out, *they need me and I'm all they have*. A small part of me also wonders if the girls coming to live with me could be the making of me. I can't deny that I haven't been lonely these last few years. It's a hard truth but life as a widow means you no longer come first with anyone.

A jolt of unease touches the base of my spine when I hear a muffled scream echoing down the landing. It takes me a moment to digest that it is real and not imaginary. Then, I'm tossing aside the satin cover and swinging my legs out of the bed, revealing my unsightly varicose veins. Hero's already wide eyes enlarge even more as a result of my panic, and he hisses in bewilderment before leaping off the bed.

Tension crackles in my voice as I call out, 'I'm coming,' while limping across the landing. Thrusting open the door to the children's bedroom; I scrabble for the light switch and flip it on to reveal Alice and Daisy in the midst of a violent scuffle on one of the beds.

'What on earth?' I gasp, as I realise that Alice, looking extremely red-faced and tearful, is struggling to get free but has one resolute fist wrapped in Daisy's long hair and is tugging viciously on it. Daisy has straddled her sister and has one hand firmly clamped over Alice's mouth to stop her from screaming. Anger and pain are visible on each of their faces.

My mind screeches at me to stay calm as I pull the two sisters apart. 'I thought you two were close. Whatever has got into you?' I gasp, as Daisy hurls herself onto the other bed, where she glowers at me. I study her face, my mind humming with questions as it dawns on me that I should have seen this coming. The atmosphere between the two girls since their arrival has been like a build-up of pressure before a thunderstorm. But what caused it, I wonder?

Blowing out her cheeks, Alice shakily swivels onto her knees and buries her head in my lap, deep sobs wracking her tiny body.

'Who is going to tell me what's going on? And who started this?' I demand, my eyes darting fiercely between the two sisters. When Daisy's guilty eyes drop away and she begins to pick distractedly at her fingernail, pulling off a strand of bright pink skin, I think I have my answer. So, I turn back to Alice and gently prompt, 'What is it, Alice? You can tell me.'

'I didn't make it up. Honest I didn't, Granny.' She sobs, clinging onto my plump body for all her worth.

'Alice, I'm sure you didn't. But what exactly are you talking about?' I run a tongue nervously around my lips, wondering what the child thinks she knows.

'Daisy says I'm lying.' Alice jabs an irate finger at her sister before wailing. 'But I'm not. I did see them.'

'You're a little liar. You always have been,' Daisy fiercely replies, looking for all the world as if she'd like to attack her sister once more. She then fixes her searing gaze on me and adds, 'You can't believe a word she says.'

I puff up my cheeks and say, dismissively, 'Well, I'll be the judge of that, thank you, Daisy.'

'Now, Alice.' I carefully lift her head off my lap to see her small indignant face. 'Tell me what you saw.'

Daisy snaps at her from behind, 'Don't,' but I take Alice's chin in my palm and turn her head so that she is staring at me alone. 'Do,' I instruct.

'Daisy said I must have dreamed it, but I didn't. Someone else was there the night Mum died.'

Shocked, I exclaim, 'In the house you mean?'

Alice nods, as if terrified of her sister's reaction, but I move to block her view of Daisy. This seems to give her the courage to proceed—

Her voice is hardly audible as if she's afraid of saying the words out loud, 'Something woke me up . . . a noise I think.' She bravely continues, 'The bedroom door was open and the landing light was on. That's when I saw them . . .' Alice stops and dares to peek at her sister over my shoulder. When I look at her, Daisy's head is bowed. Her entire body is slumped over in defeat.

Alice flinches when I put a hand on her shoulder and squeeze — perhaps a touch too tightly. I release my grasp and urge, 'Who did you see?' while attempting to sound composed, which is impossible given the situation.

I hold the air in my lungs until I'm compelled to release it in a deep, laboured breath because Alice looks paralysed and unable to speak another word. But then, she leans forward to whisper one word in my ear . . .

CHAPTER 16: THE FATHER

As I yank open the filthy, dark grey curtains to allow the light in, I think to myself that my girlfriend might as well be a vampire. Left to her own devices, Leah would live permanently in the dark. When I ask her why she keeps every curtain and blind shut in the house, she makes out she doesn't want the neighbours to see inside, but I wonder if she's experiencing the early stages of depression. Thanks to Scarlet, I'm an expert at reading the signs. It also occurs to me that she might be going through post-natal depression and that this could be the reason we're not getting on as well as we used to, or why she wouldn't have my girls come to live with us.

Given that it's almost noon and she's still in bed, in a darkened room, I decide it's an interesting theory and not one to be discounted. She might be right about the neighbours an' all because a few of them are currently outside gossiping on their doorsteps and keeping a watchful eye on our front door. They must have seen me being dropped off by the police car a few minutes ago because they never miss a trick. They'll be wondering what's going on. These days, Scarlet's murder is all anyone can talk about. Everybody and their dog believe I'm the killer. Shit, if I were a betting man, I'd put a tenner on myself being guilty.

Funnily enough, or not as the case may be, DS Mills is the only one convinced of my innocence, and that's because he now knows something most people around here don't . . . an unmatched DNA sample has been discovered at 7 The Green. They refuse to tell me where in the house it was found. All I know is that, because it differs from Scarlet's, they've ruled it out as being the children's or a family member. As a regular visitor to the house, my DNA was, of course, everywhere, and that was to be expected, but this latest information indicates they have another, so far unidentified suspect. *A person of interest*, they're calling them.

For me and Daisy, this is great news. Fantastic even. But not so much for Leah. Could it have been her DNA they found? Unlike me, Leah does not have a criminal record, so has never been fingerprinted or asked to submit a sample of her DNA. But if not Leah, then whose could it be? As far as I'm aware, Scarlet never received any visitors other than me and wasn't one for letting neighbours pop in.

Dying for a brew, I go into the kitchen-diner and put on the kettle. It's stone cold which tells me Leah hasn't been up at all. I frown as I take two mugs from the shelf, one for Leah and one for myself, and put a teabag in each, adding three teaspoonfuls of sugar to mine. When I open the fridge to take out the milk and pour it into the mugs, I realise it has gone off, so I have to start over.

As I climb the stairs, my heart is heavy in my chest and I'm not sure if this is the right moment to bring up the subject of depression with Leah. It could go either of two ways. Not good. And fucking terrible. Perhaps I should just spend the day taking care of Saffy and cleaning the house. Safer that way. But then again, I always was a coward when it came to women.

'Afternoon, sleepyhead,' I murmur, as I lower myself onto the creaking bed and set two mugs down on the bedside table that is already stained with rings.

'What time is it?' Leah moans from under the covers.

'It will soon be bedtime again at this rate,' I chuckle, trying to remain upbeat. Even though the bedroom is pitch black, a quick peek at Saffy's cot in the corner indicates that our baby girl is also taking a nap. Maybe Leah is simply worn out from being a new mum. She's still very young. Just twenty-two. Two years older than I was when I met Scarlet. We were both too young, looking back, to have settled down and got married. It's no wonder we ended up divorcing. One of the reasons that I haven't proposed to Leah is because I don't want to repeat the same mistake given her age. But, like I said, that's just one of the reasons. Another of course is Wayne.

I pull the covers away from her face. 'There's a cup of tea here for you.'

She yawns and stretches, baring her belly, and I can't help but think of a dog rolling onto its back wanting tickles. For a second or two, she blinks at me as though she doesn't know me. Or has mistaken me for someone else. Wayne perhaps?

'Where have you been?' she grumbles irritably.

'I had to go down to the police station to run through my statement again.'

On hearing this, I feel her body tense next to me. She sits up and runs a hand through her long, matted hair, which is black at the roots, before answering. 'Any news?'

'Not really,' I lie, deciding on impulse that telling her about the DNA will only make her panic. Besides, this is Leah I'm talking about. My girlfriend and the mother of my child. If she was capable of murder, I would know. Whatever her true motivation was that night for visiting Scarlet, it was not to harm her. I'm almost sure of it. *Almost.* Who, though, out of my girlfriend and my eldest daughter is most likely to have killed Scarlet? It's a question I don't have the answer to. Meanwhile everyone's pointing the finger at me. In the circumstances, it's probably better that way.

'How's Saffy been today?' I change the subject.

'Grumpy as fuck from teething,' Leah mutters crossly, casting an angry glance at the cot, which concerns me.

'If you'd like, I can take over now so you can get even more rest.'

She accepts without protest, gulping down some tea, and sliding further down in the bed before nodding. 'Okay.'

'The funeral is next Friday by the way,' I inform her, my nose wrinkling at the stale smell of sweat coming off the bed.

'Are you going?' she snaps, opening one eye.

I feel my cheeks flushing with heat as I reply, 'Of course I'm going. She's my ex-wife. Besides the girls will be there and I'll get to see them.'

When she pulls a face, I can tell that this hasn't gone down well either.

'Do you want me to come with you?'

I shudder at the thought. 'Probably best not.' I break it to her gently.

She sounds bored as she nods. 'Okay.'

With a twitch of a smile, I ask, 'Fancy anything in particular for tea tonight?'

'Big Mac. And can you bring me some toast up?'

'Okay.' I get up from the bed and go to stand over my daughter's cot. The smell of piss coming from her nappy makes my eyes water. Saffy is still asleep when I lift her up and nestle her against my neck. Leah never once looks in our direction. Her face is tight and unreadable, yet it's also weighed down with sadness or disappointment. Which one, I can't tell.

'Back in a bit,' I whisper, so as not to wake Saffy.

Her voice stops me before I even reach the door.

'Vince, you will talk to the grandmother, won't you? About keeping the children for good and helping us out financially?'

Although she doesn't use the term "blackmail" this time, my first impulse is to turn around and yell, 'No bloody way am I going down on my knees to that woman, not for you or anyone else,' but deciding that won't help, I mumble instead, 'I'll think about it.' And perhaps I will . . . if it means holding on to my baby daughter. God knows she needs me.

Leah's smile as I shut the door is just like my sleeping child's. Both have the power to manipulate me.

CHAPTER 17: THE GRANDMOTHER

Daisy, who is partially concealed beneath a large red parasol, glances up from the pages of her book and frowns disapprovingly when she catches me observing her. The solemn-faced child is wearing dull grey leggings and an oversized hoodie, despite the sun shining brightly overhead. Alice, who is the opposite of her sister in every way, is dancing barefoot around the lawn helping to water the plants. She's wearing one of the pretty new dresses we got online from Monsoon. A colourful dip-dye organic cotton dress that is even brighter than the colourful blooms in my garden. I suspect Daisy dislikes the dress as much as I do, but the choice is very *Alice* and it reflects her outgoing personality. As she pours water into the overflowing flowerbeds, she hums along to an unknown song. Her hair shines golden in the sunlight and is several shades lighter than Daisy's.

Since waking up this morning, neither of the girls has brought up the fight from last night. It's as if it never happened. Not once have they mentioned Alice's startling revelation either, which I find most disconcerting. If I'm being completely honest, I'm still in shock myself and unsure how to proceed. The girls appear unwilling to discuss it again, but

I think our new little family has to talk about it more before deciding what to do. Their ways and mine differ greatly. I would prefer to tackle problems head-on rather than act as though they don't exist. It's a challenging process as we all need to adapt to one another. Me most of all.

'It's so boring here.' Daisy sighs so hard that a thick wedge of her hair falls across her face, making her scowl even more.

'You're the one that's boring.' Alice laughs, not looking up from her watering.

Daisy groans, weary of the world. 'Why can't we go inside? It's too hot out here.'

'What's not to like?' I make a big, joyful gesture towards the expansive undulating lawn which slopes gently away before rising again. The riot of hollyhocks, poppies, delphiniums, and foxgloves create a chocolate-box effect and I recognise it's not what the girls are used to. It's not like I can claim any credit for the beautiful garden — I only inherited it — rather than helped to create it. I consider myself to be its temporary caretaker. The flawless pale stone of the cottage walls are covered in the same climbing red roses and purple wisteria blooms that are visible from the kitchen windows and the gentle and peaceful humming of bees fills the air.

Close to where Daisy is sitting at the white wrought-iron garden table, a border of herbs bursting with lavender, mint, rosemary, and thyme emits a strong, pungent perfume that I find instantly comforting. It makes me think of all the countries I've wanted to travel to but haven't. My husband and I weren't travellers. He insisted that the UK had enough natural beauty and interesting places to visit, and he detested the thought of flying. That's the price one pays for marrying a much older man who is set in his ways, I suppose. It's a shame because I would have liked to have seen more of the world and explored other countries like Vietnam, Japan and India.

Daisy's unsmiling eyes linger on me long after I've made my point but I can tell she is not convinced that this way of life is for her. I recognise that they are city children through and through but I'm hoping they will adapt to the quieter pace of the countryside eventually.

As if to prove my point, Alice suddenly and violently hurls the watering can away from her and lets out a blood-curdling scream that is bound to alarm my elderly next-door neighbour who has already undergone one pacemaker implantation this year. Before I get a chance to react, she's racing around the grass, tugging at her hair, and wildly flailing her arms.

'Get them off me. Get them off!' She squeals.

'What is it, Alice?' Leaning on my walking stick, I automatically give chase but she's too fast for me and bowls into her sister, seeking protection, which causes Daisy to scrape back her chair and spring to her feet. Now, they're both screaming and waving their arms in the air.

Daisy shoves her sister away and cries, 'The wasps are after us.' Alice then careers out of control and lands hard on her bottom on the patio slabs, causing her to burst into uncontrollable tears.

I call out helpfully, 'They're bees, not wasps,' gesturing for them to stop what they're doing. 'They'll leave you alone if you stay still.'

Daisy hisses, 'No they won't,' and bats her book aggressively at the bees before darting towards the open back door. She screams, 'I fucking hate it here,' before vanishing inside.

As the door closes with a resentful whack, I realise this is the first time I've heard Daisy swear and I'm not sure what to do about it. All I know is that this is not the time to give her grief over it. Heaven knows what Mr Burgess next door must be thinking.

Left with just one child to console, I go over to Alice and help her to her feet. Pulling a painful face, she puts a hand on her bruised bum cheek and dives into my arms, sobbing very loudly into my ear and deafening me.

'Have they gone, Granny?' She's desperate to know and keeps her kittenish nose hidden in my blouse just in case it's not safe for her to show her face. Her limbs are still twitching and quivering as though she had been stung ten times over, yet on closer inspection, not a single sting is visible.

'Yes, they're gone,' I lie, moving her away from the half dozen or so airborne black-and-yellow striped bumble bees that are still fiercely defending their patch of cyan sky. Wings angrily going ten to the dozen.

'Will I get an anaphylactic shock and die and go to heaven like Mum?' She bawls, her expression split between fear and excitement at the idea.

When I reassure her, 'You haven't been stung,' she relaxes into my embrace. 'Bees only ever sting as a last resort and are friendly to little girls. Especially ones who have lost their mothers.'

'Really?' She stares at me wide-eyed in awe as if I were someone magical and of great importance. I confess that I feel a little bit like Enid Blyton then. The emotion, though, is fleeting, for as I lead her back towards the safety of the house, with the promise of strawberries and cream, I can't help but worry that these children will be the death of me. Am I up to the job of raising them? Naturally, I have to be. Since what other option is there for them? A life spent on the Nene Fields estate, that's what, with their violent and abusive father, who I now know, thanks to Alice, lied to the police and was in Scarlet's house at the time of her murder.

CHAPTER 18: THE FATHER

I haven't worn a tie since school and even then, rarely. Truth be told, I was hardly ever in class, choosing instead to bunk off and mooch about at home or in the playground where I couldn't be bullied by the bigger kids and have the shit kicked out of me. After Mum ran off with another bloke, can't say I blame her, it was just me and Dad at home and he was mostly pissed out of his head by lunchtime. We spent our days avoiding each other. The only bit of advice he gave me came in the shape of his belt buckle and that was mostly to do with me "standing up for myself". I don't miss the old git who has been gone seven years this October. His liver didn't make it beyond fifty-three. Sometimes I worry I'll go down the same path as my old man, but I'm not an alcoholic. That's not to say I don't like a drink though.

I could do with one now if I'm honest even though it's only 10 a.m. But, since today is Scarlet's funeral, I'm feeling nervous. I can't help but wonder if the girls will be mad at me because this will be the first time in weeks that I've seen them. But as it's their mum's funeral, they're probably not thinking of me at all. On top of that, I'm dreading meeting Scarlet's mum. She's never had a good word to say about me and the feeling is mutual. I suppose I should be grateful to her for taking in my kids when my own girlfriend wouldn't, but it's a bitter pill to swallow given our history. Leah has warned me to be nice to her, but not out of respect for Scarlet. Her motive is purely selfish.

As I've thought many times before, *what Leah wants Leah gets*, and she set about trying to prove that last night by offering me a blowjob out of the blue. She didn't go quite so far as initiating sex as she seems to have gone off that these days, since having the baby, and I was tempted to take her up on her offer . . . but, call me old-fashioned I would have felt used, knowing the reason behind it. Money as usual! She's convinced herself that Yvonne Castle will give us anything we want if it means keeping custody of her granddaughters. She could be right, but I don't know, even though I've never actually met the woman I've always thought of her as cold and unforgiving, going by what Scarlet told me about her. Somehow, Leah has got the sum of £10,000 in her head.

When I sarcastically asked, "Is five grand the going rate for a daughter these days then?" she had the grace to look ashamed. I know she's already earmarked at least a grand of that money for a so-called pedigree lapdog. The rest, she'll no doubt be planning on spending on clothes and make-up.

I know I promised to think about asking the old bitch for money, but the more I think about it the more I hate the idea. I just don't think I could live with myself if I did that to Daisy and Alice's grandmother. I mean, what would they think of me if they found out? But if I do come home empty-handed, Leah is going to call me a "Fucking useless coward". Her black mood will go on for weeks and I'll be given the silent treatment. Toxic or what?

Tucking my shirt neatly into my suit trousers, I stand back from the cracked pedestal mirror, which is covered in splotches of make-up and Leah's grubby fingerprints, to check out my reflection.

'I don't look so bad even if I do say so myself,' I say out loud.

I'm growing out my cropped, borstal-boy hair and the longer style suits me. I kid myself I look like a younger Danny Dyer. Without the cockney accent. Because I'm missing one tooth, I don't smile much in public. Leah takes the piss out of me for being so self-conscious about it. It's not that I'm vain or anything, but I'd love to get it fixed. I try not to think about Mrs Castle's bank balance as I test out a grin on the mirror and sure enough the unsightly black gap is unmissable. Sighing, because there's sod all I can do about it, I realise that Leah doesn't quite get just how sensitive I am on the inside. Everyone on this estate believes that I killed Scarlet, yet my kids and anyone who truly knows me would know that I'm incapable of harming anyone. Except for today, when I'm wearing my cheap as chips, sharp black Amazon suit, I usually look like a thug, but I'm actually soft.

My shirt collar hides most of the large snarling wolf tattoo on my neck. Both the shirt and the suit, which I had to iron the creases out of, are brand new out of the packet. All I have to do now is show up at the church because I've already taken care of the three s's: shit, showered, and shaved.

'It doesn't get any better than this, my son,' I tell myself, adjusting my dark tie in the mirror.

Leah surprises me by sneaking silently into the room and saying, 'You look nice.' She's up but not dressed yet. She's wearing one of my old, crumpled T-shirts and has her hair up in a messy black and blonde streaky bun. There are dark circles under her eyes.

'Hmm and you smell nice,' Leah oozes seductively as she puts her hands on my jacket and fiddles with my tie, even though I just managed to get it exactly how I wanted it. She, on the other hand, smells rank. I don't know when she last brushed her hair, never mind her teeth. These days, she only bothers with her appearance when she goes out with her girlfriends.

'Thanks,' I say, trying not to let my impatience get the better of me. It's obvious she wants something. It's the only time she's ever nice to me.

'What time will you be back?' she asks sulkily, sensing that I've sussed her out. Because Leah doesn't give a shit what time I'll be back, or even if I return at all. Except to clean the house and look after Saffy.

I sigh and fix my tie again, saying, 'Not sure. I don't know if I'll be invited to the wake or not.'

Leah's eyes widen in panic. 'But you will go if you're asked?'

I frown at her reflection in the mirror as I remark, 'Why should that matter to you?'

'Duh,' Leah says, rolling her eyes before popping her snot-coloured chewing gum on the side of her cheek. She grins slyly then and laughingly adds, 'Because the evil, but very rich, grandmother will be there. And it's your job to charm her. Not out of her pants but out of her cash.'

When I finally turn to face her, I exclaim, 'What if you're wrong about her?'

'What do you mean?' she blusters, as though that were just plain impossible.

'What if she refuses to be blackmailed?'

'She won't. Not if she wants to keep her grandchildren.'

'And what if she doesn't?' I persist, remembering again how Scarlet described her mother. The phrase "selfish, cold bitch" springs to mind. A person like that probably wouldn't want to look after two young children long-term.

Leah screws up her face in disbelief. 'What sort of grandmother would that make her?'

'I don't know. You tell me.' When I say this, I'm thinking of the way Leah refused to take my girls in, but I'm too cowardly to admit it.

'If she won't pay up, we'll threaten to take the girls away from her. You're their father. You have rights.'

'Can you hear yourself?' I bark, angry now and unable to hide it. 'You wouldn't take the girls in even for a few nights when I was banged up in a police cell but you would take them off their grandmother for money.'

Leah narrows her eyes at me, before saying defensively, 'I said "threaten" that's all. We wouldn't necessarily go through with it.'

At that, I laugh sarcastically. 'You really do take the biscuit.'

'I don't see what's so funny,' she mutters through clenched teeth.

'What's funny, no fucking hilarious actually, is that you wouldn't let my girls come and stay with us, but you'd gladly give a home to a thousand-pound dog that will no doubt be left to piss and shit everywhere and never get walked, unless by me.'

'Oh, so we're back to that, are we?'

'It looks like it,' I scowl, realising at the same time that I'm never going to be able to forgive Leah for what she's done. Family is family in my book.

Leah juts out her chin in a challenging gesture and crosses her arms. 'Yeah, well, like I said. You're their father and you have rights. Same as I do. So, let's not forget that this house is rented in my name and I say who stays and who doesn't.'

Before I do something that I might regret, I slam out of the bedroom, shouting, 'And as usual, I don't have any say in that.'

The truth of Leah's next words cripples me. 'You were the one who abandoned your wife and kids, Vince. Not me.'

CHAPTER 19: THE GRANDMOTHER

Vincent Spencer and I have never met in person, but I could tell right away who he was based on the girls' reaction when they saw him outside the church. He's not at all how I imagined, I must say. Call me a snob, but I was expecting a scruffy, tattooed thug that stunk of cigarettes and weed. Not this smart, rather handsome, and unassuming man standing in front of me. His face lit up when he caught sight of the girls and before I could stop them, they rushed up to embrace him. He seemed genuinely happy to see them and they him, but he doesn't fool me. Not for a split second.

I know he was at Scarlet's house the night she was killed. Alice was certain that she saw and heard her father, despite Daisy's vehement denials, but I'm inclined to believe Alice over Daisy, who is unquestionably a daddy's girl. It's natural for her to want to protect her father. I understand that. But at what cost? I'm still not sure what to do about this most recent discovery. The only thing stopping me from reporting it to the police is my fear that Daisy will run away, as she threatened to do last night.

I realise I have no idea what to think anymore as I stroll over and find myself staring at him while I wait for what I anticipate will be an awkward introduction that will be about as enjoyable as discovering aphids running wild on my runner bean plants. He doesn't look like someone capable of hurting anybody. But then again, who does? Looks can be misleading as we all know. Take me for instance. My neighbours consider me to be the most kind, devout, and charitable of older ladies, yet I too have my secrets.

Scarlet's ex is considerably shorter and a lot less heavy than she was. This convinces me that someone as strong and head-strong as her could easily have given him a whipping. However, I'm forgetting all of the physical abuse he was accused of inflict-ing on her and the 999 calls she made. He must suffer from "small man syndrome", I decide rather smugly.

'Mrs Castle, I take it.' He holds out a hand with surpris-ingly clean, neat fingernails, but I don't grasp it in mine. I can't bring myself to.

'Yes, and you must be Vincent, the girls' father?' *And Scarlet's abuser!*

He nods solemnly and retracts his hand. 'I'm sorry to have to meet you in such circumstances.'

'Yes, well, shall we all go inside.' I glance pointedly at the children, dressed all in black with straightened, glossy hair hanging down their backs. Daisy has been made to wear a dress but she's less than happy about it. I keep telling her to walk straight and keep her shoulders up but she continues to slouch, seemingly intent on annoying me.

'You're coming for tea and sandwiches afterwards, Dad, aren't you? At the social club.' Daisy insists, gripping hold of his hand tightly. I try to ignore the jealous ripple that travels along my nerve endings. And the overwhelming desire to slap his hand away from hers.

'If that's all right with your grandmother,' Vince mutters humbly, glancing at his polished, inky-black shoes rather than at me.

'Of course,' I lie, for the children's sake, gesturing for them to move forward as we are currently holding up an impatient queue of mourners behind us, who are waiting to file into church. None of whom are familiar to me. We're all hot and sticky in our black mourning clothes and I, for one, itch to be inside, within St Botolph's cooling, stone walls.

I fuss over the girls like a busy mother hen once we are inside and sitting in our designated front pew seats. I make sure they have handkerchiefs and ask them frequently, too frequently, whether they're okay. Naturally, they aren't as it is their mother's funeral. But one has to ask anyway. Fortunately, we managed to lose Vincent Spencer on the way in and he is currently seated behind us. I watch, out of the corner of my eye, as he fidgets with his shirt collar and tie, as though it is too tight, and shuffles about in his seat. He appears to be just as uneasy in the church as the devil himself would be. Perhaps it's guilt. Daisy keeps bothering him by turning around to whisper loudly, and eventually, I have to point out how inappropriate this is, given where we are. After that, she sends daggers my way, but at least she does as she's told. That's mainly because her dad keeps throwing her warning glances as if advising her to follow my instructions, even though he is the cause of the disruption.

When the Reverend takes her place at the podium and motions for the congregation to stand, there are whispers and murmurs as everyone gets to their feet. Before long, all heads are turning to witness the flower-laden coffin being carried through the worn-out oak doors. That's when I realise how packed the church is. Not a single seat is empty, and several mourners are forced to stand. This seems at odds with what I know of Scarlet's later years. She was reclusive and had no friends, according to the girls and the police. As a result, I can't help but wonder who all these people are. I certainly haven't invited them. All I can surmise is that they are here out of curiosity. It's not often that a young woman is murdered in her home while her two young children are supposedly soundly sleeping close by. These people's, these imposters', filmy blue eyes and black attire remind me of waiting vultures.

I lower my head as the coffin goes by, more out of shame at the girls' choice of music than out of respect. I might be prudish and old-fashioned, but Celine Dion's 'My Heart Will Go On' is tacky and unfit for a funeral in my opinion. Although I would have preferred something more traditional, like a hymn, Daisy and Alice were insistent, so who was I to argue? Since Scarlet passed away, all of my attention has been focused on making sure her children feel welcome and have everything they need. I haven't had time to process my own feelings or even let myself reflect on Scarlet's demise. *Someone has to put those poor dear girls first for once.*

I give myself permission to cry silently now, thinking of those I have lost, while the girls' heartbroken gazes follow the path of their mum's casket. Sensing that I am being watched, I glance back three aisles to where a tall, elegant woman with caramel hair is staring at me. She looks very well-to-do in her classic black jersey dress and pearls — far more than most others here. The woman, who appears to be around my age, only much more fashionably dressed, hesitantly waves and mouths almost excitedly, "It's me." But I have no idea who she is. Her long, pointy face, thin lips and chiselled cheekbones are unfamiliar, but I have an instinctive feeling that her presence could signal danger for me.

The air around me becomes hostile and I feel suddenly cold. Who is she? An unwanted blast from the past maybe? I tear my eyes away without acknowledging her and I continue to ignore her in the hope that she will go away. I find myself fervently praying that she doesn't turn up at the wake afterwards. *The last thing I need is somebody recognising me now, after all this time.*

CHAPTER 20: THE FATHER

Yvonne Castle is not so very different to what I was expecting. The woman Scarlet once described as cold and austere is an intimidating figure. When I looked into her intelligent eyes for the first time, I sensed a ruthlessness in them that topped even Leah's. It took my breath away. And yet, her eyes soften whenever her possessive gaze alights on my daughters. This makes me think that they are her weakness, just as they are mine. Which means we have more in common than we think. That doesn't mean she doesn't scare me shitless though, because she does.

I might not buy into the tearful, grieving mother image she portrays, which has moved so many of those present, but I can admit that she has her good points. One of them is making sure my daughters are well taken care of. Everyone seems to have a soft spot for the old bat. Even Alice. Like father, like daughter, only Daisy and I remain suspicious and unconvinced. But we're probably still unfairly judging her through Scarlet's eyes. And let's not forget when it came to her parents, Scarlet could be pretty cold and unforgiving herself. As a self-confessed spoilt only child, I sometimes wonder if stubbornness and pride got in the way of her better judgement.

The one thing that gets my back up more than any other is that my former mother-in-law is capable of providing my girls with a far better life than I am. That doesn't make me want them back any less, though, but it does make me wonder if I am being selfish. If I were a better parent, I'd put their needs above my own. So far, I haven't had the balls to approach the girls' granny again, whose time is being taken up by a tall, graceful woman in a black dress who looks like she may have been a model in a past life. Meanwhile, Alice doesn't budge from the buffet and is filling her face with crustless cucumber sandwiches and miniature Melton Mowbray pork pies. When she catches me staring, she grins mischievously and I feel my heart swell.

'Dad, when can we come home?' Daisy tugs at my hand, pleading. Since my arrival at the village hall, feeling out of my depth and unsure of myself, she hasn't left my side.

'Is that what you want, love?' I ask softly, sipping weak-as-piss tea from a bone china cup — not something I'm used to. With a trembling clatter, I set it down on a table, wanting badly to get out of here.

'I don't mean *your* house. I mean The Green,' she complains, leaning into me and nearly toppling me over in the process. Even though she's just nine years old, she's almost as tall as me.

'Aren't you happy at your granny's?' I smile at her, thinking how squeaky clean and pretty she looks, which is a first for my tomboy daughter. 'Alice told me that you have a big garden to play in and your own bedroom and everything.' I'm trying to sound excited for her benefit rather than mine.

'She has a cat but she knows I'm allergic,' Daisy scowls.

I frown. 'You are? Since when?'

Daisy shakes her head and holds out both of her arms, saying, 'Since I moved in. Look. It makes me break out in a rash.'

'Hmm, maybe not today though, Daisy, huh?' I grin, seeing nothing on her milky white skin, which would suggest that she is making it up.

84

'I get asthma too from the cat's fur,' she continues in a tight voice as she deliberately coughs and makes a fake choking motion. 'It amounts to child abuse and you should let social services know.'

'Let me talk to your granny first, okay?' I offer.

Daisy rolls her eyes. 'Don't call her that.'

'Mrs Castle then,' I chuckle conspiratorially.

'Okay,' she groans. 'But seriously, when are we going to come and live with you?'

I sigh and clench my eyes shut before responding, 'That's just not possible right now.'

'Why not?' Daisy whines, pulling a face.

'Because, well . . .' I stammer.

'Leah doesn't want us,' Daisy bluntly finishes my sentence, causing me to wince.

'She's just had a baby and isn't herself at the moment,' I offer feebly, feeling my face flush.

Daisy mulls this over, narrowing her eyes the way her mother would have done. 'Do you promise that you won't leave us with her forever?' Her gaze shifts accusingly to Yvonne Castle as she says this.

'I promise.' I gulp, unsure if I will ever be able to commit to this.

'Do you swear on it? Hand on heart.' She doesn't give up easily.

'I swear.' I laugh, trying to disguise the black gap in my front teeth while placing one hand on my heart, which breaks a little more.

That at least gets a smile from her, until all of a sudden Daisy is frowning and looking worried again.

I feel a surge of alarm. 'What is it, Daisy?'

'Alice told Mrs Castle about you being in the house that night . . . you know, when we found Mum. She said she woke up and saw you . . . us.'

Something inside me dies when I hear this. As if things couldn't get any worse! But I can't allow Daisy to feel like she's in any way to blame, so I say firmly, seeming like I know what I'm talking about, 'Leave it to me, I'll explain.' *Explain what exactly.* That I lied to the police about my whereabouts that night or that I discovered Scarlet's body long before they did. Bang goes mine and Leah's alibi. *If I wasn't fucked before, I am now.*

I stealthily scan the busy village hall to make sure no one is watching, then I take out a small box from my pocket and give it to Daisy, indicating with a finger to my mouth that it is a secret. 'This is for you, so you can contact me whenever you want to . . .'

When Daisy opens the box and sees that it is a cheap, used mobile phone, she gasps. Then she glances over at her grand-mother before hissing, 'I'm not allowed a phone, she said . . .'

Shushing her, I advise, 'It's our secret. Nobody else needs to know. And even if Mrs Castle were to find out about the phone, you wouldn't get into trouble for it. I'd make sure of that.'

Daisy murmurs uncertainly, 'Okay,' while glancing around anxiously for her grandmother, who has since vanished from view.

'There's absolutely nothing for you to worry about, Daisy,' I reassure her. 'You didn't do anything wrong that night and, even if you had, I'm your dad and it's my job to keep you safe. I won't ever let anything bad happen to you.' As I say this, I also find myself glancing around for Mrs Castle, unable to shake off an increasing sense of dread.

CHAPTER 21: THE GRANDMOTHER

There's a poisonous crush of smokers outside the social club where I've come to escape the annoying woman in the black dress, who is turning out to be unshakeable. Heaven knows that I try my best to live as a Christian woman, but this, this . . . is a challenge. She won't take a hint, let alone an outright rude "excuse me but I must mingle" and follows me everywhere. Even out here. I had a hard time placing her at the church but as soon as she identified herself as Georgina Bell, the memories came flooding back, and I don't want to spend my time festering in the past.

'We must meet up for coffee soon, Yvonne,' Georgina insists, sweeping back her poker-straight hair with her left hand. A hand that boasts a trio of sparkling rings that declare she is still very much married, while I wear my wedding ring for show only.

Forcing a smile, I try to inject enthusiasm into my voice as I agree, 'We must,' but my gaze keeps returning to the door looking for an escape route. Why this woman is pretending to be a long-lost friend is beyond me. If I remember rightly, she probably only met me three times in total.

'I can't believe how long it's been.' Her plummy voice floats above everyone else's causing the huddle of smokers to turn and gape at us.

'Oh, I know,' I agree, my forehead creasing with the beginnings of a headache. 'We haven't seen each other since Charles's retirement do.'

'Goodness, that must have been fifteen years ago.'

I nod, even though she's incorrect. It was actually sixteen years ago.

'After learning about Scarlet from a friend — a dreadful business I must say — I had to come, hoping to see you, of course. By the way, I was very sorry to hear of Charles's passing. I do miss him so. We would have attended the funeral if we hadn't been travelling in Bora Bora at the time.'

Mustering a weak smile, I ask, 'How is George?' It was impossible to forget George and Georgina as a couple because of the similarity in their names. I think that was deliberate on her part. She always loved being the centre of attention. When she first started working with Charles as Head of English, she was unlikeable then, and it seems that nothing has changed. She would gossip about people behind their backs and was frequently rude. I assume that her obsession with Charles was the only reason she tried, and failed, to befriend his wife. Georgina was clearly still infatuated with Charles, despite being rejected by him years ago when they were at university together.

'Recovering from his latest heart attack, I'm afraid. Who'd have thought both of our husbands would end up with heart disease?' Georgina confides, a strained smile on her lips, before unexpectedly sniggering, 'Do you remember Charles used to joke that you would end up killing him with your love of cooking? Turns out he was right. You always were a feeder.'

I say nothing, thinking it best. It's a below-the-belt comment and she knows it. She looks me up and down, paying particular attention to my walking stick — which I know ages me — before adding with an unpleasant sneer, 'I must admit I hardly recognised you when I first saw you.'

Even though I assume she's referring to my weight gain, my skin prickles and a sense of unease slides over me. What an awful woman she is to remind me of how I've let myself go on the day of my daughter's funeral. This knowledge is like a knife in my side. 'Whereas you, on the other hand, haven't changed at all.'

She remains rooted to the spot, delighting in receiving such a compliment, which she obviously thinks alludes to her not ageing, but her eyes cloud with confusion as I declare loudly, 'I love what you've done with your hair. How do you get it to come out of your nostrils like that?'

Her steely gunmetal eyes narrow to slits at the insult, while others around us snort into their hands and look away. My temples no longer thrum with the impending headache, but I'm unable to keep the irritation from my voice as I say sharply, 'Now if you'll excuse me, I really must go and find my granddaughters.'

However, as I thrust open the door to the club and march inside, shoulders erect with tension, the smirk vanishes from my face. Was it wise of me to make an enemy of her? My stomach is in knots due to the possibility of her retaliating, but what power does she have over me? None to be precise. And even if she were to suspect me of something, what proof does she have? I have meticulously covered my tracks every step of the way and there is not a court in this land that would find Yvonne Castle — a loyal, loving, and devoted widow — guilty of harming anyone. Knowing that my secret is safe for now, I go in search of Daisy and Alice.

I spot Alice almost immediately because she's still hovering around the buffet where I saw her earlier. I can't help thinking if she's not careful, she'll end up as portly as me.

I'm about to approach her with the intention of luring her away from the calorific pastries and pies when I notice Daisy and her father exchanging secrets in a corner of the room. That's how it looks to me anyway and Lord knows I have a radar for such things. Both of them are hunched over and whispering behind their hands. When I see Daisy fumbling with a box before sliding it guiltily into her pocket, my interest is aroused, so I make my way over to them.

I startle them both, causing them to jump in alarm, when I ask, 'What have you got there, Daisy?'

'Nothing,' she declares, clenching her jaw determinedly.

Vincent's rumbled face and alert eyes catch my attention, and Daisy's irate look at being caught out has me concluding that they must think I was born yesterday. They should know not to underestimate me. Obviously, it's working too well, this sweet, harmless-old-lady persona that I put on every morning and take off only when I'm by myself in my bedroom at night.

Daisy is trying to hide something from me, but I know where she stores her precious things, so I decide to let it go for the time being, knowing I'll eventually get my hands on whatever it is. It would horrify her to know that I have already discovered the secrets she keeps hidden under her mattress. Such as the colourful friendship bracelet given to her by a former friend, a hand-written love letter from a boy called Ben, aged nine, and a photo of her parents taken on their wedding day. Another of her mother sitting on the front doorstep of 7 The Green . . . a grainy black-and-white image of a white face, a serious expression, and a worn-out smile that paints a depressing picture of mental illness in the modern world.

Daisy is prone to being secretive and mysterious, just like me. Another thing we have in common is that she doesn't give her trust or her heart away easily. If nothing else, the girl is a challenge, but am I up to it? Or will I fail her as Scarlet was failed? While Alice is easy to love, I've come to realise that love that comes easily is also easily lost. Contrarily, we put in more effort to win the approval of the more difficult, darker individuals. *Most people have a dark side and I'm no different.*

CHAPTER 22: THE FATHER

I panicked when Mrs Castle crept up on us out of the blue like that, and I'm sure Daisy did too, judging by her guilty-as-charged expression. Luckily, she managed to slip the phone into her pocket before her grandmother saw it, so I think we just about got away with it. Thank fuck. Cheeks red with embarrassment at almost being caught red-handed, Daisy then quickly ran off to join her sister, leaving us two adults alone for the first time.

'It was a good send-off,' I mumble. 'I'm sure Scarlet would have been pleased. Especially with the song choice. She loved Celine Dion and must have seen that movie a hundred times.'

Deep lines furrow Mrs Castle's brow as she asks, 'What movie?'

'*Titanic*,' I reply, but I can see from her frown that she has never heard of it.

'Anyway,' I sigh, glancing around for any sign of my daughters, who have since disappeared, 'I suppose we ought to talk about the girls.'

'I suppose so,' she agrees with an even bigger sigh, and I try not to make eye contact as her critical gaze slides over me.

'Shall we?' I gesture, in what I hope is a gentlemanly manner to an empty table and she nods sharply before leading the way. As I follow her, I can see that the majority of the mourners have already left, but Scarlet's neighbours, who make up the remaining group of about twelve, are still present at the free bar, making this a proper Nene Fields turnout. "Waifs and strays," she used to call them. You can't beat an old-fashioned, working-class wake. I doubt the church would have done well out of today's congregation though. I smile when I consider that half the people here are more likely to have nicked the cash out of the church collection box than contribute to it. Also, I can't help but wonder what happened between my ex-mother-in-law and the woman I saw earlier; the latter who disappeared out of the door a few minutes ago in a flood of tears. But that's to be expected at a funeral, I suppose. I'm not sure what her connection to Scarlet is though. More likely she's a friend of Mrs Castle's . . .

'Can I get you a drink?' I offer politely as she settles into a chair.

She responds with an unpleasant smile. 'I don't drink but please don't let that stop you. I expect you're dying for one.'

The bitch is right, of course, but I'm not going to let her know that, so I sit down stubbornly. My legs feel like jelly but the rest of me is rigid with pent-up anger. She was bang out of order for talking to me like that.

Her voice quivers with emotion when she eventually mumbles, 'I'm sorry. I was completely out of order for speaking to you like that.'

It's like she can read my mind. But maybe I misjudged her. She doesn't have to apologise, and if our roles were reversed, I doubt I would.

I'm the one who breaks the long silence that stretches between us, by saying shakily, 'That's okay.'

'What specifically did you want to talk about?' she prompts efficiently.

I have to avert my eyes as I explain, 'Well, as you're probably aware I'm in no position at the moment to have the girls come and live with me. But I'm hoping things will change in the future . . . you know, when I get a job or someone gives me a break.'

Am I testing her? Is that what I'm doing? Putting my toe in the water to see if she'll help me out. Man, how low can I go? Scum, that's what robbing a defenceless old woman would make me.

'Anyway, in the meantime, I was hoping to have them at the weekends,' I finish lamely, wanting the floor to open up and swallow me.

'To stay over at your house?' she interrogates, picking up one of the cardboard beer mats and ruthlessly shredding it.

'No. We don't have room for them at ours, not with a new baby an' all.' Our eyes lock as I say this and I swear she can tell I'm lying because there's no way I'm going to admit that my live-in girlfriend won't allow it. 'Just during the day on a Saturday or Sunday, if that works for you.'

Mrs Castle leans back in her chair and appraises me, as if I were a rival competitor at a village vegetable show, before announcing, 'Daisy, Alice and I are still getting to know one another, therefore I would much prefer it if they didn't spend the night in any case.'

My heart thuds in my ribcage as I mutter, 'Good. That's settled then?'

She nods. 'Will you take them to your house for the day? I'd like to know what your plans are.'

I squirm in embarrassment as I admit, 'They won't be coming back to mine because of the baby, so I'll be taking them out for the day.'

'That sounds expensive,' she acknowledges.

'I'll figure it out somehow.'

She rolls her eyes. 'I'm sure you will.'

I'm not sure if she's taking the piss out of me or not, but before I can reply, she beats me to it—

'I'll give you a hundred pounds every Saturday when you collect them so you can do something nice with them.'

93

To say I'm gobsmacked is no exaggeration. She's just handed me a get-out-of-jail-free card because now I can go back to Leah feeling like a winner.

'That's very kind of you,' I manage to say.

'Oh, there's nothing kind about it.' She easily brushes me off, puffing out her cheeks in annoyance. 'I want my grandchildren to be properly looked after, that's all. And I shall want to see the receipts, mind. Meals. Petrol. Any admission fees to parks or museums, that sort of thing.'

Fuck. And bollocks. They say never look a gift horse in the mouth and I had done exactly that. She's a wise woman, I'll give her that. She must have guessed that some of that money would have gone on fags and beer or cash in my pocket for Leah to buy cosmetics. Even nappies for the baby.

'May I be frank with you, Vincent?' she asks, narrowing her eyes at me.

'Please do,' I sigh, wondering if I will regret it.

'You must know that I never approved of my daughter marrying you. My late husband didn't think you were good enough and I shared that view.'

'Because I was poor?' I grumble at the injustice.

'Not just because of that, although I admit it was a factor. But once we found out about the drug use and the abusive behaviour . . .'

I can feel my cheeks growing hot with shame. I won't interrupt this time because I don't have anything to defend myself with. Rather, I let her keep destroying my reputation. Such as it is.

'As you are aware, I vowed not to speak to Scarlet again until she came to her senses about you. But she never did, or if she did, she was too proud to admit it. You'll be thinking that she gets that from me no doubt, we were both as stubborn as each other.'

I nod thoughtfully, watching her draw circles on the floor with the end of her walking stick. 'I can see that.'

'In any case, I can't undo the past but I do regret how we treated her. We made a mistake cutting her off like that, and

I intend to make up for it.' Tears sparkle in her eyes as she sits up straighter in her chair.

'So, you are human after all?' I jest, thinking there's a small chance we could wind up getting along. Not exactly friends, but friendly. Her next words wipe the floor with me.

'But I'm no pushover, so don't expect to receive any more money from me, other than what we've agreed upon today.'

CHAPTER 23: THE GRANDMOTHER

Even though I have just accused the man in front of me of being after my money, I do wonder whether my suspicions are unfounded. Does he want money, or does he genuinely have feelings for the girls? It's hard to figure him out. But Vincent Spencer must have some positive traits to have captured Scarlet's heart. She obviously saw something special in him to want to spend the rest of her life with him as well as bear his children.

The girls do not speak well of their so-called stepmother but neither has a bad word to say about their father. That must have some significance. It's not like I can stop him from seeing them anyway. Since he is their biological father, the girls have a right to visit him and vice versa. More's the pity. He might not come across as the villain I've always pictured him to be, but I will remain on my guard until I discover what his true motives are regarding the girls. A sickening sense of guilt consumes me whenever I think of Scarlet and what happened to her. Therefore, I've vowed to do all that I can to keep her children safe.

When Vincent suddenly scrapes back his chair and heads to the bar, I don't expect him to come back, but he does, a few minutes later, with a pint of frothy Guinness and an even bigger chip on his shoulder. He lowers himself onto his seat, takes a big mouthful of his drink, and uses the back of his hand to wipe his mouth. There's something grey and depressing about him. His pale face and shattered eyes remind me of Daisy.

As though he were going to make a big announcement, he shuffles forward in his chair and places both palms on the table. When he sees me staring at the snarling wolf tattoo on his neck, just visible beneath his collar, he goes still and his chin jerks upwards. His voice has a hard edge to it as he says, 'I was hoping to talk to you about the cat.'

I blanch at this. 'Do you mean *my* cat, Hero?'

He nods and clears his throat, observing, 'Interesting name for a cat.'

Rattled, I shoot back, 'What has my cat got to do with you?'

He switches his attention back to his pint glass and murmurs, 'Daisy is allergic.'

'Since when?' I bark, louder than I intended.

I feel his body tense next to me as he stammers awkwardly, 'Since she moved in apparently.'

My mouth curls into a grimace as I reply, 'Nonsense. The social worker would have informed me if that were the case.'

'Maybe she's always been allergic, but since we never owned a cat, it went unnoticed,' he suggests reasonably.

But I can tell he doesn't believe it any more than I do. Either way, he has me wrapped around his finger — or rather, Daisy does — and he is aware of it. Because I will not be allowed to keep my beloved cat if he is the source of Daisy's medical condition.

'What symptoms does she have, and why didn't she tell me?' I insist.

He explains patiently, 'I think she was too scared to say anything in case it upset you, but she reckons his fur is giving her asthma and bringing her out in a rash on her arms and legs. I'm surprised that you haven't noticed she goes out of her way to avoid him.'

Even if he is right about Daisy's aversion to Hero, I can't help but glower at him. My voice crackles with rage as I launch my counterattack. 'Are you implying that my granddaughter is frightened of me? Or that I'm neglecting her general health?' *How dare he criticise me when he's an absent parent, cheater, smoker, and former drug addict?*

He recoils from me as if I've just punched him, before sighing, 'Hey, don't shoot the messenger, okay?'

My mouth is as dry as sand as I explode, 'Well, I also have a message for you, Vincent Spencer.' Before I wade in any further, I pause for breath.

'The girls told me you were at the house the night Scarlet died.'

He keeps his voice low, his look furtive as he replies, 'Everyone knows I was there that day and that we had an argument about child maintenance. All of this is documented in my witness statement.'

Hearing this, my brain jerks into action, realising that he has just tried to pull the wool over my eyes. 'But the police are unaware that you returned to the house later that night when the girls were asleep in bed.'

'This isn't news to me, Mrs Castle. Daisy told me what Alice said to you about me being there. But I can assure you she must have dreamed it—'

'No. I don't think so,' I interject sharply. 'You were there and the fact that you lied about it makes you a person of interest again.'

He lets out a long exhale. 'I swear on the girls' lives I never touched Scarlet.'

'Isn't that what you used to tell the police after giving her a black eye?'

'That was different,' he sulks as if he knows he is beaten. 'How?'

His eyes flash with something like regret as he explains, 'Your daughter could be violent. I had no choice but to defend myself at times.'

Rolling my eyes, I sneer, 'And you expect me to believe that?'

With a challenge in his eyes, he demands, 'So how come you haven't gone to the police with this already?'

'Because we both know Daisy will never forgive me if I do,' I hiss, my face crumpling. 'Besides, I figure that if it *was* you that harmed Scarlet, the police will catch you in the end without any assistance from me.'

At that moment, the girls decide to dash over to the table. Breathless and with rosy cheeks, they both laugh uncontrollably as they hurl themselves into Vincent's arms, and he responds by acting as though they are overpowering him. As Alice settles on his lap and Daisy hangs onto his hand, my insides twitch with envy as I realise I've come to regard them as *my girls*. For want of a better word, they appear content. But that's only because their father is present as there's no getting away from the fact that today is a sad day for them as they are burying their mother.

'It looks like I'll have you all to myself on Saturday, girls. What do you fancy doing?' he remarks casually, without looking at me.

Daisy fixes her bright green eyes on me, and asks, 'Are we allowed?'

'Of course,' I chuckle as if the idea were as delightful to me as it is to them, even though nothing could be further from the truth.

'Thank you, Granny,' Alice playfully shrieks, wriggling on her father's lap, trying to escape his tickling hands.

'Maybe we ought to double the fee given the circumstances?' Vincent mutters while glancing at me.

Perplexed, I enquire, 'What do you mean?'

'How about we call it two hundred pounds a day instead?' With a deliberate sideways glance at the girls, he remarks, 'I think they're worth that much, don't you?'

His words are like a weight around my heart and I have to press a palm to my chest to stop it from pounding. It appears that his true intention is to blackmail me after all now that he knows I have no intention of reporting his late-night visit to Scarlet's house to the police. Which means I'm not the one calling the shots anymore, and I don't like that one little bit. I underestimated him and I won't be making the same mistake again.

Relief rushes through me when he remarks with a devilish laugh, 'Hey, relax, Yvonne, I'm just kidding. You didn't take me seriously, did you?' He acts shocked as he continues in the same vein, 'That would make me a common criminal, someone capable of blackmail. Or worse.'

CHAPTER 24: THE FATHER

I've come home to an empty house *again* and had to open all the curtains and blinds to let the light in, thanks to my blood-sucking shapeshifter of a girlfriend. For all her talk this morning of me asking the girls' grandmother for money, Leah didn't stick around to find out the outcome. To make matters worse, the sink is full of dirty dishes, the bin is overflowing and the entire house stinks of fried food, so I open the down-stairs windows to let some fresh air in. And then tackle the washing-up so I can make myself something to eat, because there are no plates left in the cupboard.

Fifteen minutes later, I'm wolfing down a fried egg sand-wich with a dollop of tomato sauce on top and wondering if Leah has gone shopping as there's hardly any food in the fridge. Since it's the last day of the month, our combined uni-versal credit payment should have been paid today. Our bank balance was down to a pitiful £3.92 when I checked it last night. That's not even enough to buy a tin of baby formula.

We'll live like kings and queens for a week as usual, then spend the rest of the month being piss-poor. It's no way to survive. But at least payday gives us something to look forward to. I can top up my phone, restore our Netflix account, order a Chinese takeaway, and grab a few beers for tonight. There'll be a new Babygro for Saffy and Leah will treat herself to a lip gloss or a fake designer purse. It's not like she needs any new stuff but if it makes her happy, even for a short time, that's what it's all about, isn't it?

Since Leah insisted I stop paying child maintenance when Scarlet passed away, I'm curious as to whether it will be diverted to Yvonne Castle instead. It's not like the rich old bag needs my £15.40 a week. As Scarlet loved to tell me, "You couldn't keep a dog on that money." *Expensive dog*, I'd once commented unhelpfully, but at least I paid something, or rather the government did since it came out of our benefits.

I probably shouldn't have wound Mrs Castle up about wanting more money — just for seeing my kids — but she asked for it by insinuating, *a big word for me*, that this had always been my plan. Fuck knows I'm better than that. Even though I've had arguments with Leah over it, I'd already made up my mind that I would not stoop so low as to blackmail my children's grandmother. I won't pretend it hadn't crossed my mind though, more than once, but I wouldn't want Daisy or Alice to think badly of me. They're good kids at the end of the day and given the chance, I think I could be a decent dad to them. All I need is a good job to set me up for the future. But there's fat chance of that happening. Not when I lack any sort of qualifications, skills or experience.

I scroll through the employment sites on my phone and search for "no skills needed jobs in Peterborough", as if to prove this to myself. I'm quickly notified of a bunch of care and production vacancies, but none of them pay nearly as much as our benefits package, so I wouldn't be able to afford the rent, let alone anything else. Although I don't fancy washing old people's arses, I could pack fresh produce into boxes. How hard can it be? Given that we have a baby, I'm sure the government would boost our income if it doesn't pay enough to cover all our bills. As a working man, Leah would have to show me some respect then. But when I consider how much she is struggling to cope with Saffy at the moment, it doesn't seem like such a good idea leaving her alone every day.

Instead, I could consider volunteering one or two days a week, perhaps working for the Samaritans, to gain experience. If Leah ever finds out that I've called them in the past just to have someone to talk to, she'll piss herself laughing. I've even sobbed down the phone before. I've never felt suicidal exactly but I sympathise with those who do. That's probably because I lived with Scarlet for so long and witnessed her desperation up close. I regret not helping her more, but since I was burnt out myself, I felt I had to prioritise my own needs. Selfish, I know. If I could have my time again, I would never have left her with two young children to bring up. But I can't regret having Saffy. She means as much to me as Daisy and Alice. I wished I'd done better at school so I could have gone to college or university and trained to become a mental health nurse or something like that. Helping people must be so rewarding and I think I'd be good at it . . .

Leah is right when she accuses me of being a "daydreamer". She's got me all figured out too when she says I'm too soft for my own good. If I were the big, tough man she seems to want me to be, like Wayne, then I would have no qualms about blackmailing an old woman. But I'm forgetting one thing. Yvonne Castle has something on me. Nothing is stopping her from informing the police where I was the night Scarlet died. Then I'll be screwed. Not only me but Leah too for giving me a false alibi in the first place. It would be just our luck if poor Saffy ended up with both her parents behind bars. Some people around here, Leah's mother being one of them, might think that was better for the baby in the long run. She could be right.

I wish I could shake off the gloom of my situation, but then I realise that Mrs Castle could be in as much trouble as I am for not informing the police of my real whereabouts. Hasn't she perjured herself by not doing so? My best bet is to try and persuade Alice I wasn't there that night and that she must have dreamt it. To convince her, I'll need Daisy's help.

I mustn't forget her involvement in all of this. Protecting her is my top priority.

Morally speaking, I have the upper hand over Mrs Castle because, if she really believes that I killed Scarlet, she has demonstrated, by not dobbing me in to the police, that she would rather allow her daughter's killer to walk free than risk losing custody of her grandchildren. Why would she do that? More out of spite than anything, I'm guessing, because she doesn't come across as a caring, loving granny, let alone a grieving mother. She makes out that she's a kind, harmless old woman but she doesn't fool me. She's a cold bitch that one. Her excuse for not grassing me up to the police when she must be dying to do so doesn't ring true. Worrying about upsetting Daisy is a pathetic lie. This implies that she must have another reason for wanting to avoid talking to the police. But what could a well-respected, law-abiding citizen like her have to fear from the cops? What is she hiding?

CHAPTER 25: THE GRANDMOTHER

I jump in alarm and drop the key on the floor when from behind me a small inquisitive voice demands, 'Why do you keep that door locked?'

Daisy is standing just behind me, staring at the door to my attic office, as I turn to gawk at her. She's biting her lower lip and her arms are crossed over her chest in a defensive stance.

'Daisy! You scared me half to death,' I exclaim, clasping a hand to my racing heart while leaning against the wall for support. I've misplaced my pesky walking stick again. My hip is on the mend so I don't need it quite as much as I used to. But shocks like this, I'm not up to.

'Sorry,' she mutters, colour creeping up her neck to match her hair shade. But she doesn't *sound* sorry.

'It's where I store all my important documents. That's why the door is locked. To keep them safe,' I explain amicably, pondering why she doesn't move. The child seems determined to obstruct my path.

'From me and Alice?' She scowls.

'Not at all,' I bluster, thinking, "pot calling kettle" when I've found out the little minx is concealing a secret phone under her mattress that her father must have given her this afternoon. 'Would you like to see inside?'

She nods after initially seeming uncertain, as though this was not the reaction she was expecting. I stoop down, grab the key, and open the door while indicating that she should follow. There are a few carpeted steps leading up to the room and then we are inside. Daisy looks around in wonder, at the beamed apex ceiling and large Velux windows which bathe the room in matching stripes of sunlight. There is a built-in bookcase full of books at one end. A polished oak desk sits under one of the windows, guarded by two squashy oxblood leather armchairs.

'Wow. Who owns all those books?'

'I do,' I answer.

'But you said you weren't a reader,' Daisy protests, as if owning all those books and not reading them were a crime.

'I used to read years ago when I was a child,' I tell her, as I cross over to the book cabinet and take a small hardback from the shelf. 'But I admit the majority of these belonged to your grandfather.'

Daisy joins me and looks down at the book's cover. 'He must have liked reading a lot.'

I chuckle and say, 'Well, he was an English Head before he was ever a headteacher. You've most likely inherited his love of books.'

'I must have,' she grins sheepishly, obviously happy with the link. 'Grandfather Castle,' she tries out his name for the first time, even though she's yet to address me by my title, "Granny".

She gasps at the title of the book, *The Lion, the Witch and the Wardrobe*, and then runs her pink fingertips over the early edition's faded cover, which has tattered corners. 'I've read this,' she confides.

'Oh, me too, many years ago, of course. Would you like to read it again?' I ask, holding out the book as if it were a peace offering.

I'm not sure if she shrinks away from the book or from me, but she's reluctant to take it, protesting, 'It's old. Isn't it worth a lot of money?'

'Possibly,' I admit. 'But just because it's old doesn't mean it shouldn't be put to good use. What good is a book on a shelf, Charles used to say.'

'I think I would have liked my grandfather,' she says animatedly.

'And he would have adored you,' I confirm and offer the book to her once more, but she still seems wary of accepting it. Perhaps because she doesn't trust my motives for giving it to her and believes I will expect something in return. Like friendship. It is quite upsetting for someone her age to be so distrusting. I blame her parents for this. Both of them.

'Take it. It's yours,' I insist in a no-nonsense voice. 'And any others you might want to read as well. When you've finished with that one, just let me know and I'll bring you in here so you can choose another.'

She takes the book and holds it to her chest, murmuring, 'Thank you,' without looking at me. And then, 'I promise to look after it.'

'I know you will, Daisy.' I nod as I make my way over to the desk. The poor love is close to tears, and if I don't watch out, she'll have me crying too. To distract us both, I open a desk drawer and show her where all of my paperwork is kept. 'If it weren't for these documents — wills, birth and death certificates and the deeds to the house — I would keep the door unlocked so you could come in whenever you'd like, but as it stands . . .' I trail off, feeling like I don't sound very credible. Because let's be honest, I have more than just a few documents to conceal.

'It's okay—' Daisy pauses and seems to struggle for words before settling on, 'Mrs Castle,' and then goes on to explain, 'I have a younger sister so I know how important it is to have a safe place to keep your things.'

Is it just me, or does her tone sound accusing? If I didn't know any better, I would assume she's worked out that I know where she hides her secrets, but I quickly brush that thought aside. I've been sneaking about covertly for years without ever getting discovered. A child wouldn't be able to figure me out, in my opinion, if the police still can't after all these years.

I tell her, arching my eyebrows, 'You don't have to call me Mrs Castle. For now, will you please call me Yvonne?'

'Yvonne?' she repeats, frowning.

'Yes, if you're happy with that. Mrs Castle seems so formal, considering we're family.'

Daisy looks down at the book in her hands once more before unexpectedly smiling and lifting her bright gaze. 'Okay, Yvonne,' she agrees.

'Excellent.' I smack my lips in approval and pat my apron pockets in celebration. 'Now let's go and see what we can find for supper.'

She dutifully follows me out of the room and waits while I lock the door.

'You go and find your sister and I'll see you back in the kitchen,' I suggest.

'All right, Yvonne,' she says with an innocent smile and goes in search of her sister while calling out loudly, 'Alice, it's supper time.'

Once she's gone, I gently open the door to the dining room and slip silently inside. With its gleaming, gothic dining table and chairs and ornately carved cabinets brimming with diamond-cut glassware, this little used room is noticeably darker than the rest of the house. The thick, floor-to-ceiling brocade drapes are partly drawn, adding to the mood of gloom. As I approach the Victorian tiled open fireplace, the almost black, polished wooden flooring creaks beneath my feet.

As I'm about to put the key to my office back in its hiding place — inside the open grate of the fireplace — where no one would ever think to look for it, I hear a squeaking sound behind me, as if someone else had just entered the room and stepped on the same creaking floorboard as me. I take a deep breath, wondering if Daisy has sneakily crept back to see where I hide the key so she can access my personal belongings when I'm not there, perhaps as payback for my doing the same to her. When I turn around, intent on catching her out, nobody is there. Yet, I could have sworn . . .

CHAPTER 26: THE FATHER

We're all together as a family for a change, lazing on the sofa and tucking into our Chinese takeaway. Saffy is in her bouncy chair, gummily chewing at her knuckles and blowing milky bubbles. When I hear someone knocking loudly on the front door, I almost shit myself in case it's the police. Until I can persuade Yvonne Castle that I wasn't at the house the night Scarlet was killed and that Alice was mistaken when she thought she saw me there, the threat of being arrested, or even charged for murder, is never far away. I obviously can't count on Mrs Castle staying silent forever.

As I climb to my feet and creep over to the door, I put a finger to my mouth and shoot Leah a warning look. With a sweet and sour chicken ball paused halfway to her greasy mouth, she silently mouths the question that is mirrored in her panicked eyes, 'Pigs?' Shrugging helplessly, *because how the fuck should I know*, I close the inner door behind me. Before I can answer the front door, the letter box rattles open and a smoky, familiar, once-dreaded voice bellows, 'Spencer, get your arse out here.'

'Gaz,' I utter with astonishment, and a hint of alarm when I open the door to discover none other than Gary Pearce on my doorstep. As usual, he has a shaved head, a face full of stubble and is kitted out from head to toe in urban streetwear, with a pop of gold bling at his bull-sized neck.

'How are things? I hear you're quite the celeb these days,' he drawls in a practised, phoney Jason Statham accent. He's all about the street cred is our Gaz.

'Huh?' I scowl, feigning ignorance.

'Heard you were pulled in by the pigs because of what happened to your ex.'

'I was just helping them with their enquiries,' I sigh, my humiliating ordeal at DS Mills's hands still vivid in my mind.

'If you say so.' He shrugs disinterestedly as he peers behind me and into the hallway, seemingly attempting to determine whether or not I am alone.

'Leah's in,' I tell him pointedly.

With a furtive nod, he says, 'Okay, mate,' lowering his voice appropriately.

'What can I do for you?' I cut to the chase, worried that Leah might decide to help herself to my beef chow mein while I'm not around. I wouldn't put it past her.

'Got a job for you if you're interested?' he blurts out, taking a drag from his cigarette. Unlike me, he can afford to buy proper fags.

'What sort of job?' I ask suspiciously.

He coughs into his hand before murmuring, 'Commercial premises.'

'You sure it's commercial?'

'Mate, would I lie to you?' He chuckles dirtily. It's the kind of laughter that if you heard it in the pub you'd snigger along. But not when somebody as dangerous as him is standing on your doorstep.

'You know I don't do over people's homes, right?' I hiss, before grinding out, 'Or jobs where anybody gets hurt.'

'Says the honourable thief that could end up doing life for murder.'

'I told you I was just—'

'Helping the police with their enquiries, yeah I know,' he cuts in sarcastically, rolling his fentanyl-infused, bloodshot eyes.

Squinting, I look him up and down, wondering if he's for real. With someone as slimy as him, you can never tell.

'Can I trust you, Gary, because after last time—'

'Kick a man in the balls, why don't you? Fuck,' he mutters in jest, then reaches into his pocket to pull out a bundle of twenties. I close the door behind me so Leah can't hear him as he begins to count out the notes loudly. I swear that girl can smell money a mile away. But if this job goes ahead, she won't be getting her greedy hands on it. I have other plans.

Out of cowardice I haven't broken the bad news to her yet, that Mrs Castle is already on to me and won't be parting with her money any time soon. Instead, I rattled off some lame excuse about warming her up to the idea and left it at that. But when I admitted the daft old bat was picking up the £100 tab for me having the girls every Saturday Leah was dead chuffed, claiming it was a "good start".

Meanwhile, Gary is bragging, 'I'm a man of my word and if that isn't good enough for you, then have a ton on me as a goodwill gesture.'

I shake my head and pull a doubtful face. 'I don't know, Gary.'

'Then, call it two tons.' He counts out another hundred as if it were Monopoly money. 'An advance, if you like.'

The notes are in my hands before he's even finished counting. I don't want to give them back now they're in my possession. Nothing beats the texture of a crisp crease-free note. Or the smell.

'Two hundred quid is a lot of money,' I observe warily, glancing across the street at one of our neighbours who has stopped to admire Gary's shiny black pickup truck. The engine is still running and the driver's window has carelessly been left down. Always on the lookout for trouble, Gary turns to see what I'm staring at and offers the guy a friendly thumbs-up. It would never enter his head that anyone would have the audacity to steal or damage anything that belongs to him.

'Plenty more where that came from,' Gary sniggers, turning back to me and stashing the rest of the notes back in his pocket. At a guess, I'd say he's walking around with at least a grand on him, but once again, somebody like him is in no danger of being robbed. Everybody knows Gary Pearce. And with good reason because cash won't be the only thing he's carrying on his person. I'll bet he's got a four-inch blade on him somewhere too.

My nerves spike as I ask, 'How much is the job worth?'

'Twenty grand four ways.'

'And the other three?'

'You know the score,' Gary reminds me, frowning. 'You'll find out who they are on the night. You in then, or do you need to think about it?'

Do I need to think about it? Five grand for one night's work would be enough to put down a deposit on a rental *and* pay a solicitor to help me get the girls back. But what if something went wrong and I ended up getting caught? I'd go to prison then, for sure, as I've used up all my chances with the courts. There'll be no more fines or community service for me. A conviction for robbery will get me a four or five-year stretch inside. If that happens, I can say goodbye to my girls forever. Leah and the baby too most probably. Who am I kidding? Wayne would be moved in straight away.

They'd probably be better off without me. Daisy. Alice. Saffy. *I'm a waste of space and always have been,* just like Mrs Castle told Scarlet all those years ago. But, if I do manage to pull this job off without getting myself arrested, I'll be quids in. Who knows, I might even get laid.

Before I can change my mind, my fingers instinctively close around the notes and I find myself mumbling, "I'm in."

CHAPTER 27: THE GRANDMOTHER

It's too soon . . . is all I can think as I watch the children clomping downstairs in their immaculate, pressed-to-within-an-inch-of-their-lives school uniforms. While Daisy, predictably, has chosen grey trousers, a white short-sleeved shirt and a purple and grey striped clip-on tie, Alice is dressed in a purple gingham checked summer dress with white ankle socks. Both girls wear plain black sensible shoes and have long ponytails that swing from side to side like a horse's tail.

'You look amazing,' I beam, clapping my hands together in admiration. It's all I can do, to be honest, not to cry. I've come over all emotional and am feeling overwhelmed with pride, which has taken me completely by surprise. *Silly old fool.* Never mind that Daisy is rolling her eyes and shrugging her shoulders like a stroppy teenager. Alice, on the other hand, is now strutting down the last of the steps like a catwalk model.

Following numerous discussions about what was best for the girls, the social worker had overridden me and insisted that they enrol in their new school for the remaining weeks of the summer term, as she claimed it would aid in their healing process. I was inclined to disagree, especially when you consider the poor dears have only just buried their mother, but I decided in the end that it wouldn't do me any good to get on the wrong side of her. But my goodness, the trouble I've had with Daisy over this! As you can imagine, Alice is ecstatic to be starting at her new school and is looking forward to making friends, but beneath Daisy's bored posturing and sour looks, I suspect she is terrified by the prospect. I am too, *for her*.

'I've made your favourite breakfast of scrambled eggs,' I announce in what I hope is a cheerful, encouraging voice, even though I'm feeling anything but. I'm so worried about Daisy. How ever will she cope?

'I don't like eggs. They're disgusting,' Daisy sulks.

'You know that's not true, Daisy. You said you loved them last week,' I tut, marshalling the two girls into the kitchen.

Alice sits down at the table and immediately takes a swig of orange juice. Daisy remains standing, her arms folded tightly across her chest.

'It's stupid having to start at a new school when the term ends in a couple of weeks,' Daisy vocalises for the hundredth time.

'I don't disagree,' I say with a heavy sigh, thinking *not this again*. I then pull out Daisy's chair and tell her to, 'Sit down, love.'

Slumping onto the chair, Daisy swipes a hand across her eyes, which are glittering with unshed tears and then she hangs her head.

As I dish up platefuls of scrambled eggs and toast, Alice instantly tucks in and gives me an eggy grin as I sit down next to her. Daisy refuses to touch her food, but when I squint at her and advise, 'You have to eat something,' she snatches up her knife and fork and begins to viciously stab at her breakfast, decimating it.

'What time are we leaving?' Alice wants to know, seemingly unaware of the tense atmosphere around the table.

After taking a sip of my Earl Grey, from a china cup and saucer, I respond, 'Not until twenty-five to. It's only a short walk.'

Daisy complains, 'I don't see why Dad can't take us.'

In an attempt to be helpful, Alice remarks, 'He lives too far away, silly,' but it's not the response Daisy wanted, and she makes this known by pulling an ugly face. Hunger seems to have got the better of her though, as she starts to nibble on the edge of a slice of toast.

'Dad always takes us to school,' Daisy persists with a clenched jaw.

'Saturday is only a few days away. You'll see him then,' I remind her.

'I want to see him now,' Daisy erupts, slamming down her cutlery and causing bits of scrambled eggs to fly off her plate.

Alice darts a concerned look at her sister, as if to say, "You're in trouble now." But instead of reprimanding Daisy, I ask as gently as I can, 'Would it help if you gave him a quick call now before we leave?'

A tear leaks onto Daisy's cheek, but her eyes soften as she expresses gratefully, 'Yes, please.'

'Go on then, love. You know where the phone is.' When I say this, I'm referring to the landline in the living room not the secret mobile phone she keeps under her mattress, which I'm not meant to know about.

Daisy scrapes back her chair and makes an apologetic attempt at cleaning up bits of scrambled egg from the table before exiting the room.

Alice then mumbles, 'Granny, I'm beginning to think Daisy doesn't want to go to school,' and shakes her head as if the idea were unthinkable.

'You don't say.' I burst out laughing, realising what a delight Alice is and how happy she makes me. Although she's not the most perceptive child, it must be said, not like her sister.

Then, thinking I might have time to load the dishwasher before we have to leave, I get up from the table. Alice is still chattering nonsensically behind me, but I have to admit that I tune out most of it. She would talk non-stop if you let her. But my ears do prick up when she says—

'Granny, where's Hero? I haven't seen him today.'

I freeze on hearing this, but I don't turn around, since I'm afraid I will give myself away. Instead, I chastise, 'Don't talk while you're eating Alice, there's a good girl,' with a mock-serious tone.

'You're not even looking at me,' she objects, sounding deeply offended. 'So how can you tell if I'm eating and talking at the same time?'

This causes me to smile, and I begin stacking the dishwasher as I retaliate with, 'I can tell. That's all you need to know.'

There's a pause behind me as Alice swallows down the rest of her food before asking again, 'So where is Hero?'

Sliding my hand inside my apron pocket, my fingers sentimentally wrap around the blue velvet collar that has a fish-shaped metal ID tag with the word "Hero" engraved on it. Squeezing my eyes shut, I stifle a sob, before uttering, 'I'm sure he's around somewhere.'

CHAPTER 28: THE FATHER

I brush a tear from my eye as I see all the kids walking through the school gates. Normally, I would be one of the parents dropping their kids off, but instead, I'm slouching against a wall with my hands in my pockets feeling like an outsider. Daisy and Alice went to school at the Nene Fields Academy on Soke Drive and I'm the reason they're not here today, surrounded by their childhood pals and favourite teachers. They are going to attend a new school instead where they won't know anyone. I'm told it's a Church of England school and much smaller than this one, which is something at least.

'Come on, Saffy,' I grumble, grabbing the buggy handle and steering it in the direction of The Green. I felt that it would be best if we cleared off for a bit and allowed Leah some quiet time since she's having one of her migraines. Who knows how long we're meant to stay out of the way? I've prepared multiple bottles of formula just in case. Saffy is currently asleep, but if she wakes up and won't settle, we can always drop in at Leah's mum's. In any case, I need to keep busy because I know if I don't, I'll wind up overanalysing everything. Scarlet. The girls. My relationship with Leah. Waiting for Gary Pearce's call to find out when *the job* is going to take place is also messing with my head but I'm a dead man if I chicken out now.

Even though it's the middle of summer, as we turn the corner, the heavens open and it starts pissing down with rain. I almost fall arse over tit on the wet pavement as I run for cover. By the time I reach number 7's front porch, I'm completely soaked. More rain is on its way and there are sporadic cracks of lightning and thunder overhead. When Saffy starts to cry, I realise that rain has seeped into the buggy onto her face. Fuck. Now what? It's just my luck to get caught out in a freak storm with a bawling baby. I feel like I've won the lottery when I realise that I have on the same shorts I was wearing the day Leah gave me back the spare key to my old house. Sure enough, I still have the back door key in my pocket.

We just need to make one more wet dash to the rear of the property, that's all. Once we're inside and Saffy is in my damp arms, I grab one of the still-warm bottles of milk and start feeding her. Her pale blue eyes are fixed on me as she sucks hard on the teat of the bottle. She brings out the caveman in me. I would do anything to keep her safe. As I would every one of my kids. I continue to cradle her in my arms as I check the downstairs rooms for signs of damage or forced entry. The irony of me doing that isn't lost on me considering what I've just signed myself up for . . . another of Pearce's break-ins. As the police have now concluded their searches, I'm no longer in danger of getting into trouble for being here. Observing the damp, mouldy ceilings and flaking paint, I wonder what will happen to the house. Will the council relet it or is there a possibility they might let me have it back? As far as I know, Scarlet never requested that my name be removed from the tenancy, even though I was no longer paying the rent.

But what would happen to me and Leah then? She's unlikely to agree to us living apart for the sole purpose of me getting custody of my kids, while also being in a relationship with her. I'm no longer certain I even want that. Yet I can't just abandon her. After treating Scarlet the way I did, I've learned my lesson. But I can't help resenting Leah for forcing me to choose between her and my children. Then again, I wouldn't hesitate if it was just Leah by herself. Daisy and Alice would come first every time. Except they hadn't, had they? Because I'd walked out on them when they needed me most. And for what? Talk about selfish. I will never forgive myself for what I did to their mother and them. And now I'm having to choose between my baby and my two older girls since I cannot have one without the other. A man can only have one home . . . and although the two houses are identical, I've always felt more at ease here than at Leah's. Odd that.

This place would look brighter with a coat of fresh paint, I decide. Why did Scarlet paint the walls a deep shade of purple? It's far too dark. Depressing even. I wonder whether this was done on purpose to match her mood. Although Scarlet was a neat freak and kept her house spotless, I could have helped her make it nicer, for the kids' sake if nothing else. It wouldn't have hurt me to do some DIY around the place — put up some shelves, mow the lawn, that sort of thing — even though it wouldn't have gone down well with you know who. My phone pings with an angry message from Leah as if she had just read my thoughts. I have to juggle Saffy so I can read it. "Paracetamol!!!" her text screams. I respond with my own one-worded response and just as many exclamation marks, "Okay!!!"

Now that Saffy has contentedly gone back to sleep, I can't bring myself to disturb her by winding her or changing her nappy, so I return her to her buggy. I head upstairs then, and my heart is thudding in my ribcage as I arrive on the landing. The door to Scarlet's bedroom is shut and blood sings in my ears as I push it open, scared shitless in case someone or something should suddenly jump out at me. Leah takes the mickey out of me for being a scaredy cat over anything remotely spooky. It's true that I cannot sit through a scary movie to save my life. Maybe that's the reason I avoid going inside. Hovering in the doorway is enough to bring it all back again.

Tears cloud my vision as I recall Scarlet's lifeless body on the bed and the incriminating mark of the pillow left behind on her cheek. The faint creak on the landing had prompted me to turn to see what was causing the noise and my heart twisted in my chest when I saw Daisy standing there in her pyjamas, cradling a pillow against her waist. She looked right through me, as if she couldn't see me, clearly traumatised, and then let out a spine-tingling scream, "I killed her. I killed Mum," that I have tried and failed to push from my memory, and which woke her little sister up.

In a very *Stephen King*-like moment, the ghostly clanking of the letterbox downstairs followed by the dull thud of something falling onto the doormat scares the living daylights out of me. After a fright like that I almost take a tumble down the stairs. I take several deep breaths and force the tension from my body. For a minute there, I believed it was a message from the dead. An indication that Scarlet wanted to talk to me and alert me to a potential threat. How stupid is that? I don't even believe in God, let alone ghosts. I need to get a grip.

Hurrying down the stairs, desperate to escape the gloom of the bedroom, I grab the flyer that has just landed on Scarlet's doormat. When I see that it is an appeal for volunteers from the Samaritans, I start to doubt my atheist beliefs. Considering that I was just thinking about joining, how can this be a coincidence? "Every ten seconds we help someone turn their life around" the poster claims. Surely, it must be a sign from Scarlet urging me to right the wrongs of the past.

CHAPTER 29: THE GRANDMOTHER

It has been rather satisfying, I must say, to have the house all to myself. I have come to adore Daisy and Alice, but raising two young girls is not without its difficulties. One of them was getting them ready for school this morning. After waving off a smiley-faced Alice and an unhappy Daisy at the gate, I returned home and threw myself into the washing, ironing, hoovering, and dusting. Keeping busy was the only antidote to not fretting about Daisy. Currently, I'm pottering around in my garden, weeding, watering, and dead-heading flowers. Aside from baking, this is what I enjoy most, though it pains me that I'm without my usual companion. Every time I catch myself instinctively searching for Hero in his typical hiding places — peering out from among the flowers, grooming himself beneath the shade of the apple tree or hunting for mice in the log store — my eyes sting. That cat is going to be sorely missed, but I had to give him up. He couldn't become a barrier to me keeping Daisy with me.

Time has run away with me I see, because a glance at the large garden wall clock tells me it's almost time to pick the children up. I step into the cottage and use the oval wall mirror in the hall to tweak the ends of my hair before putting coconut lip balm on my thinning lips. The last thing I do before leaving the house is swap my gardening clogs for sandals and fetch my purse. The girls deserve a treat from the village store after school.

It's a lovely day and the sun is warm on my crepey skin as I walk past the church and the cemetery on my way to the school, which is located on Church Street. I feel a sense of belonging and pride in my village as I nod to other caregivers who, like me, are on their way to pick up their charges. Though the proximity of the cemetery and the lopsided, unreadable gravestones give me the shivers, I'll be the first to admit. I'm hoping not to run into the vicar coming out of the church because I've missed Sunday services a few times lately, but once I explain about the children and my new responsibilities as a grandparent, I'm sure she'll understand.

Ryhall is a charming place to live and I couldn't be happier here. I especially love all the character stone-built properties and the idyllic village pond that attracts flocks of ducks that the younger children enjoy feeding. It's a safe, almost perfect place to raise a family. Unlike Peterborough. I shudder whenever I think of Daisy and Alice having to grow up on that awful city housing estate with its high crime rates and overcrowded schools. They're much better off here. With me.

The girls' Church of England school has been awarded "Outstanding" status by Ofsted. With less than 200 pupils ranging from reception class to year six, they should do well here. Each student is assured of receiving outstanding care and attention along with top-notch teaching. I've been informed that Daisy is in Tolethorpe (year five) and Alice is in Burghley (year three). I've previously met Miss Chase and Miss Nightingale, their class teachers as well as the head teacher, who, as I reach the school gates, I notice is striding purposefully towards me with train-wreck eyes.

His unnerving stare can't possibly be directed at me, can it? I crane my neck to peer beyond him, hoping to catch a glimpse of Daisy or Alice, but they're nowhere to be seen, even though the bell has rung and other children are leaving the building, walking out of the gates hand in hand with their parents.

'Mrs Castle,' the head teacher skids to a stop in the gravel immediately in front of me, gnawing at the inside of his cheek. He's tall, slim, and reasonably attractive but he is partially cross-eyed which I find disconcerting, as it's hard to know where to concentrate one's gaze.

Settling on the bridge of his nose, I ask sharply, 'Is everything all right, Mr Redbond?'

He mutters darkly, 'I'm afraid not. Will you come this way? I'll explain everything once we're inside.'

I go to follow him and realise people are openly staring at us. Ignoring their gazes and inhaling deeply, readying myself for the worst, I follow him inside the building, taking sharp turns this way and that until we arrive in a quiet corridor outside his office where Daisy and Alice are seated. They glance up with puffy, wet eyes as I approach.

'Granny,' Alice sobs, hurling herself into my arms. When Daisy comes to stand beside me and places her trembling hand in mine, my jaw drops open. Things have to be bad for her to reach out to me.

'Whatever is it? What's happened?' I rattle off, flummoxed.

'We hate it here,' Daisy scowls, treating the head teacher to a particularly savage glare.

Nodding in agreement, Alice murmurs tearfully, 'We want to go home.'

Daisy angrily declares, 'They picked on Alice and called her fat.'

'Who did?' I ask, confused.

'The bitchy girls in her class.'

'That kind of language isn't helpful,' the head teacher corrects before smarmily complaining, 'And what you're saying is not strictly accurate . . .'

Daisy's jaw clenches at that, which is never a good sign and then she lets the head teacher have it. 'It fucking well is,' she explodes.

123

'Daisy!' I cry in embarrassment, but as I turn to apologetically face the head teacher, I find that he has been shocked into silence.

'Let's go into my office,' he suggests coldly, gesturing to the door.

After we enter, he moves to the other side of his desk and settles into his leather chair, leaving the girls and me standing.

'How about that explanation you promised me?' I demand tetchily, placing a protective arm around the girls. While Daisy's temper shows no sign of diminishing, Alice continues to weep hysterically.

'I'm afraid there was an incident in the playground during break time when a group of year three girls refused to let Alice join in with their game.'

'That doesn't sound very inclusive, or *outstanding*,' I mutter, frowning.

'Quite,' he replies, wincing in response to my dig at the Ofsted award. 'One of them happened to comment that Alice was, well . . . a little on the plump side. As you can imagine this was very upsetting for her.'

'Quite,' I parrot, being deliberately sarcastic. However, as I study Alice more closely, I realise that the girls in her class have a point. Since moving in with me several weeks ago, she has gained quite a bit of weight, and I must accept responsibility for that. It's true what they say, children can be cruel. Take Scarlet for instance, whose cold indifference to her parents from a very early age led to a ten-year estrangement that never healed.

'But that's not all,' Daisy interrupts, her eyes narrowing to mere slits as she goes on. 'When I told them off for calling my sister names, they called us council house scum.'

Her words slap me in the face. *How dare they?* Daisy was right to call them bitches. I second that. Feeling myself tense with indignation, I turn my outraged gaze on the head teacher before demanding, 'Is that right?'

He coughs nervously into his hand before replying, 'While I'm not suggesting Daisy is exaggerating or lying, I'm struggling to comprehend that children as young as seven would use such language to describe . . .'

'Describe what?' I interject huffily, blowing out my cheeks.

He gulps several times as if he's afraid to say the wrong thing before going on to explain, 'Families that come from social housing backgrounds.'

I respond, wide-eyed in disbelief, 'What a dreadful thing to say!'

'It doesn't matter because I'm never coming back to this shithole ever again,' Daisy wails, jabbing an irate finger at the head. 'And you can't make me. Nobody can. I'll only run away if you do.'

Alice stomps her foot, crying, 'And I'll come with you,' in solidarity with her sister.

CHAPTER 30: THE FATHER

We're on. It's happening tonight. And true to form, I'm crapping myself. Even Leah, who doesn't show me a scrap of affection these days, sensed something was up. She didn't say anything. Just kept giving me odd looks. But since Scarlet died, she no longer questions my every move, so she accepted my excuse that I was "nipping out for a bit to help a friend". And now, here I am, with said friend. Or rather three of them. In a black van with a fake number plate. I'm the driver. And a good one. Gary wanted me on board for that reason. Quick getaways are what counts. I know two of the guys, Skid and Spud. The other one, Zoom, is a stranger. He has a straggly man bun, shot eyes and tribal face tattoos. They're all fake names, of course, just like the plate. Mine is Tank for the sake of tonight's job.

We've pulled up outside Booker's cash and carry in Woodston under the cover of darkness. I've manoeuvred the van so that it's just a few feet away from the staff side entrance door, which will act as an invisible shield between us and any-one who might try to enter the car park. We're masked up and are wearing gloves. Armed with crowbars, Skid and Spud exit the van first and attack the door while I stand guard. As soon as the door has been prised open, Zoom disappears into the darkened building, the sound of the entry alarm beeping behind him. He has precisely thirty seconds to locate the alarm system and disarm it otherwise we're screwed. I keep the engine running, just in case. When the beeping is abruptly cut off, I punch the air in relief. I hadn't realised I was holding my breath the entire time.

'Kerching,' Skid and Spud exclaim simultaneously and give each other a high five before stepping inside the building.

I open the rear doors of the van and light a roll-up to calm my nerves as I train my mind on that five grand. We have fifteen minutes at most. That's the amount of time it should take the cops to detect movement from the CCTV and dispatch a car. But the wait is already killing me. My nerves are shot, like Zoom's pupils. I'm too old for this. I've promised myself this is the very last time and that I'm going straight from now on. Gary will just have to find someone else in future. I can't go to prison. My girls need me.

Instead of standing out here by myself with nothing to do but think, I'd rather be inside helping the others. Then I wouldn't be imagining I can hear the siren of a police car racing towards me every time I stare blankly across at the car park. I break out into a sweat and end up scaring myself when I climb back into the cab and catch a glimpse of my reflection in the rearview mirror. My eyes spark like headlights in the dark. I check the time on my phone non-stop for the next ten, eleven and twelve minutes, light up another fag, gulp down a can of Red Bull, and go cross-eyed from peering into the darkness. *Where the fuck are they? We're running out of time.*

Relief floods through me when Skid, Spud and Zoom burst through the smashed door like ghosts in the dusk. I immediately jump out of the van to help load the stolen goods into the back of the vehicle. It's quite a haul and I feel myself doing a double take when I calculate the sums in my head. The cigarettes and tobacco alone must be worth a quarter of a million. Never mind the cases of whiskey and what was found in the cash till.

We pile into the van after the last of the boxes are loaded. Skid and Spud beside me. Zoom in the back. When our eyes meet in the rearview mirror, I have to look away. There's something off about him. I can't put my finger on what it is but I just don't trust him. When I hear the police siren in the distance, I know I'm not imagining it this time, so I put my foot down.

'It's too far away to concern us,' Spud mutters, ripping off his mask.

With a curt nod, I drive towards the main entrance gate which has been left open for us to make our escape. Zoom broke the padlock when we arrived on site. So as not to draw any attention to ourselves, the van lights are off. I won't switch them on until we reach the main road.

With the siren getting closer, I'm picking up speed all the time and I think we must be doing around sixty-five in a forty-mile limit. At this time of night, there is no other traffic on the road. Except for the police car, which is probably entering the opposite end of Morley Way right about now. Once they arrive at Booker's we'll be long gone.

'Fuck, look out!' Spud screams, putting up a hand as if to avoid a blow.

I brake sharply, panicking. 'What is it?'

Though I can't see what Spud is seeing from his side window, I can feel the bone-crunching scrape of flesh on metal as the van crashes into something, sending us careering off the road and mounting the pavement before coming to a sliding halt.

Terrified, the four of us silently lock eyes, trying to make sense of what just happened. I don't move from my seat. Not one inch. It feels as if my muscles will never unclench again. And then I'm begging in disbelief, 'Tell me we didn't just hit someone.'

'You mean *you* hit someone,' Zoom sneers from behind. From the moment I met him, I could tell he wasn't a team player.

Spud looks at me with pitiful eyes, as he says, 'It was an old guy walking a dog.'

Skid is beside himself. 'Why the fuck would anybody be walking their dog around here at this time of the night.'

'Wait. Where are you going?' Zoom demands, placing a restraining hand on my shoulder as I unbuckle my seatbelt and open the driver's door.

I shrug off his hand with a grimace, and mutter, 'To see if he's all right.'

'Of course he's not all right. You hit him with a three-and-a-half-tonne piece of metal,' Zoom argues.

Ignoring him, I stagger out of the van and I go limp with fear when I see the lifeless shape of a body on the ground twenty metres away.

'Can you see anything?' A pale-faced Spud slouches over to join me.

'Fuck. He's not moving.' Skid observes, putting his head in his hands.

'You don't say.' This is from Zoom.

All four of us shuffle over to stand over the body. An old boy. Around seventy I'd say. He's on his back, staring up at the charcoal sky with dazed eyes. His face is smeared with dirt and blood and is wet and sticky in places.

I exclaim in horror, 'He's fucking dead,' fearing that I'm about to pass out and join him on the concrete. *It's what I deserve.*

'There's nothing we can do. We should get out of here,' Zoom is adamant, and he glances around agitatedly as the police siren intensifies.

I turn on him, yelling, 'We can't just leave him.'

'Why not?' He shrugs dismissively.

'Because he's a human being,' I stammer, shocked by what I'm hearing.

'Zoom's right,' Spud murmurs more reasonably, sounding as though it pains him to agree with the piece of garbage that is Zoom. 'We need to leave now before the cops show up.'

'Come on, Tank.' Skid pats me encouragingly on the back. 'There's no point doing time for a corpse that no longer gives a shit.'

'It doesn't feel right,' I persist doggedly, even though he's right. But I know I'm on my own when I watch Zoom whip around and slink off without another word and the other two follow him back to the van.

My eyes well with tears as I murmur, 'I didn't mean to. It was an accident. I'm so sorry,' to the deceased. And I'm about to leg it back to the van to join the others when a small, fluffy white dog approaches me and wags its tail. A lead is attached to its collar, so I'm guessing it's the man's dog and that it somehow miraculously escaped being hit.

When it begins to yap and paw at the old man, as if it wants him to get back up, I impulsively grab it and tuck it protectively under one arm. I might not be able to help the dead guy, but there's no way I'm leaving a little dog out here by itself at night. Anything could happen to it.

I respond with a, 'Don't ask,' to the three men who are staring at me with wide eyes as I slide inside the van and prop the dog up on my lap.

CHAPTER 31: THE GRANDMOTHER

'We've come to apologise,' the woman at my door announces with a warm if slightly apprehensive smile. Her chiselled cheek bones burn with humiliation as she extends a French manicured hand in greeting, 'I'm Rosalind Knowles. And this,' she looks down at her exceptionally pretty, blonde, doll-like daughter, who shyly peers out from behind her legs, 'is Verity.'

Puzzled, I find myself instinctively shaking the woman's hand, which is sticky with hand lotion. 'And I'm Mrs Castle. But what are you here to apologise for?' I enquire briskly, glancing behind me when I hear a sharp intake of breath and frowning when I see Daisy and Alice staring at our visitors in horror. They obviously recognise Rosalind or her daughter whereas I don't think I've ever seen them before. Before I can say a word, they scamper away again. I turn my attention back to our visitors.

'Verity told me what happened at school. I'm afraid she was among the group of girls who were unkind to your granddaughters,' Rosalind goes on to explain, her face reddening further.

At that, I gather myself to my full height, put my hands on my hips, and mutter in an unfriendly tone, 'Well, you'd better come in then. I'm not one for airing my dirty laundry in public.'

It's an old-fashioned saying, and I can tell Rosalind doesn't get it as she follows me inside, nudging her child to follow. It's also clear she's displeased with her daughter. I would be too. There is an awkward moment when I motion for them to remove their shoes but they comply without hesitation. Although I do detect a surliness in the little girl's gaze. This leads me to believe that she isn't quite as sorry as her mother wants her to be.

'This way,' I instruct, breaking the tense silence, before stomping into the living room. Mother and daughter follow, their identical blue gazes riveted on their surroundings as they take everything in.

Once I'm seated in my imposing armchair and Rosalind has finished inspecting the room, presumably to make sure it is safe and hygienic for her little princess to sit in, they settle side by side on the large sofa.

'This is such an unpleasant situation,' Rosalind remarks, averting her gaze. Then she lets out a sigh and admits, 'I can't think what got into Verity or the other girls. They are usually so friendly and welcoming.'

A sudden surge of anger bubbles to the surface and I find myself grinding out through clenched teeth, 'Are you suggesting their appalling behaviour was somehow my grand-daughters' fault?'

'No, of course, not! That's not what I meant at all,' Rosalind backtracks, appearing mortified and wringing her hands. 'I just don't want you thinking that it's normal for my daughter.'

'And what is normal for her?' I pose this somewhat cynically.

Rosalind's lips open and close, unable to form the right words, until they finally do . . . 'Might we meet Daisy and Alice so Verity can tell them how sorry she is?' There's a hint of Essex in her voice.

'You're not from around here,' I observe caustically.

Seeming astonished, she answers, 'No. Dagenham.'

'Takes one to know one,' I smile conspiratorially at her.

'No way,' she exclaims, scooting forward in her seat, clearly eager to continue the conversation. Meanwhile, her daughter rolls her eyes, bored.

'Whereabouts?' I enquire.

She gives her daughter a cautious look, then drops her gaze and replies feebly, 'Becontree.'

My pulse quickens as I confide, 'I know it well.'

'Did you grow up on the estate too?'

But I've said too much already, so I stand up and go over to the door to shout, 'Daisy. Alice. Would you please come down to the living room?'

While we wait for them to thunder down the stairs, I berate myself. One mention of my former home and I've naively let my guard down. No one can ever know where I came from. And I dare say the young woman seated across from me experiences as much shame as I do, though it does help explain why she is so upset over the attack on Daisy. Rosalind Knowles will not be unfamiliar with the term "council house scum". Becontree is possibly the worst council housing estate in the entire country. Far worse than Nene Fields. Another thing I have in common with Daisy and Alice is that I grew up in social housing, though they will never hear about it from me. I didn't spend years rebuilding my life only to expose myself now.

Sadness fills my chest as the girls grudgingly enter the room. When I see the doll dangling from Daisy's hand, I sigh inwardly. Verity has noticed it too. The smirk on her face seems to suggest that she considers this ammunition for more bullying. I do wish the child would give the doll up, but I don't want to be too hard on Daisy, or Alice, as they'll have heard us talking and will be aware that they are going to have to confront their tormentor — who is casually swinging her legs against my sofa as though she doesn't have a care in the world and isn't in trouble.

I don't beat about the bush, declaring, 'Verity is here to say sorry for the nasty and cruel way she treated you.'

Rosalind's body goes rigid at that, as if slightly offended, but I can live with that. 'Isn't that right, Rosalind?' I torment her further.

'Verity,' Rosalind prompts, motioning for her daughter to stand up.

To be fair to the child, she gets up willingly enough and shoots a curious glance at Daisy and Alice as if to check if they will accept her apology.

'I'm sorry for calling you plump, Alice, because you're not really, but the other girls used to call me that all the time, and worse. So, I thought maybe after you came along, they wouldn't call me the fat one anymore.'

Brave girl, I think, almost wanting to applaud her. Still, I reserve judgement, as this might yet all be an act. She exudes a precocious aura, does that one. I'm not at all surprised as I watch Alice's expression change from one of defiance to sympathy and something more than that . . . a yearning to connect. After all, she's the nicest, kindest, most forgiving child I know. That's not the case with Daisy, though, and as soon as I lay eyes on her, I can see that her walls are not going to come down so easily.

Seeming intimidated by the eldest sister, Verity isn't immediately forthcoming with an apology for Daisy, so Rosalind jumps in. 'Verity explained to me that while she joined in with the other girls' taunts, she didn't understand what she was saying. She'd never heard the term *council house* used before, never mind the other unpleasant word.'

'You mean *scum* so why don't you just come out and say so?' Daisy challenges.

'Daisy, there's no need for that,' I reprimand sternly. 'Rosalind and her daughter are here to apologise and are guests in our home.'

Suitably chastised, Daisy hangs her head and my heart aches for her. She has such a hurricane of emotions whirling around inside her. I then turn to Alice and Verity, who are eyeing each other up and half-smiling at each other, and say,

'Alice, why don't you show Verity your bedroom while Daisy and I make tea for everyone?'

The girls timidly exit the room together, but it isn't long before we hear them chatting above our heads as Alice gives her new friend a tour.

'How do you like your tea, Rosalind?'

Noticing the way I'm leaning on my walking stick, she says, 'I don't want to be a bother.'

'It's no bother,' I cluck, as if I were a fluffed-up broody hen.

'White with no sugar, then please,' she says with a polite smile. Happy now that her daughter has done the right thing.

'And I imagine carrot cake is your favourite,' I smile effortlessly, even though the pressure from maintaining my harmless-old-lady mask is building.

'It is. How did you guess?' Rosalind chuckles, impressed.

I don't say what I'm thinking — that carrot cake is so middle-class that it is the obvious choice for anyone trying to shake off their working-class background. I should know.

'Oh, and Mrs Castle, I'm sure there aren't any in your lovely carrot cake but no nuts for Verity, please. She has an allergy.'

Brow furrowing in concern, I observe, 'How unfortunate.'

'Thankfully, nothing too severe.' Rosalind obliges me with a fuller explanation, going on to say, 'But even though it's a mild allergy, Verity develops a rash and gets swollen lips if she accidentally eats one. Sometimes it makes her vomit too.'

'Poor thing,' I reply, radiating sympathy. Then, taking a pop at Daisy, I remark innocently, 'Children suffer from so many allergies these days.' And of course, I'm thinking of my cat Hero when I say this.

'Can't you get rid of them?' Daisy hisses as soon as we enter the kitchen and are alone together.

'In due course, Daisy,' I assure her, boiling the kettle and slicing up portions of cake, before finding nice crockery to display it on. Daisy watches spellbound as I open a packet of ground nuts and carefully sprinkle them on the largest, too-impossible-to-resist slice of cake.

Daisy asks, her eyes wide with incredulity, 'What are you doing?'

I wink at her. 'You remember what Rosalind said about Verity having a nut allergy.'

CHAPTER 32: THE FATHER

I shake my head in disgust and push the dish of unappetising sausages, beans, and chips away, complaining, 'I can't eat a thing.'

Leah, at the other end of the kitchen table, narrows her eyes. 'That's not like you.' Never one to miss a trick, she also reaches greedily for one of my burnt sausages.

Scraping back my chair, I gulp down my glass of Coke and belch loudly, before groaning, 'I think I'm going to be sick.'

And with that, I vanish out of the back door and puke into the sun-scorched, dying grass by the bins. The little white dog follows me, as it's done since I brought it home with me in the early hours of this morning.

'Fucking gross,' Leah mutters from inside the house.

'Give me a break,' I yell, 'I would never have made it upstairs to the bathroom.'

Leah comes to stand in the doorway, hands on hips, and watches me with mean eyes. 'What's got into you? What happened last night?'

'Don't even go there,' I warn. It's best she doesn't know. She couldn't keep a secret to save her life.

Hands covering her gaping mouth, she squeals in horror, 'Shit! Is that dog eating your sick?'

'Lucky, get out of there,' I command, gently shoving the dog's messy little snout away from my foaming vomit.

'Lucky!' Leah scoffs. 'What's lucky about that dog?'

That dog is what Leah has called the scruffy little cross-breed since I presented it to her, with an unwise, 'Surprise,' in bed this morning.

'You said you wanted a dog,' I sigh, dragging a hand through my hair. A scream echoes through my mind. *An old man's scream.* Followed by the crunch of bone on metal. My head hurts from reliving the scene of the bloodied and battered body stretched out on the road.

Eyes popping, chin out good and proper, Leah protests, 'I *said* I wanted a chihuahua.'

I retaliate with, 'Well, we don't always get what we want, do we, Leah?' And I'm thinking of my girls when I say this, but I don't say so. It's a sore subject.

Her chin wobbles, never a good sign, so I pick up the dog and tuck it under my arm for protection in case she takes her temper out on it, and say more softly, 'I'm sure you'll grow to love him and he's good with Saffy.'

On cue, Saffy wakes up and starts to cry. Leah looks upwards at the open bedroom window where the sound is coming from. 'Great,' she mutters, then turns, and stomps away.

'I'll go,' I offer, trying to appease. But she ignores me. Doesn't even toss her head in anger or call me "a useless unemployed slob", which is currently her favourite term of endearment for me. I know of no one who can "bitch" like my girlfriend. Ironically, though, a bitch and a killer go well together. *We make a great team.*

Truthfully, though, I wouldn't intentionally harm a fly. Only in self-defence, like I sometimes had to do when Scarlet drunkenly attacked me. Why didn't I get her the help she needed instead of bailing out on her when things got too difficult? I'd do things very differently if I could go back in time. Put her first for once instead of being a self-centred cunt. She was a bloody good woman. The best. I see that now. When it's too late. I have to live with that mistake for the rest of my life. As do my kids.

A tear rolls down my cheek when I think of them. I must have grown soft in my old age. If you can call thirty-two old. Leah seems to think so, but I'd say I'm in my prime. She thinks I'm washed up and I can't argue with that. Not when I've no job and no prospects either. All I can look forward to is a life on benefits. Of getting by. And watching my kids follow in my footsteps. No fucking way do I want that for them. As for me, I'll be lucky if I don't wind up getting banged up for good. For lying to the cops about my whereabouts the night Scarlet died and running an old man down while fleeing from the scene of a crime.

As I carry Lucky back inside, he tries to lick frantically at my mouth, which undoubtedly still tastes of sick. I put him down on the stained, ripped linoleum floor and offer him a bowl of fresh water. When I give him a pat on the head and say, "Good boy," his tail wags tenfold.

The first thing I notice when I walk back into the kitchen-diner is how gloomy and depressing our house is with all the curtains and blinds shut. A haze of cooking oil smoke fills the room, which also stinks of fried food. The uneaten food is congealing on chipped plates on the table and I find myself wondering if the man I killed lived in a rundown shithole like this or if he came from a nice neighbourhood. Life on Nene Fields is all I've ever known but I've always dreamed of something better. For Daisy and Alice. Saffy too. Leah at a pinch. But only because she's Saffy's mum. I keep scrolling through the local news on my phone, but the hit-and-run hasn't been mentioned yet. It won't be long until someone misses the dead man and contacts the police about his disappearance. It's possible they've already identified the body and called the man's widow or his grown-up children. He could be a doting grandfather of many for all I know. I can't help but imagine what his poor family must be going through. Because of me!

It's not like I can turn myself in to the police and confess what I've done, so the old man's family would know it was an accident and that I didn't run him over on purpose just to make a speedy getaway . . . because what good would that do? If I did or said anything that implicated Gary Pearce or his gang of crooks, I'm a dead man. Besides, I'm not a grass. Nor is Leah, but she's got a big gob on her and isn't to be trusted, *in so many ways*. And there's no way she's getting her hands on that five grand. She wanted me. She got me. She wanted a baby. She got a baby. She wanted a dog. She got a dog. But for once, Leah won't be getting what Leah wants. I was going to use that money to hire a solicitor to help me fight for my kids, but I'm thinking twice about that now. Should I give it to the deceased man's family instead? The least I can do is make an anonymous contribution towards the funeral costs. But what of Daisy and Alice? I'm screwed without that money. As it stands, I'm not entitled to legal aid to fight Mrs Castle for custody. And in any case part of me believes they're better off where they are rather than with me. *A loser.* Except there's something about their grandmother I don't trust. I just can't put my finger on what it is.

I'm spared from making an extremely difficult decision when I see the headline "Breaking news" on my phone—

A prolific paedophile convicted of abusing dozens of young children who spent twenty years in a maximum-security facility has been discovered dead in Peterborough. Ralph Setterfield, 69, a native of London, relocated to Woodston following his release from prison in 2020. He was killed in a questionable hit-and-run in Morley Way early this morning. Police suspect he was deliberately targeted after discovering hordes of child pornography at his single-occupancy residence.

Whoa, what the fuck. It sounds as though I've done the world a favour by taking out that sick bastard. Who'd have thought that a useless, unemployed slob like me would ever become a super hero?

CHAPTER 33: THE GRANDMOTHER

'How is she doing?' I ask in earnest while extending my peace offering — a large punnet of strawberries picked from my allotment. 'Alice told me Verity loves strawberries and I thought they might cheer her up.'

Rosalind looks up at me, eyes wide and enquiring. 'Oh, Mrs Castle, that's very kind of you. She's feeling a lot better now the vomiting has stopped. Won't you come in so she can thank you herself?'

'I can't stop, I'm afraid,' I say, shaking my head. 'The girls are out looking for my lost cat and I don't want to be away from them too long. I just wanted to see how Verity was. I feel so bad about yesterday . . .'

Rosalind interrupts, her eyes flickering in alarm, 'Oh, please don't. It's not as though you gave her the nuts. She must have accidentally consumed some at school earlier in the day. You can never be certain of ingredient labelling these days.' She tuts before continuing, 'Yet the school is usually so good at that sort of thing.'

'You should complain to Mr Redbond,' I suggest, as wily as any coyote. I would welcome any attempt to put the head teacher in his place, given the way he spoke to me and the girls.

'Don't worry, I intend to,' Rosalind threatens, crossing her arms.

Behind her, I glimpse a world of white wooden panelled walls, beige carpets, gold chandeliers and elegant mirrors. This spacious, beautiful stone house is a far cry from where Rosalind Knowles grew up. I imagine she prefers keeping her past private, just as I do. Her husband, I understand, is an architect. The girl from "Corned beef city" has done well.

'Verity should be back at school tomorrow with a bit of luck.' Rosalind pauses mid-sentence as if unsure of herself, before asking, 'Will your granddaughters be there?'

'Alice yes. Daisy no,' I admit frankly.

She frowns. 'That's a shame.'

'It is, because she's very intelligent and loves reading, but I've been advised homeschooling might be a better option for her.'

'If she loves reading so much, she can always come to my book club, Mrs Castle.'

'Yvonne, please,' I insist.

She offers me a tired smile. 'Yvonne then.'

'You run a book club?'

'Actually, it's the village book club. Not mine,' she chuckles. 'We meet in the village hall every Wednesday at seven. Everyone's welcome. Even nine-year-olds. We're very inclusive.'

With a wave of appreciation, I reply, 'If Daisy can be persuaded, we just might come along.'

'That would be lovely.' Rosalind beams, sounding like she means it.

I feel guilty then . . . about Verity. But it's not as if the child didn't deserve to be punished for how she treated Daisy and Alice. Still, lesson learned. Except I haven't really learned anything, have I? Because I told the girls a big fat lie when I finally admitted that Hero had gone missing. And now they're out searching for him when they haven't a hope in hell of finding him. Why didn't I just tell them that I'd rehomed him? When it comes to avoiding the truth, I seem incapable of resisting.

Saying my goodbyes, I trudge back down the very long path and let myself out of the gate. Tap, tap, tap goes my walking stick on the decorative cobblestones. I glance up at the house, and that's when I catch sight of Verity glaring at me from an upstairs window. She is a picture of defiance with her comical little frown. Unlike her somewhat gullible mother, she is not as trusting and looks like she blames me for her sudden bout of sickness. Somewhat childishly, she sticks her tongue out at me and I covertly stick up two middle fingers in retaliation. I was right all along when I called her precocious.

After a quick stroll home, I hear squabbling as soon as I let myself in the front door. *What now?* I've only been gone ten minutes and they promised they would be fine on their own. My heart rate increases as I march into the kitchen where the shouting is coming from.

Alice is launching an attack on her sister, screeching, 'It's all your fault!'

She is bright red in the face and the force of her anger is impressive. Daisy, on the other hand, appears cowed. Her cheeks burn when she sees me standing there.

'What's Daisy's fault?' I ask wearily, clasping a hand to my forehead in frustration.

Alice points a finger at her sister and rages, 'She wanted him gone, and now he has.'

'Who?' I ask, puzzled.

Alice's eyes blaze with indignation as she mutters, 'Hero. I've looked for him everywhere. In all his usual places. And I've called him loads, but . . .'

Tears come easily to Alice, and she tries and fails to blink them away.

'It's not my fault we couldn't find him,' Daisy protests stubbornly.

Alice's body ripples with anger as she yells, 'No, but it's your fault he went missing.'

'How so?' I scowl.

143

'Daisy was mean to him *and* she pretended to have an allergic reaction even though there was nothing wrong with her,' Alice accuses, tearing her gaze away from mine to fiercely glare at her sister. 'You made it up so Granny would have to get rid of her cat, which you knew she loved. Because of you, he ran away.'

My mind numb with disbelief, I bark, 'Is this true, Daisy?'

Startled and appearing cornered, Daisy struggles for words. 'I, er . . .'

'See. I told you!' Alice explodes.

Voice sharpened in anger, I address Daisy. 'I'm very disappointed in you.'

With a crimson face and bulging eyes that seem like they might pop out of her head, she looks away from me and droops her head. 'I'm sorry, I didn't mean to—'

Jaw clenched with anger, I order, 'Go to your room.'

Astonished by my feral tone, both girls turn to face me

'Now,' I repeat, taking a menacing step towards her. 'Before I drag you there.'

Blinking away tears, Daisy bolts from the room, slamming the door behind her. Her sobs can be heard as she thunders upstairs.

I turn to face a visibly trembling Alice, who has stepped back from me as if I were the worst grandmother in the world. And perhaps I am.

Softening my voice, I admit, 'Alice, I haven't been entirely honest with you about Hero. I should have told you the truth from the start.'

144

CHAPTER 34: THE FATHER

Daisy whispers the terrifying words, 'We're not safe here,' and I feel the sweat sticking to my back and the hair on my arms standing up.

Before I can reply, she hisses urgently, panic in her voice, 'I've got to go. I can hear her coming up the stairs and I'm scared she might . . .'

When the phone suddenly goes dead, I bite down on my tongue till I taste blood. What was Daisy about to say? Was she scared her grandmother might hurt her? Hit her? As I mull over what Daisy has just told me, my heart thumps loudly in my ribcage and my body remains rigid with righteous anger. Daisy has now confirmed what I already suspected about Mrs Castle — there's something off about her. That woman, who has fooled everyone into believing she's a nice, harmless old lady had threatened to forcibly remove my daughter from the room if she didn't do as she was told. What loving grand-mother would behave in such a way? *The evil old bitch.* Scarlet would turn over in her grave if she knew.

The beer bottle is only inches from my lips when I impul-sively hurl it across the living room where it shatters satisfy-ingly against the wall. I'm back at 7 The Green in my old home, sitting in the dark. I needed some peace and quiet so I came here to escape Leah's nagging. I've had it up to here with her going on about Wayne's new job as a bouncer at Angels' lap dancing club. *Is it too much to hope that he hooks up with a stripper or gets an STD?* The dog gave me a perfect excuse to get out of the house for a bit. Lucky seems unfazed by my violent outburst, but then again, he must have witnessed the worst of humanity having lived with a sick paedophile. I can't believe I wasted a shred of sympathy on that scumbag, let alone considered covering his funeral expenses. Anyone who sexually abuses children can go to hell for all I care.

Hauling myself to my feet, I come to a decision I should have taken a long time ago. 'Right, that's it,' I growl. 'Time to fight back.'

I won't let Scarlet's mother get away with this. Not now she's proven the girls are actually better off with me. First thing tomorrow I'm going to find a solicitor who will help me get them back. Though, realistically, I know custody won't happen overnight, it will at least get the ball rolling. Until then, I'm left with no choice but to leave them where they are. *Their grandmother wouldn't really hurt them, would she?* I hate to think of Daisy and Alice living in fear of her but social services won't take any action or consider removing them unless there's concrete evidence that Mrs Castle is an unfit carer. And who are they going to believe? Me, a down-and-out known to the police or a respectable widow. Even if Daisy could be persuaded into telling them what happened, Mrs Castle will blame it on trauma and grief, claiming that it's a ruse to get Daisy sent back to her dad, who she will argue is a violent drug addict and a criminal to boot.

Well, I'll show the old bag, *see if I don't*, and I'll also prove the courts wrong by becoming the person I've always wanted to be. I know I have it in me. Scarlet believed in me and told me I could succeed at anything I put my mind to. Fuck, she even chose me over her parents when they badmouthed me to her face. She said she knew in her heart that I was a decent person and that's why she loved and supported me through the difficult times. It's a shame I didn't show her the same loyalty.

Feeling sick to my stomach, I stagger into the kitchen and drain a pint glass full of tepid water. I haven't turned on any lights because I don't want to alert the neighbours to my presence. So, I'm having to steal about in the dark like the thief I am. But not any longer. I can never go back to that chapter of my life. Or the drugs. My whole focus from now on will be on creating a home for the girls and being a good dad. But part of me longs for revenge. There's a reckless voice in my head urging me to jump in my car and head over to Mrs Castle's house right now — regardless of the repercussions — and bundle my girls into my car. But a second, wiser, more cautious voice, which I like to think is Scarlet's, advises me to "think things through", warning me that if I go through with this, I may not only lose Daisy and Alice for good but also have my visiting rights withdrawn.

Feeling the rage drain out of me, only to be replaced with a feeling of complete helplessness, I shuffle into the living room and flop on the sofa with my head in my hands. How did I allow things to get to this point? With my children being threatened? Why didn't I put my foot down with Leah and insist that the girls move in with us? Am I as weak as she says I am? A big softie. *A coward*, my dad used to call me, for not standing up to the bigger boys. Bullies like Gary Pearce who are still controlling me today.

'Think man. *Think*,' I urge myself, clawing at my hair in desperation. Though I'm itching to tell that woman what I think of her, I can't afford to let my anger get in the way. I have to play the game for the time being, which means complying with all of Mrs Castle's requests . . . picking Daisy and Alice up at the agreed time on Saturday while acting as if nothing had happened. I'll also need to keep my side of the bargain by accepting her money and taking the kids out on a fun outing. It won't be easy, but it's the only way to protect Daisy while she's living under her grandmother's roof. If Yvonne Castle finds out that her granddaughter told me anything about this incident, Daisy will be in even greater risk of danger.

But I'll be working behind the scenes to turn my life around. I've decided I'm fully prepared to move back into 7 The Green and become a full-time dad if need be. And to hell with the consequences. My name is still on the tenancy so what can the council do? They can hardly evict me when I explain that it's the only home the girls have ever known — until they went to their granny's that is — and that they are coming back here to live . . . with me, their biological father, and a transformed man. When that time comes Mrs Castle won't know what hit her.

CHAPTER 35: THE GRANDMOTHER

'Daisy, please don't raise your voice. You'll disturb Mr Burgess next door and he hasn't been at all well.' *Nor have I*, I'm tempted to add, leaning heavily on my good leg and wishing I hadn't had the hip operation. Knowing my bones are failing me at sixty-five makes me feel old and decrepit.

'But you told Alice that Hero hadn't gone missing. That it was a lie and you had really given him away!' Daisy protests vehemently, holding out my cat's blue collar between her thumb and forefinger. Dangling it at me as if it were evidence.

'That's right, I did. And we both know why,' I insinuate, letting out an irritated sigh. I then continue in a more consoling manner, 'He went to a lovely home with a retired church friend of mine two villages away.'

'So why did I find his collar in the bin?' Daisy squeals in frustration and jiggles the collar beneath my nose.

As much as I'd like to swat it away, I squeeze my eyes shut and count to three. When I blink them open again, my gaze automatically swings to the wheelie bins that are housed in an attractive grass-green trellis store. *What on earth was the child doing rummaging about in the trash?*

I chew my lip and point out sensibly, 'Because it has my postcode on the tag which is no use to his new owner.'

'And why have you got all those scratches on your arms?' Daisy demands, squinting at me.

That child doesn't miss a trick, I can't help but think. The sun is directly in her face and her knotty waist-length hair, which hasn't been brushed yet, makes her appear feral. In contrast, little Alice left for school this morning looking perfect in her pigtails, gingham dress and shiny shoes.

Grimly, I tug at the arm of my blouse in a feeble attempt to hide the claw marks on my wrists. Hero hated being put in a cat carrier and, although normally docile and placid, he would hiss, spit and claw at me whenever I tried to force him into one. I'll never forget the reproachful look of betrayal in his gorgeous green eyes when I left him at his new owner's home. His pitiful meows had followed me down the path.

Huffily, I reply, 'I don't know what you're trying to imply, Daisy, but you have no idea how painful it was for me to give up Hero when he was my only companion for years before you and Alice came along.' Just saying his name out loud brings a tremble to my chin.

When Daisy next speaks, her voice is not much more than a whisper, but her green eyes flash with suspicion. 'You didn't hurt him then?'

'Of course not,' I gasp. 'How on earth could you think that?' Sadness blooms in my breast as Daisy continues to eye me warily, appearing to consider her next move. I don't have to wait too long.

'You made Verity sick by giving her nuts when you knew she was allergic,' my granddaughter accuses.

I surprise her by chuckling, 'Did I?'

'You know you did,' Daisy argues, her voice quivering just a little.

'But if memory serves me right, you were the one who gave her the piece of cake. Everyone saw you. So, it could just as easily have been you who sprinkled it with nuts. You had a

150

good reason to want to get back at her for calling you *council house scum*. Isn't that right, dear?' I ask sweetly.

Daisy's mouth gapes open, but it doesn't take long for her jaw to stiffen and her eyes to narrow. *That's my girl.* Scowling, she mutters through clenched teeth, 'I hate you,' in a way that's intended to wound.

And then she's barging past me into the cottage. I don't try to stop her, but I do throw over my shoulder, 'Don't forget we have an online religious education lesson at ten.'

Pent up with anger, Daisy shouts loudly from somewhere behind me, 'I don't give a fuck about religion or God,' while stomping up the stairs.

'Nor do I, Daisy,' I mumble, not loud enough for her to hear. 'But then again, I didn't sign up for homeschooling you either. Or any of this . . .'

Heaving a sigh, I go and pick up Hero's collar from the patio where Daisy tossed it and run my fingertips over his engraved name tag. A wave of emotion floods through my chest and my eyes well up.

Daisy is clearly taking her frustration out on me because she blames herself for the cat's fate, having faked an allergic reaction to it in an attempt to hurt me, knowing I'd have to rehome him. Now that I know this was a lie, I realise everything I put myself and Hero through was in vain. And that's hard to forgive. What with the uproar at the school and Daisy's refusal to go back, the girls' constant squabbling, the endless tears, and having to say goodbye to my precious cat, I ask myself, *Could this week get any* worse?

I have my answer when the back gate unexpectedly opens and I catch a glimpse of silky caramel hair at exactly the same time as a high-pitched voice trills intrusively, 'Cooee, Yvonne, it's only me.'

To make matters worse, just as I figure out that Georgina *bloody* Bell is paying me a visit and wonder how in the world she tracked me down, the head of a grumpy, elderly man pops up from behind the garden fence to complain, 'Mrs Castle, your granddaughter's swearing needs to stop. This was a nice neighbourhood before—'

I stop listening to my next-door neighbour when an angry buzz fills my ears that has nothing to do with the bees flying around my garden. Rubbing at my temples with my fists, I yell, 'Oh fuck off,' at a startled Mr Burgess.

CHAPTER 36: THE FATHER

I feel like I'm on top of the world when I return home from town at midday. For once, Leah is up and dressed and is actually sitting outside in broad daylight with Saffy on her lap, working on a tan by the look of it. She doesn't see me at first because she has her eyes closed. Her long hair is billowing out behind her and her head is tipped upwards at the blazing yellow sun. Her pale white skin is starting to turn pink already.

'You'll burn if you're not careful,' I say stripping off my top to reveal my own white skin shot through with blue veins and a sparse sprinkling of black chest hair. Channing Tatum I am not.

'Who are you, my mother?' Leah pouts, opening one eye. And then somewhat suspiciously asks, 'What's up with you? You look as if you've won the lottery.'

'Almost,' I gloat, aiming for a casual tone.

Leaning towards me, she parrots, 'Almost?' while arching her eyebrows.

'I got a job,' I announce, spontaneously pulling her into a tight hug.

'Seriously,' she gasps, shoving me away so she can look me in the eye. 'You're not kidding?'

'I'm not kidding,' I laugh. Then, when she leaps to her feet and starts bouncing barefoot around the garden, startling Saffy, I laugh even harder. 'That's fantastic news!' she tells me, affectionally patting my shoulder as I extend my arms to take Saffy from her. The drowsy baby immediately nestles into my neck and, as always, I feel a rush of love.

'Where?' Leah asks animatedly, almost as excited as I am.

Not wanting to spoil the mood, I avoid answering her question straightaway by volunteering, 'I start next week,' and sit down in the spare plastic patio chair.

As though realising that I am deceiving her in some way, I watch her sharp little face darken as she resumes her seat next to me. 'How much are they paying you?' she asks.

'They're going to train me up and everything, but it will only be for a few evenings a week at first,' I prattle, my inner voice pleading with her not to ruin this for me.

Her voice drips with disappointment as she comments, 'Not full-time then?'

'No,' I admit, shrugging off my discomfort as I fidget in my chair. 'But it might lead to something more.'

'Something more, huh?' She sounds sceptical and bored now. She's popping chewing gum and her teeth are yellowish and unbrushed. It occurs to me that I've never once seen her mouth empty. It usually contains something. A roll-up, chewing gum, sweet and sour chicken balls, chip shop mushy peas, insults, and lies . . . Wayne's dick, most probably.

I should have known that she would quickly burst my bubble. Though I would have preferred to pretend for a little while longer, I knew it was coming. So, I reluctantly confess, 'There's one downside—'

She interrupts me before I can finish, furiously wading in with, 'They're not paying you, are they?'

She's quick. I'll give her that. But then again, she knows me. Too well as it turns out, because the joy and confidence boost that I experienced earlier when I was away from her, is slowly being nibbled away at.

A hard knot forms in my stomach but I know my eyes have a determined glint as I finally admit, 'It's a volunteer role with the Samaritans.' I try to remain enthusiastic as I paste on an unconvincing smile and add, 'I'm going to help people turn their lives around, Leah.'

She throws back her head and laughs spitefully, before turning to glare at me. 'Is that what they told you?' Teeth bared, she's more vicious than any guard dog. Even Lucky hides from her. Her voice is a harsh whisper when she goes on to attack me with, 'I always said what a useless piece of shit you were. How stupid can you be?'

Heat flashes up my neck and onto my cheeks, as I angrily respond with, 'Stupid enough to leave a good woman for a . . .'

Instead of finishing what I was about to say, I clamp my mouth shut. It's just not worth it.

'A what, exactly?' she screams in my face, unconcerned that our neighbours might hear us arguing.

'It doesn't matter,' I mutter, my gaze hitting my grass-stained trainers. But I'm cringing inside, pissed off. I made a promise to myself earlier that I would finally have it out with Leah and put my foot down with her where my kids were concerned. So, I take a big breath before saying something I might live to regret. When I open my mouth to speak my voice comes out surprisingly gentle and patient. Emotions I'm not feeling inside.

'That's not all. I have something else to tell you. I've been to see a solicitor and she's agreed to help me fight for custody of my girls.'

Leah's icy blue eyes crinkle at the corners in surprise. 'And how are you going to afford that when you're not eligible for legal aid?' she demands, folding her arms in a way that makes me think of a school bully. My girlfriend would be deadly if she were a man.

'That's my business,' I mumble, avoiding her cold gaze once more by staring at my trainers — which, up until now, I had no idea were so fascinating. A vein throbs in my neck and

I imagine it makes the snarling wolf tattoo come to life. It's a shame it can't attack my girlfriend.

'Is that so?' she drawls. And pop goes the gum in her mouth again. It's a measure of her fury, I realise. Right now, on a scale of one to ten, I'd rate her as a seven or eight.

'And where are you planning to live, if that works out for you?'

I bristle at that, but try to remain calm as I explain, 'The way I see it, Leah, I have two options.' I take a moment to snuggle Saffy closer because I need to feel her soft skin against mine.

'Go on then, hit me with option one,' she sniggers maliciously.

I'm trying to appeal to her more sympathetic side but I'm also feeling conflicted because I wonder if I'm the arsehole for asking her to take on two more children on top of a newborn. But it's not as if I'm expecting her to raise my girls. I'm their dad and I'll be the one taking care of them.

'It wouldn't be for long because the council would have to re-house us eventually,' I say encouragingly. 'Just think. We'd most likely end up in a much nicer house than this one, with three or four bedrooms. Then, we could truly be a family.'

Leah seems to mull this over for a while before rejecting the idea. 'Saffy is all the family I want,' she finally snaps. 'And you'd have to offer me a mansion before I agreed to take on your kids.'

'This is as much my home as it is yours,' I object lamely, gesturing with my head to the house behind us.

'Is that right?' She taunts provocatively. 'Well, that's where you're wrong because your name isn't even on the tenancy.'

'But it's me who pays the rent,' I argue hopelessly, knowing I'm on a hiding to nothing.

'You don't pay shit. It comes out of my benefits.'

'*Our* benefits, which are in both our names,' I remind her, tapping my chest in an ape-like motion. 'So you wouldn't be able to stop me from moving the girls in.'

She gets in my face then with a jailbird look in her eyes. 'If you do that, I'll tell the police you've been knocking me around and get you thrown out. You wouldn't be allowed within a foot of me and Saffy then.'

Horrified, I step back from her. 'You'd do that?'

'Watch me,' she snarls, getting in one last barbed-wire dig.

I made a mistake about her being a seven or eight. She rates a solid ten out of ten when it comes to anger. I've never known anyone else use the sweetest of voices to say the cruellest of things. The saddest part is that she would be believed by everyone, especially the cops. If Leah ever did what she's threatening to do there's no way I'd get my kids back.

Her words stab at my heart, but I manage to grit my teeth and respond with, 'Fair enough. Option two it is then.'

CHAPTER 37: THE GRANDMOTHER

Flustered, I bustle about the patio table, pouring coffee from a cafetiere into minuscule cups and accidentally splattering some onto Georgina's white quilted handbag, which she pretends not to notice. I'm so startled by her swanlike presence that my hands won't stop shaking, even when I give them something to do, like arranging jewel-coloured macaroons on a plate.

Georgina repeats, 'I came to check if everything was all right,' as if I hadn't heard her the first time. I knew I shouldn't have insulted her at Scarlet's funeral. I felt it in my varicose veins at the time. Now I'm paying for it. Until she wins this argument, she won't leave me alone.

'Why wouldn't they be?' I scowl at her from over the top of my glasses.

'Call me a daft old woman, but something keeps bothering me about the last time I saw you and no matter how much I try to shrug it off I can't.'

'You always were tenacious.' Recognising that flattery is effective on high-maintenance women like her, I intend to ingratiate myself into her good books. Anything to get her to stop glowering at me with suspicion. As if she knows something.

She responds belatedly by giving the smallest of nods. 'Quite.'

Now that I've run out of things to do, I sit down across from her and pin on a smile. I get the chance to observe her as she squints at the patch of brilliant blue sky above us before slipping on glittery shades. She has a habit of tucking her hair behind her ears and her fingers constantly toy with her creamy peach-rouged face. I tuck my short, soil-caked fingernails under the table when I see her long, elegantly manicured talons.

Her almond gaze finally lands on me, and her glossy mouth curves into a triumphant grin. 'I wanted to ask you about Charles,' she announces in a conspiratorial whisper as though we were close friends sharing a secret.

Deciding to play dumb, I say tetchily, 'My husband, Charles, you mean?'

Her lips twitch in annoyance at that, as if she doesn't appreciate being reminded that he was married to someone else and not her. This doesn't come as any surprise. I've known all along that she had the hots for him.

'It's a rather sensitive subject,' she acknowledges, blushing.

'But you won't let that stop you, will you, Georgina?'

Her cheeks flush red once more. That's when I notice the musty old-lady odour emanating from all around us. Rouge. Powder. Lily of the valley. Vanilla. Lavender. It's as if God gave women our age our own particular scent so that we might find each other. The same is true of our monogrammed hand-kerchiefs and elastic waistbands.

Averting her gaze, Georgina observes casually, *too casually for my liking*, 'I can't get over the fact that I would not have known you if I'd passed you in the street, as I believe I mentioned at Scarlet's funeral.'

'Is that a polite way of telling me I haven't aged well?' I pull a face, putting her on the spot.

'No of course not,' she backtracks, giving a strangled laugh.

'Ask away about Charles.' I shrug my shoulders and sigh, acting as though bored, but in reality, her visit has made me anxious and hypervigilant.

Taking a sip of her drink, her eyes meet mine over the coffee cup as she reminisces. 'It was such a shock to find out he'd passed away.'

'Is it still a shock after three years?' I reply bluntly, noticing the way her eyes have gone all watery as if they were stinging her.

Her voice falters as she says, 'It's just that he was so healthy and virile.'

There's a telling pause between us, and I'm willing to bet that she's thinking back on their past sex life. I was never sure before whether their relationship was platonic or not, but now I am convinced they were having an affair. The former Head of English sitting next to me with her sewn-on smile probably rode Charles like a bucking bronco while quoting snippets of Shakespeare. On that thought, a headache begins to throb at my temples and I realise how bone tired I am. The coffee isn't helping.

Looking around, flustered, Georgina goes on, 'His heart attack was so sudden and unexpected, I assume there was a post-mortem?'

Baffled, I shake my head. 'No, it wasn't necessary. He suffered from heart disease and had several minor heart attacks in the years leading up to his death.'

'Oh, I see,' she gasps. 'I wasn't aware of that.'

I can tell that she's stunned by this news and is probably feeling hurt that he kept this from her.

She fiddles with the pearl buttons on her silk blouse, before observing, 'He never mentioned it to me, and I thought he would have done, considering how closely we worked together.'

I huff at the understatement. 'How close exactly?'

Her face seems to collapse at this point, and the powdery, cloying scent of her fills my nostrils, making me want to vomit.

'Just friends, nothing more,' she insists haughtily, her cheek twitching in irritation. When she risks a sly sidelong glance at me, I know she is lying.

I feel inappropriate laughter bubbling away inside me as I retaliate with, 'Exactly, because Charles only shared that information with those he loved.'

It's a below-the-belt comment but well-deserved and I feel perfectly entitled to my moment of smugness when I see the ripple of sadness wash over her. The lying, cheating old witch. When Daisy and Alice moved in with me, I felt like I was beginning a new chapter in my life and that the past was behind me, but then this woman appears out of nowhere to threaten my existence. She has no idea who she is messing with.

'And were you with Charles when he died? Was it just the two of you or were there other people present? Maybe a paramedic or doctor? You did call an ambulance, right?' The questions all centring suspiciously on Charles's death are fired out of her like bullets aimed at my skull.

'Georgina, what exactly are you accusing me of?'

CHAPTER 38: THE FATHER

All the way to The Green, Leah's spiteful words continue to stab me in the back. "I'll tell the police you've been knocking me around. You wouldn't be allowed within a foot of me and Saffy then," she'd screamed. But would she actually carry out her threat just to get her own back on me? I was too angry to pack a bag, thinking it best to escape the house before either of us said anything else that we might regret. I'll fetch the car and my belongings tomorrow when we've both had a chance to calm down. My last glimpse of Leah, before I slammed out of the house with the dog tucked possessively under my arm, was of her sneering at me. The cow.

Option two was always to move back into 7 The Green and deal with what the council had to say about it later. If it weren't for leaving Saffy behind, I could even feel happy about this decision, although the place will constantly remind me of Scarlet. Her absence will be felt in all of the silent, empty rooms, but most of all in her bedroom, where Daisy and I came across her lifeless body. The image of which is permanently etched into my brain. Glazed-over eyes. Slack jaw. Head turned ever so slightly to one side, seemingly looking at the door. The pillow fibres visible on her blue lips. Worst of all, the indentation on her cheek caused by the pillow pressing down on her face. Daisy's cries, "I killed Mum."

When the lead goes slack in my hand, I look down to see Lucky has come to a stop and is growling, his tail sticking out stiffly behind him. 'What's up, boy?' I ask, frowning. But when I glance up, I realise why he is reluctant to move forward. I don't blame him. Gary Pearce and his massive dog are strutting cockily towards us, occupying most of the pavement.

The dog has enormous, muscular shoulders and is built like a heavy-weight wrestler. Although everyone knows it's an American Pit Bull — a banned breed — Gary likes to make out it's a harmless Staffordshire Bull Terrier. Known as Butch, it has a reputation for terrorising the neighbourhood and although it has a heavy gangland chain around its neck, it is off the lead and allowed to roam where it pleases. Right now, it is eyeing my scruffy little dog with something like ridicule. Just as I think it's about to pounce on Lucky, Gary puts a restraining hand on its collar.

He grimaces, as though Lucky were guilty by association. 'Is that the dead pedo's dog?'

'Someone's been gossiping,' I remark drily, thinking that it had to have been Zoom. I could tell he wasn't one to keep his gob shut.

'Nothing new there,' sniggers Gary.

I hang back, not wanting the dogs to get too near to one another. With one bite, Butch could easily snap Lucky's spine in two. But Gary persists in encouraging his dog to "say hello" appearing to find it funny.

When Lucky suddenly corrects the much larger but much younger dog with a targeted bite, effectively putting it in its place, Gary and I are both shocked as fuck. Butch yelps in fright and cowers in a submissive gesture after that, his tail between his legs. I'm made up by this, but Gary seems to take it personally. Humiliated, he yanks at the dog's chain and hisses 'Puff,' at it. I feel sorry for Butch, but can't resist commenting, 'Size doesn't always signify courage.' This is a dig at Gary for having beaten the shit out of me years ago for being a scrawny short arse.

Gary forces a smile. 'I hear you're thinking of going straight from now on. Is that right?'

My stomach gives an unpleasant lurch because his voice is laced with menace. Or am I imagining it because I'm so paranoid? Always thinking everyone's out to get me when that's not always the case. The solicitor is clearly on my side and thinks I have a strong chance of obtaining custody. I liked Rachel Winters. She wasn't stuck-up and didn't look down her nose at me. She didn't come out with any of that legal jargon either that I wouldn't have been able to understand. It helped that she was also easy on the eye. But I've learned my lesson where attractive women are concerned and won't be fooled by a pretty face again. But back to Pearce—

Pressing my lips into a firm line, I take a deep breath before wading in with, 'About time, don't you think? I'm thirty-two now with three kids.'

Disappointment pulls the smile from Gary's lips, but he brushes it off with a dirty chuckle. 'Good on you, mate. If I had a kid, I'd do the same.'

This was not the reaction I expected from him. I wrongly assumed he would try to *persuade* me otherwise in the way that only Gary Pearce can, with threats and bribes. He surprises me further by taking off down the street without saying another word, as if we no longer know each other, which suits me down to the ground. His dog follows obediently, going out of its way to keep a safe distance from Lucky, whose hackles are still up. I bite my lip as I watch them go, my mind racing off in another direction.

Could it be that things are looking up for me at last? With a solicitor on my side, a job of sorts, a home of sorts, and free of Gary's criminal influence, I think I have a real shot of getting my family back and turning my life around, just like the Samaritans promised to do. Though Leah pissed herself laughing at me for that, I genuinely want to become a better person. For my girls mostly. Above all, though, to atone for the harm I caused Scarlet. She was a beautiful person, despite her mental health problems, and didn't deserve to be treated the way she was. I wish I could tell her that abandoning her was the biggest mistake of my life.

Karma got me in the shape of an angel-faced woman who was more skilled at manipulation than a room full of Tory MPs. Wincing, I feel the brutality of Leah's attack all over again. All morning, I'd worried about her reaction to me accepting the unpaid role, but I hadn't expected it to blow up in my face quite that badly. It only goes to show that you never truly know someone. Even your nearest and dearest. For instance . . .

Who was Scarlet on the phone to that evening that caused her to become afraid for her own life, *and with good reason*. And why had Leah decided to visit Scarlet that same night? Did she really return afterwards just to look for a lost ring? Most important of all, could my kind, thoughtful, beautiful daughter, who is only nine, have killed her own mother?

CHAPTER 39: THE GRANDMOTHER

Daisy smiles like butter wouldn't melt in her mouth as I tuck a stray lock of her silky, coppery hair behind her ear. She doesn't recoil from my touch for once. And I suspect that's because her dad is outside in the car waiting for her and she doesn't want to do anything that might prevent her from leaving. Since our fallout yesterday, neither of us has mentioned the cat or the incident with the nuts. Only Alice, out of the three of us, is acting naturally and as one would expect from a seven-year-old. Daisy and I may have called a truce for now, but I worry that our relationship is getting worse rather than better. This is something I am committed to working on, starting from today. I make an awkward attempt at it now by saying, 'I hope you and Alice have a lovely day with your dad and I want you to know that I have a special dinner planned for you when you get back later.'

'Is it spaghetti bolognese?' Alice whirls into the kitchen excitedly, like a miniature Tasmanian devil. I swear she can hear any mention of food from a mile away. In my next breath, I sweep that thought away as uncharitable.

'No, it isn't, Miss Nosey,' I joke.

'Mac and cheese then?' Daisy mumbles, in an attempt to match my effort at making up.

Impressed, I remark, 'Clever girl.'

Daisy peers up at me from under her pale eyelashes and nods as if to say, "And don't I know it." She hasn't yet been able to outsmart me, though.

'Now, girls, have you got everything you need?' I fuss.

They both nod. Alice then flings herself into my arms, squeezing me tightly and noisily kissing me on the cheek. I'm not yet entirely comfortable with such exaggerated displays of affection, but Alice doesn't appear to notice when I skilfully peel myself out of her grasp. The child can be a little too intense at times. Daisy, on the other hand, has already left the house and is racing towards her dad's car. For once she doesn't have that raggedy old doll with her.

'Off you go, love,' I say, following Alice to the door, where I stand forlornly and watch the girls get into the bashed and rusted piece of metal that their father drives. Lord, my heart turns over when I think of them riding around in that. I wonder if the car even has airbags.

'Be careful,' I shout after them, then, for Vince's benefit. 'And don't be late back.' But he doesn't even acknowledge me. Rude man.

Back in the kitchen, I wipe away a stray tear and feel a sense of loss creep up on me. What will I do without the children for a whole day? I'm self-aware enough to know that if they weren't spending the day with *him*, I wouldn't be nearly as concerned. Without his influence, I'm convinced Daisy wouldn't resent me so much. Nothing would make me happier than for Vince to just disappear. Smirking to myself, I wonder if there are any paid assassins for hire in our picture-perfect village. But on a more serious note, Daisy would have to come to rely solely on me if her dad was no longer on the scene. What we lack is trust, and since I'm mostly to blame for our issues, I'm my own worst enemy. I should really remember to take my medication more regularly in future because failing to do so seriously lowers my mood and causes me to act out of character. Without the concoction of beta blockers and antidepressants, I become extremely irritable and revert to my old melancholy ways.

We both know that I was the one who added the nuts to the cake, so it was mean of me to tease Daisy about being the guilty one. It's a shame she can't take a joke and I wonder if she will ever forgive me. I'm not sure what gets into me at times — *the devil, most probably* — like now, when I should be concentrating on cleaning the smudges on the windows that are visible in the gleaming sunshine . . . but instead I'm considering getting into my car and following Vince and the girls so I can keep an eye on them and make sure they're safe. But what if they saw me? *I'll be careful*, I tell myself. After all, watching people without their knowing is what I do best. Some might deem this spying. Whatever you want to call it, I've been getting away with it for years without ever being discovered.

There's still time. They won't have made it out of the village yet. Impulsively, I grab my keys, walking stick and handbag, take off my apron and slippers, put on some comfortable walking shoes, and head out the door. My automatic, almost new island-blue Mini electric is parked at the side of the cottage next to the charging point. In hindsight, I probably should have offered to lend Vince my car. At least that way I'd know the children would be safe. It's too late now. After sliding into the front seat, I shift into drive and the car starts effortlessly and I'm soon driving across the charming white bridge over the pond and taking a left onto Ryhall Road.

Not knowing exactly what direction they'll be taking, I'm left with two options. I can either take the A1 into Peterborough or keep going on this road into Stamford. Assuming that Vince is heading back to Peterborough, I join the A1 and almost instantly spot his beat-up vehicle. They must have got off to a slow start because he's only three cars ahead of me. I tuck my car behind the one in front so I can keep a close eye on them without them seeing me. The fumes being pumped out of Vince's exhaust make it incredibly easy to follow.

I spend the next forty minutes listening to a boring Radio 4 play while gritting my teeth and cursing under my breath at lorry drivers who keep driving up my arse. One even has the audacity to pip me for not driving fast enough. He probably believes the reason for this is because I'm an elderly, grey-haired lady driving a Mini, but it's mainly because Vince is driving so damn slowly. *Honestly, he's as useless as the "ueue" in queue.*

When the next impatient lorry driver speedily overtakes me and casts a mean sidelong glance my way, I yell, 'Fuck you, arsehole,' while raising two fingers. His expression when he sees me is priceless and it makes me chuckle. But my laughter soon dies when I realise where we are heading . . .

CHAPTER 40: THE FATHER

Daisy is helping me paint the living room a cloudy light blue after changing into some of her old clothes from upstairs. Alice, who has zero interest in decorating, is binge-watching Disney films and munching on a family-sized bag of Maltesers. If Daisy or I so much as exchange words, Alice brutally shushes us, before turning her attention back to the princesses on screen, which makes me smile every time. I can tell they're really glad to be back home, even though their mum died here. At first, I was nervous about taking them to 7 The Green as it's impossible to keep kids quiet. But then I thought, so what if the neighbours hear us? Let them. The sooner everyone finds out I've moved back in, the better, as far as I'm concerned. There will be uproar if the council tries to kick me out, especially when people realise that I intend to bring the girls back here to live. Once I've won my court case that is.

Earlier, Daisy presented me with an envelope with my name on it, saying, 'I was told to give this to you. She also said something about receipts.'

My oldest daughter always calls her grandmother "she", never Granny. 'Thanks, love,' I'd murmured noncommittally while trying to figure out how long I could get away with not handing over any receipts for the cash inside. What a cruel joke it would be to use Mrs Castle's own money against her in court. A hundred quid a week soon adds up and solicitors like Rachel Winters don't come cheap even when working for a fixed fee.

Sitting down to a big plate of fish and chips was a bad idea before attempting the painting, I realise now, as I'm feeling stuffed, but already the house looks so much brighter. The old grotty carpet has been ripped up and all the grimy fingerprints and smudges on the walls have been covered up with fresh paint. Later, I've promised the girls I'll take them to the cemetery to visit their mum's grave before taking them back to their grandmother's. This might not be the day out Mrs Castle had in mind for the girls when she offered to fund my weekly visits but I'll be blowed if I'm going to waste money on trips out right now. Not when I need to buy things for the house to make it nice for the girls.

'I'm bored,' Alice suddenly declares from the sofa, rolling onto her back and sighing.

'I thought you were watching your video.'

Alice rolls her eyes dramatically. 'I've already seen it hundreds of times.'

'Why don't you play with Lucky in the garden?'

On hearing his name, the little white dog's ears prick up. He was an instant hit with the girls who fell head over heels for him, and he them, just as I predicted they would. We've never been a cat family.

'Okay,' Alice grudgingly agrees, as though she had been asked to go down a chimney and sweep it. Rising to her feet, she cries, 'Come on, Lucky,' and they both disappear out of the back door.

Now that I'm finally alone with Daisy I'm not sure what to say. There are so many things I want to ask her, like *Did you kill your mother?* But I'm afraid of how she might answer. Whatever she's done, I'm still her dad and the way I see it, it's my job to keep her safe.

'So, Daisy,' I make a start. 'How have things been going with your grandmother since we last spoke?'

When Daisy rolls her eyes, she really rolls her eyes, outdoing her sister.

'Has she said or done anything else to upset you?'

'No.' Daisy's eyes hit the floor and I assume from this that she's lying. But why lie to me when she knows I'm not a fan of Yvonne Castle? Kids are complex creatures though, my daughter especially so. She's always been extremely sensitive and has a habit of internalising everything.

'You would tell me if she hurt you in any way?' I urge, wanting to hold her in my arms, but Daisy already thinks she's too old for cuddles, so I normally let her come to me when she wants love and attention.

'Dad!' she objects, acting as though she'd rather talk about anything other than her grandmother. I take the hint and change tack.

'So, what do you think of me coming back here to live?'

Daisy gives a contemplative shrug and asks, 'What about Leah?'

'It's complicated, but I think it's probably best we part ways.'

Daisy looks alarmed. 'But what will happen to Saffy?'

She's right to be concerned about her sister. It's what I'm thinking about too, but I don't say so. I've been worrying myself sick over how Leah will cope on her own with the baby. We haven't talked yet, but I'm going to stop by there later when the kids have gone, to see if we can come to a compromise. I know she loves Saffy and would never intentionally hurt her, but she also struggles with her at times and this can result in her being neglectful. I'll happily have Saffy half the time if Leah is agreeable. But I suspect her mum will have something to say about that. Like Mrs Castle, Leah's mum has never liked me. *What is it with mothers-in-law?*

'Dad? Dad . . .'

When I realise Daisy is trying to get my attention, and is annoyed that I've zoned out on her, I shake my head in an attempt to try to get rid of all the anxieties and fears inside it. No such luck.

'Yes, Daisy,' I stutter, watching her frown deepen.

Daisy mumbles, 'Can I tell you a secret?'

Oh my God. This is it, isn't it? The moment I've been secretly dreading when my daughter finally confesses to murder. What the fuck? I take it back what I said earlier. I'd prefer not to know.

I swallow what feels like a giant marble as I spell out, 'Of course, Daisy, you can tell me anything. You know that.'

Daisy glances out of the window, checking her sister is still out there before hissing, 'But you mustn't tell anyone. Otherwise,' she hesitates before mysteriously adding, 'I could be in a lot of trouble.'

Fuck. Balls. Buggering balls. And bollocks. Mustn't forget the bollocks.

'Cross my heart and hope to die,' I tell her, putting my palm on my pounding heart, which at this moment is all hers. My Daisy. My lovely daughter. Whom I'll never stop loving no matter what. If anyone is going to take the blame for killing Scarlet, it's going to be me. Never her.

You could knock me down with a feather when Daisy comes out with, 'I think *she*, Mrs Castle, poisoned a little girl from school.'

CHAPTER 41: THE GRANDMOTHER

Observing the tired-looking row of grey houses with their ugly concrete facades and worn regimental front doors, I realise that my brand-new car is as much out of place in The Green as I am. Spiky metal railings guard the properties that are packed in as tight as old peoples' dentures and some also have broken cars and rusting fridges on their driveways. Bins left out for too long spill over onto patches of littered grass.

On the drive here, I passed a Spar shop that had groups of teenage hoodies swarming around it, who eyed up both me and my car. Fortunately, I'm just someone's harmless old granny so they quickly lost interest. I've said it before and I'll say it again there are benefits to being invisible, because old, grey-haired ladies go unnoticed and that suits me just fine. Still, it's a depressing place to live with little chance of escape for those who are interred here. The Nene Fields estate is like a scab that's become infected after being picked at too many times.

However, having grown up on the Becontree estate, I am accustomed to poverty and hardship, and since these people *are* my people, I can hold my own among them. Not that they would ever know this. The fact that people are shocked and upset when elderly folk don't act in a way that is expected of them never ceases to amuse me. Take the young, slim blonde woman pushing the buggy, who I nearly ran over when I momentarily lost Vince's car and had to jump the traffic lights to catch up . . . when she saw me speeding through the red light without giving a thought to her or her screaming baby, she couldn't believe her eyes. She even stopped chewing her gum to stare open-mouthed at me.

And now I'm parked five doors down from Scarlet's old address, concealed behind a large white van with a missing number plate, wondering what the hell Vince is doing at 7 The Green with the girls when I was told he was taking them to Ferry Meadows. I'm about to step out of the car and investigate further — it wouldn't be the first time I've spied in other people's windows — when there's a loud rap on my window.

A bald man dressed all in black with gold chains dangling around his bull-sized neck is staring curiously at me. Next to him is a massive, slobbering dog that looks as if it eats people for breakfast and who has a matching chain around its neck. Despite feeling apprehensive, I wind my window down an inch to peer out.

'Are you on a stakeout or something?' the man asks, sniggering.

'Very funny,' I respond sarcastically, then immediately hit the button to wind my window back up. The man is obviously an idiot. I know his type. Hard as nails. Drug dealer. Thief. With a list of convictions as long as your arm. But what I can't tell is if he's a threat to me or not.

'Plain clothes, then?' He shouts through the glass, as though he wants to hold my interest and keep me talking.

He thinks he's hilarious, which makes him extremely irritating, so I wind my window down again and enquire politely, 'Do you have an off button?'

He frowns. 'A what?'

I nod, and cuttingly add, 'I thought so.'

His expression darkens, and I understand then that he's onto me . . . aware on some level that I am taking the piss out of him. In an attempt to regain control, he sneers, 'You're obviously not from around here, not in a car like that. Are you visiting someone?'

'How may I ask is that any business of yours?' I complain haughtily, although secretly I'm rather enjoying myself. It feels liberating to let the mask slip for once, where it doesn't matter because no one knows me.

He growls. 'Look, lady, we take care of our own around here—'

'And you think someone like me poses a threat to the local criminals, rapists and convicts?' I comment innocently.

He snorts, puffing out his muscular chest like an emperor penguin. 'I've never seen you before, which means you're not visiting family.' He then continues in a decidedly aggressive manner, 'So why are you here?'

Narrowing my eyes, I remark, 'I was going to give you a nasty look, but I see you already have one.'

'Don't you be giving me no beef, lady,' he warns, narrowing his eyes.

'Luckily stupidity is not a crime.' I throw him a charming smile and begin winding up my window at the same time, saying, 'So you're free to go.'

It's evident to me that he is absolutely clueless about what to do. He has clearly never come across someone like me before. On the one hand, I'm a harmless old woman — an old fart, a coffin dodger, a dinosaur, an old fogey — but on the other, I've insulted him. Not once, but three times. He might be stupid; but he isn't so dumb not to know when he is being made fun of. It could go one of two ways. He could drag me of my car and give me a black eye or he could decide I'm not worth it and walk away. His public image would suffer though if he was caught beating up a defenceless old woman. He goes for the second option—

'The world is full of Karens,' he mutters, sloping off with his dog in tow, kicking out at a piece of loose trash as he goes.

Keeping one eye on him in my driver's wing mirror, I let out a long sigh and ask myself what on earth am I playing at. Why do I keep taking such risks? Then, reaching into the glove compartment, I fumble around for a packet of pills. Usually, I have some spares stashed in here somewhere. Yes, they are right here. Propranolol and Sertraline, prescribed in equally high doses. "Widow's medicine" I call them.

I throw two of the pills to the back of my throat and swallow them down without water. Hardcore. Like me.

A while later, just as I'm starting to feel relaxed from the medication, I notice Vince and the girls coming out of number 7's front door, so I duck down in my seat to hide. They're not glancing in my direction, and it's obvious they haven't seen me . . . so when his beaten-up old car indicates and pulls out of the street, I start my car and follow.

This time, though, I drive more slowly and don't feel the need to yell at other drivers or raise my fist in frustration. I even allow an old pensioner with a walking stick to cross the street in front of me, waiting patiently for him to reach the other side while continuing to belt out the hymn we sing at church the most: 'Give Me Joy in My Heart (Sing Hosanna)'.

CHAPTER 42: THE FATHER

There is no shortage of greenery in the Eastfield Road cemetery, which features a tree-lined avenue that looks out over brick-lined graves in the older section and black glossy headstones in the newer part where Scarlet is buried. Daisy has hurried ahead to kneel next to her mother's grave so she can arrange the flowers in the stone vase that has "For Mum" printed on it. We got the brightly coloured bouquet from the garage where we filled up the car using Mrs Castle's cash.

Alice, quiet and thoughtful for once, walks beside me holding my hand. Every so often she glances up at me as if about to ask me something.

'What is it, Alice?' I prompt, squeezing her hand.

'Dad, who is Jesus?' she ponders, frowning.

Thinking that's an easy one for once, I reply confidently, 'The son of God. I thought they taught you that sort of thing at school.'

'If he was the son of God then why did his dad let him die?'

Okay, I have to admit that one is not so simple. But I think my credibility is saved when I explain, 'So he could save us all.'

'All of us?' Alice pulls a cynical face.

An atheist at seven. What is the world coming to? 'That's right,' I reply.

Alice shakes her head before protesting, 'But if he died to save us then why do people, like Mum, still have to die?'

Noticing how Alice's eyes are now glistening with tears, I feel my own eyes well up. As my mind starts working faster, wondering what is going on in her head, the thought of any of my children dying makes me shudder.

'I don't know,' I answer truthfully, gazing at her for a moment.

'Why not?' she insists.

When you're a dad it's kind of implied that you should know everything, but in my case, nothing could be further from the truth. I'd like to bet that Daisy and Alice are both smarter than me, given that I dropped out of school at sixteen with zero qualifications, not even one GCSE to my name. Just a lot of old wounds that, despite what people may say, never heal.

'Nobody does,' I sigh, wishing I had all the answers. One of the amazing things about being a parent is how much your kids worship you while they're young, but it's heartbreaking when they start to grow up and realise that you're just like everyone else. An adult who lies and is untrustworthy. If only I could pretend for a while longer to be the all-knowing God-like figure in my children's lives. But I can't even solve the most uncomplicated of mysteries, like— *What the hell is that bloody woman doing here?*

Following my appalled gaze, Alice exclaims excitedly, 'It's Granny,' while jumping up and down on the spot.

I was right then, about her following us. All along, I'd felt like someone was watching us, but every time I glanced over my shoulder, I saw nobody. I did, however, see a bright blue car in my rearview mirror once or twice, but didn't mention it to the girls in case I was mistaken. I watch Mrs Castle act all startled, as though she's stunned to see us in the cemetery, but as she hobbles towards us — the irritating tap, tap, tap of her walking stick disturbing the peace and quiet of the graveyard — her cold, difficult-to-read expression gradually returns.

'Fancy seeing you here. I got such a shock when I realised it was you,' Mrs Castle remarks, beaming at Alice, who instantly wraps her arms around the woman's waist to greet her, almost unsteadying her in the process.

Nice recovery but you don't fool me, I'm tempted to say. Instead, I paste on a fake smile for Alice's sake, and observe cynically, 'Exactly what I was thinking.'

Looking mildly uncomfortable, Mrs Castle turns to face me and pointedly exclaims, 'I thought you were spending the day at Ferry Meadows.'

Do I imagine it or does her tone seem slightly accusing? Unless she followed us to 7 The Green, and I wouldn't put it past her, she wouldn't know *where* we actually spent the day. I decide not to say anything when I see Alice nervously hopping from one foot to another, clearly indicating her discomfort. It's one thing for me to tell a whopping lie but I don't want my daughter to be caught out doing so. She would hate that.

When Mrs Castle's alert eyes alight on her eldest granddaughter, who has stopped arranging flowers to stare hostilely at us, she remarks, 'I see Daisy has brought flowers for her mum's grave. How thoughtful.'

It occurs to me how odd it is for Mrs Castle to have come here empty-handed. It's unusual for somebody of her generation not to bring flowers. I catch her gazing down at her empty hands as if she too were thinking the same thing and I'm about to comment on this but Alice beats me to it.

'Have you come to see Mum too?' she asks eagerly, as if keen to avoid the subject of Ferry Meadows and the lie that accompanies it.

'Yes, but now that you're here, I'll make myself scarce.'

'You don't have to do that,' I protest weakly, feeling it's expected of me.

She shakes her head emphatically, 'No, it's fine. I was going to visit Charles anyway.'

'Who is Charles?' Alice asks, screwing up her nose.

'Your Grandfather Castle.'

Alice's eyes widen on hearing this. 'Can I see where he is buried?'

For some reason, Mrs Castle appears dumbfounded by this question and her face takes on a worried expression. I get the distinct feeling that she is trying to hide something from us. But what could that possibly be?

'I don't want to take you away from your father,' she mumbles, avoiding my gaze. This convinces me that she's definitely up to something.

'Not at all.' I go for casual, but really, I'm grinning inside, especially when the old woman's lips start to twitch in annoyance. Her patience frays even more as I slyly add, 'We can all go once we're done visiting Scarlet.'

She begins, 'No really—'

But Alice cuts her off, insisting, 'Yes, Granny. We'll all go together. Like a proper family.'

Both mine and Yvonne Castle's eyebrows soar at that. Alice then puts one hand in her grandmother's and one in mine, and the three of us, joined in the middle by Alice, awkwardly make our way over to Scarlet's grave where a furious Daisy is waiting for us.

CHAPTER 43: THE GRANDMOTHER

'I could have sworn it was this one,' I admit feebly, feeling my chin drop onto my chest in defeat as I run a wrinkled, blue-veined palm over the chilly gravestone of a stranger.

'How can you not know where your dead husband is buried?' Daisy asks irritably, and with good cause, I happen to think. Because she's right. How could I have forgotten where Charles was buried? What sort of widow does that make me? Not the grieving kind one could argue.

'I took a sleeping tablet last night after a very unexpected and upsetting visit from an old friend,' I lie, fearing if I tell the truth that I will be judged for using antidepressants while driving. 'I think I must still be feeling the effects of it. It's either that or I'm going senile,' I attempt a joke, but it back-fires on me when I notice them exchanging concerned looks, as though they truly believe I'm suffering from dementia. That wouldn't necessarily be a bad thing, I decide because it would excuse my most recent erratic behaviour, *and surely Daisy would have to forgive me then*.

Taking advantage of the chance to play on their sympathy and therefore avoid suspicion, I let out a small sob while stumbling on my words, 'It's not much fun getting old and losing your memory. When you're young no one warns you that you eventually forget both the good and the bad times.'

'You're not old, Granny,' Alice, God bless her, comes to my rescue, just like I knew she would. Counted on it even.

As I gaze across at the hundreds of named gravestones scattered throughout the cemetery, tears slide down my cheeks. 'Where are you, Charles?' I whimper. But Vince is the one who reaches out to steady me when I stumble and almost fall. 'Careful,' he warns, sounding sincere. Funny that, when I imagine he'd love nothing more than to be rid of me. How ironic would it be if, due to my advanced age, I was deemed unfit to raise Daisy and Alice only for them to be brought up by a liar and a cheat? Never mind thief and ex-drug addict.

'It must be this dreadful heat making us all wilt,' I tell him.

'I'll help you find Grandfather?' Alice offers, biting her lower lip, as though seeing me distressed and disorientated upsets her.

'Thank you, sweetie,' I gush, tilting my head to one side as if I'm suddenly experiencing hearing loss too.

'I'll help too,' Daisy murmurs.

Moved by her offer, my face creases into a grin when I see the concern in Daisy's eyes. Her hand is just inches away from reaching out to touch me. At last, I sense she feels something other than anger and distrust towards me. Seizing the moment, I grasp her arm and lean into her, as if I didn't already have a perfectly good walking stick to hand.

'I think I can just about find the strength to get going again if you let me lean on you, sweetheart, while Alice goes to look for Charles's grave.'

Daisy dutifully obeys, while Alice skips on ahead, reading aloud the names on every grave she encounters. Vince, meanwhile, gives me the cold shoulder as though he doesn't buy into my newfound vulnerability.

'Richard Wright, Anne Clarke with an E, Jane without the Y Armstrong,' Alice musically pings the names off one by one.

'Now that I have you to myself, I have something to show you,' I tell Daisy, but I say it loudly enough for her father to hear. It's important that he does in case Daisy has confided in him her fears about the cat. She's being nice to me for once, and I mean to make the most of it.

'It's about Hero,' I go on to explain, pulling a crumpled envelope from my pocket with my free hand and presenting it to her. Her body tenses immediately on hearing the cat's name, but her eyes soften when I say, 'It's a note from his new owner letting us know how well he is doing in his new home. She even sent a picture. Look.'

I risk a glance at my granddaughter then, noticing how her expression has changed from doubt to relief. She obviously believes me. Thank goodness. At last I am exonerated from the unimaginable crime she has suspected me of — that of harming my beloved cat. I may be bad and capable of very dark deeds, but even I'm horrified by this suggestion.

Without removing the support of her arm, Daisy hesitantly takes the letter and the photograph and runs her inquisitive eyes over both. 'Hope White, is that the name of his new owner?' she asks.

'Yes, dear,' I nod.

'It seems like he's really happy where he is,' Daisy observes quietly, gazing up at me with eyes that are no longer angry.

'Seems that way,' I agree with a smile meant just for her. 'Although your father was absolutely right to insist on us getting rid of him.'

Daisy gives her father a shrewd narrow-eyed look, obviously not realising that he'd already spoken to me about this. I can almost imagine her mind whirring with all of the other things he might not have mentioned to her. Seeing her stare at him as though everything was his fault certainly makes a change. It's a small victory but I'll take it, nonetheless.

Over my shoulder, I mumble to Vince, 'We couldn't risk any harm to Daisy, could we?'

'Of course not,' he points out in a scratchy voice, as if he had been wrong-footed.

'After seeing those awful rashes on Daisy's arms and legs and hearing her cough and wheeze, the poor love, we were left with no choice but to rehome Hero.'

At that Daisy's eyebrows shoot up her forehead. Another falsehood, she'll be thinking, but the look I give her warns her to *bear with me*.

'It was simply one of those unfortunate things. Nobody's fault at all. Isn't that right, Daisy?' I pitch innocently.

After a pause, during which she studies me intently, Daisy accepts the gift I'm offering her — of not being to blame for Hero's disappearance — she gives me a goofy, lopsided smile and nods enthusiastically. 'Yes, Granny.'

The look on Vince's face after that . . . well, let's just say I've had bowel movements more attractive.

'I've found him! I've found Charles,' Alice's voice pipes up enthusiastically from behind one of the shiny black headstones.

'You run along,' I encourage Daisy, graciously waving her away, adding, 'I'll catch you up in a minute.'

She then bounds off, but not before giving me a gentle pat on the hand to let me know that what I did for her won't be forgotten. Vince chases after her because, understandably, he doesn't want to be left alone with me. As they assemble around the late Charles Castle's grave, my memory, which is absolutely fine by the way, transports me back to the time I visited this cemetery and first met the woman who would change my life forever.

The real Yvonne Castle . . .

CHAPTER 44: THE FATHER

With my hands stuffed in my pockets, I trudge dejectedly along Saxon Road, dodging loud sweary kids on bikes as I go, before turning into Roman Court, a place where anti-social behaviour and theft are as common as dogends and garbage. I lived at number 79 up until my old man died. Leah lives at number 46 . . . my home too until a few days ago. Overcrowded houses. Overflowing bins. Peeling paint. Graffiti on garage doors. Boarded-up windows. Rusty, flimsy scaffolding climbs every other house as though they are the only thing holding the crumbling walls up. The neglected street looks like a crash site. As if a jumbo jet had ploughed through it. I've never flown. Just one of the many things I've never been able to afford to do. I feel like a bit of a wreck myself, though. It's hard to remain positive when your life turns to shit. Screw that, let's call it by its real name, diarrhoea.

Seeing the change in Daisy, when her granny came over all funny like that as if she were about to pass out, was difficult for me to take. It made me question once again, am I doing the right thing in battling to take them away from Mrs Castle? The truth is she can provide them with so much more than I can — a safe environment and a good school. Under her roof, the girls want for nothing. Aside from their dad, that is. Until today, Daisy hadn't fallen under the woman's spell like Alice had, and I felt she was on my side. But seeing her granny frail and in need of help seemed to move her in the same way she'd taken care of her mother. Daisy is unable to help herself. She's a natural caregiver.

In my opinion, Mrs Castle is a talented actress who knows when to turn on the waterworks to make the girls feel sorry for her. The trouble is, it's working, and this means I'm in for an even bigger fight than I imagined. Because what if the girls decide in the end that they want to stay with their grandmother? But if I'm wrong and the frailty isn't an act, and she's really losing the plot and going senile, this could also play in my favour. Not even a high court judge could argue I'm not the best person to raise my kids then. It's not as if I'd wish dementia on my worst enemy, but just when I thought everything was going my way she had to go and outsmart me.

When she claimed to have seen Daisy's rashes and heard her wheezing, I could see the smug look on her face as she sided with her granddaughter on the fictitious allergy to cats. This was a blatant lie, and it makes me wonder how many more tricks the devious old bat has up her sleeve. Despite everything Daisy has told me about her grandmother, she is definitely going soft on her. I swear Mrs Castle took the kids back with her just to spite me, knowing I'd lose a precious hour of my time with them.

Pursing her lips in that prudish way of hers, she'd prat-tled, 'It's no trouble and it will save you a journey,' as if she were doing me a favour. By this stage, my two girls were almost holding her upright and she was leaning against them as if afraid she might fall. When I saw that, I have to admit, all I wanted to do was rip them away from her.

Still, I've now got an extra hour to try to sort things out with Leah. Not that I'm holding out much hope on that score. But now that we've both had some time to cool down, there's no reason we can't get along . . . for Saffy's sake if nothing else. But all that goes out of the window and I see red when I turn the corner and see Wayne's shiny, freshly washed and polished, piano-black BMW coupe parked outside her house.

I hammer on the front door glass, almost breaking it, and it reminds me of the time I punched out the glass at Scarlet's house to make it look like someone had broken in. I did this to keep my daughter safe. Later on, I also shielded Leah when I caught her letting herself out of 7 The Green under the pretext of searching for a lost ring and she confessed to being at Scarlet's the night she was murdered. If it weren't for me, Leah would have been arrested, possibly even charged for entering a crime scene and for lying to the police about our alibis. And this is how she repays me.

Intent on keeping me at the door as if I were a stranger, Leah peers at me through an inch gap in the door and hisses, 'What do you want?'

'What's going on, Leah?' I demand, gesturing to Wayne's fancy car on the road. I know he's inside my house somewhere, hiding. Leah probably would have insisted he stay out of the way, not wanting any trouble. He'd better keep his grubby hands off the remote control for my precious 40-inch flat-screen TV, which . . . ahem . . . fell off the back of a lorry, much like most of the stuff in our house. Losing your woman to another guy is one thing, but your LED Ultra HD smart TV . . .

She lets out a long sigh and runs her fingers over her newly bleached hair, which looks clean for once. Her black roots have gone and she's wearing a new jumpsuit that looks expensive. 'We're not together anymore, Vince.' She shrugs as if she doesn't owe me any answers. And perhaps she doesn't after I walked out on her. But my ego knows best so I protest—

'And how long did you wait before replacing me? An hour? Half a day?'

'He has a job,' she replies in a matter-of-fact voice.

'*I* have a job,' I point out indignantly.

'He gets paid for his,' she huffs, raising one eyebrow. I can't help wondering if Wayne dislikes heavily pencilled-on eyebrows as much as I do.

'All I wanted to do was help people,' I argue, cringing at the way I make myself sound like a victim.

Hackles raised, she scowls, 'What about helping me and Saffy?'

'I do my fair share.'

'Who decides what is your fair share?'

She has a point, although I don't say so.

'You were going to leave me and Saffy alone at night to help other people. Pissheads and crackheads. People who don't want to live anymore.'

'I can make a difference to those people's lives. I know I can,' I state, trying to impress on her how important volunteering is to me.

Leah growls, 'Try making a difference to your family,' and then adds sulkily, 'Anyway, Vince, I'm done. You and me are over.'

'Clearly,' I sneer sarcastically, but then I decide that Wayne and Leah don't matter and that it's my pride that's hurt, not my heart. 'Fair enough, but—' and I'm about to say "We still need to talk about Saffy" because I'm determined to remain a hands-on dad even if her mum and I are no longer together when I see the glittering diamond on Leah's engagement finger.

'Is that the ring you lost at Scarlet's house?' I ask, stunned.

She looks at the ring in disbelief as if she has no idea how it got there, and her attitude instantly shifts from boredom to humiliation.

'It's just that I haven't seen you wear it before.' As she stares at me in shock, unsure of how to respond, the truth rushes at me like a Pitbull with bared teeth. 'If I didn't know any better,' I venture, not quite ready to believe it yet, 'I'd assume Wayne gave you that ring, which is why it was so important to you, and that you two are already engaged.'

I know I'm right when she opens her glossy lips but no words tumble out. A knot forms in my stomach making me want to puke. Confirmation of her cheating *does* hurt. And since this is precisely what I did to Scarlet, she comes to my mind right away. That's why I deserve to experience the same suffering. They say Karma is a bitch, and they're too bloody right.

Leah's eyes linger on me for a time before softening and she eventually whispers, 'I'm really sorry, Vince. I didn't mean for this to happen. You can't help who you fall in love with, can you? Or back in love with in my case.'

Her words stab at my heart because, word for word, that is exactly what I said to my wife the day I packed up and left 7 The Green. If it weren't for me, Scarlet would be alive today. I'm convinced of that. I might not have harmed her, but make no mistake, her death is on me.

CHAPTER 45: THE GRANDMOTHER

Georgina Bell is starting to become a serious problem. She has left two messages on my answering machine since her visit the other day, stating that she'd like to see Charles's death certificate as she still feels that things don't quite add up. The nosey mare! There was definitely a threat to her tone, which I did not appreciate. I'd be happy to oblige, but, of course, then I'd have to kill her. I chuckle to myself at the thought. The children are asleep in their separate bedrooms while I'm sitting up in bed after a very long day, sipping my glass of brandy. I could tell Georgina, once again, that she is barking up the wrong tree and that there was nothing at all strange or suspicious about Charles's death, but I doubt she would believe me. Hmm. How am I going to handle this situation? That's the burning question. She'd better watch out, that's all I can say. She has no idea what I'm capable of.

If I told her my real story, she'd have to believe me . . . since I've never had the pleasure of meeting Charles Castle, much less harmed him. However, that's not possible. I haven't been Nancy Tyrrell for a very long time. As for Yvonne Castle, the gentle, sweet and kind-hearted widow I encountered at the cemetery, she certainly wasn't capable of plotting her husband's death. I recall that she talked about him all the time. When we first met, we were both widows, but her tears went on long after mine had dried up. Although we were both grieving our husbands — in our own ways that is — who were buried in the same cemetery, it turned out hers was significantly wealthier than mine, and she was left in an enviable position with a generous pension, a mortgage-free home, and savings, whereas my husband Ted had been in prison for ten years prior to his death for a string of offences including robbery and murder. As far as I was concerned, those years by myself were the happiest years of our marriage.

Sleepily, I rub my eyes, trying to erase my thoughts because guilt nags at me whenever I think of Yvonne, who quite honestly wouldn't have hurt a fly. We became immediate friends. Inseparable for a while. And why not? She was both lonely and alone, if you know what I mean. Her spoilt, ungrateful only daughter refused to have anything to do with her and Yvonne had no other family. Except for her two grandchildren, of course, whom she had never met. I discovered all there was to know about the widow's life in the months that followed. She took great pleasure in sharing all the personal information and anecdotes about her early years, her marriage to Charles, her experiences as a mother, her concerns for Scarlet and her children and most of all, her love for her daughter and husband.

It was me who persuaded her to sell the grand house on Thorpe Road in Peterborough and move to the charming cottage in Rutland, where she, meaning *I*, could have a fresh start in a place where no one knew me. Even though she was more attractive than I was, we were similar in height and build, so "Becoming Yvonne" as I liked to call it, wasn't nearly as difficult as you might imagine. But before my transformation could take place, there was one more daunting thing left for me to do . . . I had to make Yvonne disappear. I refuse to traumatise myself further by remembering the gory details. I still struggle with flashbacks whenever I run myself a bath.

Before that though, I deliberately isolated Yvonne from her former friends and made myself everything to her — friend, confidante, helper, advisor — so I could steal her identity, but she allowed it to happen. She never once asked herself why I was so interested in her life. Generally speaking, people don't. They think others find them fascinating, even when that isn't the case. In many ways, she was everything I was not — a homemaker, expert baker, avid gardener, and an active charity fund-raiser — all of which I had to emulate. Some hobbies, like baking and gardening, I've taken to more than others, but having to attend church every week is tedious. Committees and social groups are also not my thing.

However, there was one big difference between Yvonne and me. She was weak and a pushover, *a timid old thing*, whereas I was quite the opposite. *Hard as nails*, Ted used to call me. It's true nobody could pull the wool over my eyes. But Yvonne's self-centred daughter — who deserved to be cut out of her parents will; something I later made sure of — treated her like trash and Charles, who everyone declared a saint but wasn't, had an affair with that awful Georgina Bell right under his poor wife's nose. I detest that woman for what she did to Yvonne, who didn't deserve to be treated that way. The whore is deserving of nothing less than a public whipping if you ask me. If Ted had done that to me, I would have beaten his dick with a rolling pin until it was black and blue and fell off.

The peachy rouged creature has temporarily disturbed my peace of mind and I haven't yet figured out what to do about it, but aside from that, I have everything I've ever coveted thanks to the Castles. A beautiful home and a charming life of privilege. In contrast to Yvonne, I was left penniless and my only son, Teddy, died in his sleep when he was three months old. Cot death they called it back then. It was the saddest day of my life.

Now I have a family of my own. What a surprise that has turned out to be. Two lovely, intelligent girls who I have come to think of as my real granddaughters, and whom I adore. I won't give them up for anything. Alice has been devoted to me since day one but after today, I suspect even Daisy is finally starting to trust and love me. Who knew she was such a sucker for a sob story. Having to part with my cat is the one thing I regret about all of this. Hero was mine. All mine. Similar to how my grandchildren belong to me, so it killed me having to give him away to somebody else, no matter how deserving they might be. The only thing more unbearable would be handing over my grandchildren to their father. Over my dead body is what I say. I'll do whatever is necessary to keep my grandchildren with me. So Vince Spencer and anybody else who gets in my way better watch out.

CHAPTER 46: THE FATHER

The curtains are drawn as usual and there isn't a black BMW parked on the street today but I know Leah is home because I can hear Saffy crying inside. Leah will be pissed to see me back so soon, especially after I stormed off yesterday, calling her a "cold-hearted bitch" but I want to see my kid. I've never been apart from Saffy this long before, except for those two horrible days I spent in a police cell while they were investigating Scarlet's murder. I've heard that her killer is still at large. My brain refuses to dwell on *why*.

I knock gently this time. 'You again,' Leah scowls when she eventually comes to the door. She has a tearful Saffy on one hip but when my daughter sees me her little face explodes into a happy smile and she holds out her arms, making Leah scowl even more.

'I thought I could take Saffy off your hands today,' I offer, longing to feel my baby girl's skin against my neck and her warm breath on my face.

Leah swings Saffy away from me, out of reach, and says in a tight voice, 'I don't think that's a good idea.'

'Why not? I'm still her dad even if we're not together anymore.'

Leah averts her gaze and turns her face away, mumbling vaguely, 'Yeah, well . . .'

As soon as I spot the bruising on her face my jaw drops open and my body goes limp. Despite her attempts to cover it up with concealer, it remains noticeable.

'Did your new boyfriend do that to your face?' I growl.

Her hand flies to her face and she gasps, 'What? No.'

Although she acts horrified, fear is what I really see in her eyes. That bastard Wayne must be knocking her about already. The Waynes of this world come and go and Leah will have to find that out for herself but I'll always be there for Saffy and to some extent her.

I move in closer because I need her to know this, and I whisper, 'I'm not angry with you, Leah, but I need to know that you and Saffy are safe.'

'Of course, we're safe,' she responds defensively, but her eyes darting back and forth give her away. Her gaze is anywhere but on me. Because she is aware that I can see straight through her lies.

Frustrated, I run my hands agitatedly over my face, before hissing, 'Do you really want to be with someone like that?'

Her eyes immediately fill with tears and she bites down on her bottom lip as though considering this. For a split second, she's the girl I fell in love with, albeit fleetingly. It's true what I said though, I'm not angry with her. How could I be? She's so young and let's face it, we were never really a match. There is goodness in her and there was all along, I realise now. But I didn't bring it out in her. I failed her just as much as I did Scarlet. But I won't fail my kids. And Saffy is still my daughter no matter what.

I screw everything up by saying so, 'Saffy is still my daughter no matter what and I won't let that fucking bully hurt her.'

'Is that right?' Leah sneers. Now that her back is up, the softer woman she could have been has disappeared. As if to demonstrate this, she pushes her face into mine and demands, 'And what are you going to do about it?'

'I mean it,' I mumble, holding my ground, 'I'll kill him before I let him hurt you or the baby.'

'Like last time, when he beat the shit out of you,' she scoffs.

I wince. 'Thanks for the reminder.'

Leah's eyes suddenly widen in alarm and her focus is on the street rather than on me when she urges me to, 'Just go will you.'

With a sickening thump in my chest, I turn to see what's grabbing her attention and my heart lurches as Wayne's car turns the corner. *The piece of shit.* I can't decide whether I should leg it to avoid getting into another scrap or bash his good-looking face in because I know that I won't win a custody battle from prison. In the end, I do something extremely stupid. I'll tell myself later that it was a desperate attempt to keep my child safe, but in all honesty, I believe I acted out of blind panic.

I snatch the baby from Leah's arms, while growling menacingly, 'I'm not leaving her here with him.' She resists and tries to hold on to Saffy, but she doesn't react quickly enough and I win the battle.

'Vince, give her back. You can't just take her!' Leah screams hysterically, slapping at my hands.

'Yes, I can,' I yell, cradling my sobbing baby daughter in my arms to soothe her. 'She's as much mine as she is yours.'

Then I take off down the path, and Leah chases after me, pulling at my T-shirt to try to stop me. Although she lacks the physical strength to prevent me from leaving, her words do the trick . . .

She comes at me like a wrecking ball by shouting, 'She's not yours. She never was. She's Wayne's.'

'What?' I freeze. My heart is pounding. I have blurred vision. Everything slows. Did I hear her right? Has my day, my life, my world just got a hundred times worse? Blood pulses in my ears. A vein throbs agonisingly on my forehead. *Thrum. Thrum. Thrum.* I can't move from this spot. Or feel anything. Not my hands or my toes. My feet no longer function.

I'm still reeling from this revelation when Leah staggers towards me, a hand clasped over her mouth as if she can't believe she's finally told me the truth. When she plucks Saffy out of my arms, I'm too numb to resist.

'I'm so sorry, Vince.' Leah shakes her head pitying me and sighs. 'For everything. For Wayne. For lying to you about Saffy when Wayne broke up with me. And you leaving your wife and kids for me. But she's not yours. She's Wayne's. He's had the DNA test and everything.'

'Wayne's?' I mumble as the big man himself swaggers up the path as if he owns it.

I'm caught off guard when he pulls a sympathetic face as if in solidarity with me, before muttering, 'Sorry, mate,' as though he might actually mean it. It dawns on me that he might not have wanted to get saddled with a kid in the first place. Let alone his ex-girlfriend.

It breaks my heart to see Leah handing our baby girl over to him when his hands are monstrously big and capable of shattering her skull. I have to force myself look away before I do something even more stupid.

Instead, I turn to Leah in tears and cry, 'But I love that kid so much.'

'I know,' she says, her voice breaking as she wipes away her own tears, before admitting, 'And you were the best dad ever.'

I panic as another more distressing thought pops into my head, and before I know it, I'm pleading, like the loser I am, 'I'll still get to see her, won't I?'

Lines of pain appear on Leah's face as she squeezes her eyes shut and shakes her head. 'No, that's not possible. And, Vince, you have to leave now.'

Wayne then puts a protective arm around Leah's shoulders, claiming full possession of my family and my home, as he leads her back inside.

CHAPTER 47: THE GRANDMOTHER

As we join the crush of people filing inside the church, storm clouds gather menacingly overhead, but no one appears to notice them but me. Our feet crunch on the gravel path and I imagine there's a smell of death in the air as well, but I attribute that to my mood of melancholy because today would have been Teddy's fortieth birthday, had he lived. I wonder, as I often do, what kind of man he would have become. Hopefully, not like his father. I like to think of him as a thoughtful introvert, someone who played chess and cared about the environment. He would have had dark hair, serious eyes and worn plain, academic glasses. His face would have glowed though whenever he saw me. We would have been like two peas in a pod, and just like me, he would have secretly hated his father. "No girlfriend will ever take your place," my son would have boasted to anyone who would listen.

Noises flood the entrance as the girls and I shuffle forward in an excruciatingly slow manner, held up by the queue. With their conservative, lace collar dresses and well-groomed hair secured with Alice bands, their father would not recognise them. They look like a pair of identical Victorian dolls but their white unsmiling faces are more ghostlike. On that unpleasant thought, I let out a weary sigh and keep as still as possible as if I too were dead. My nose is filled with the musty dampness of the stone walls and, once we are on the move again, my feet lightly echo on the tiled floor, like a reluctant bride escaping through the church door on her wedding day.

I brush a few loose grey hairs from my shoulders and try to ignore the imaginary whispering sounds that fill my head . . . churchgoers sniggering behind their hands as secrets, best kept hidden, are shared. Sweat prickles my skin as the sun pushes through the stained-glass windows and tiny dust particles glitter in the shafts of light, appearing to spell out Teddy's name. My breath quickens upon noticing that the eerie fifteenth-century carved human heads also seem to be peering down at me from the high walls, as if passing judgement on me alone. It's not like I blame them.

Fear gnaws at me, like the dusty church mice would, given the chance, when I realise that I have once again forgotten to take my medication. *Deary me, what is to become of me?* I've become forgetful in my old age. Sadness settles around my shoulders like an ash cloud might, similar to those that rain down on grieving families at crematoriums. The peal of church bells calling people to worship creates an ominous thrum in my head, like a painfully slow heartbeat. *Will these flashes of grief ever stop? As for those awful memories of Yvonne Castle . . .*

As we settle into our worn-smooth-with-age wooden seats, I observe the vicar scurrying this way and that, always keeping her head down in reverence. Her dark hair and long beak-like nose make her resemble a velociraptor. However, as she greets her parishioners, her voice has a hypnotic calmness about it. Despite being a regular churchgoer, I do not class myself among the good Reverend Fleming's flock. The Lord himself knows I have no right to be here. Not when I carry the devil on my shoulder.

An insistent tug on my sleeve and an urgent whisper in my ear causes my body to stiffen. Impatiently, I slump in my seat and let out another weary sigh, feeling like it's all too much.

'Yes, Teddy,' I mumble exhaustedly.

'Who is Teddy?' A sharp voice demands.

I squint to see where it came from. However, Daisy is the one gazing up at me with an inquisitive, expectant face — not Teddy. The deep anguish of losing him is suddenly difficult to bear.

Why on earth did I think Daisy was my son? I chastise myself before muttering apologetically, 'No one, Daisy. Take no notice of your silly old grandmother who doesn't know what she's talking about.'

Daisy gives me a faint smile and fondly rolls her eyes, but she seems satisfied enough with my explanation. I must be losing the plot to have mentioned my boy's name out loud. I need to be more careful. I mustn't give myself away or I could lose everything. Including Daisy and Alice.

My brow is clammy with sweat as I turn my attention back to the vicar who has clapped her hands together and is now preaching—

'Welcome to this Sunday morning service on what is already a glorious day filled with sunshine and not a single cloud in sight. We are gathered here today at St John the Evangelist to talk about God's creation of the family and His wish for it to be a strong and wholesome institution. Even if your children are grown, and your family is broken, it's never too late to start being a strong force for good . . .'

The vicar's holier-than-thou smile is like a beam of hope, but as her words echo in my head, I am drowning in a sea of blackness and regret. So, I rest my forehead against the worn pew in front of me and close my eyes, as if deep in prayer. It's Yvonne Castle I'm thinking of in this moment. Her, with her shattered family and unending charitable efforts to do good. *And look where that got her!*

Beside me, I sense Daisy giving me a worried look, but my eyes are tired and heavy — as if I've been drinking — so I ignore her. Every cell in my body groans with weariness. Before I know it, my head is lolling on my chest and I find myself dozing off for a second or two. The sound of my own snoring startles me awake and I jolt upright in panic to find people staring at me, including Daisy and Alice, eyes wide with disbelief.

As one would expect, Daisy wears a judgemental frown and shakes her head in mock despair while Alice smothers a laugh. I can always count on my youngest granddaughter to find any situation amusing.

Clasping my hands together in my lap, I prop myself upright, my spine rigid with humiliation. When I glance over my shoulder to find out who else might have witnessed my embarrassment, my heart skips a beat. Towards the back of the church, I glimpse a defiant toss of caramel hair and rouged cheekbones that I recognise. My throat tightens with a lump of fear.

That awful woman is back! Georgina bloody Bell.

CHAPTER 48: THE FATHER

Our diverse group of five is huddled around a circular table in the staff room. Gusts of dry air from the air conditioning units blast in our faces to help cool us down on what must be the hottest day of the year so far. Mind you, I'm still sweating my bollocks off in a T-shirt and shorts. On the other hand, Dave, the sixty-year-old trainer is in a shirt and tie and looks as cool as a cucumber. Lucky sod. He's been a volunteer with the Samaritans for over twenty years and is a retired accountant. He's also recently widowed, poor bastard. Once I've completed my training, he's going to be my mentor. Then there's Ajay, who is in his early forties. He lives just a few doors away from the Lincoln Road office and works in IT. Everyone here has a job except me.

Lexy is a twenty-something accounts assistant who wants to pursue a career in counselling. She has bundles of energy and I'm in love with her already . . . but not in *that* way. After what happened with Leah, I intend to steer clear of women for a while, but *not forever*, especially the younger ones. And last but not least, there's Holly, who is about my age and has a large birthmark on one side of her face that you don't notice after a while. Despite being the quietest person in our group, everyone pays attention to her when she speaks. She has a very soothing quality. For some reason I can't explain, being around her makes me feel safe.

'What about you, Vince, what type of calls do you think will be the most challenging?' Dave asks.

Caught off guard, I immediately tense and shift in my seat, but as soon as I look across at Holly, whose long brown hair is poured over one shoulder in an attempt to conceal her disfigurement, my shoulders relax. She told us earlier that ever since she was a child, she has been the target of bullying.

Deciding that some people have it far worse than me and that there's no point in feeling sorry for myself, even if I have just been dumped by my cheating girlfriend and told I'm not the father of my child, I answer as enthusiastically as I can, 'When people ring up feeling suicidal, I suppose. It must feel like a huge responsibility for the volunteer, because what if they're unable to help and the caller ends up taking their own life anyway.'

This had been my fear when Scarlet was alive but in the end someone else had taken her life. *Could it have really been someone as close to home, as say, her own daughter? Or my ex?* The nodding going on around the table convinces me that I'm not the only one who is nervous about taking such a call from a member of the public.

'It's a common fear among new volunteers, but suicidal calls happen less often than you might imagine,' declares Dave. 'Naturally, you will receive all the training and support needed to handle challenging circumstances. Someone more experienced is always on hand though to help in this kind of situation.'

'That's a relief,' I sigh, relaxing for the first time since my encounter with Leah earlier today. My heart might be broken but amazingly I'm not beat yet. Even with a Saffy-sized hole in my heart. Although I can't bring myself to think about my baby daughter just yet, strike that — *Wayne's* baby daughter — there's still my girls to fight for. And the chance to do something good for a change. Who knows where volunteering might lead? Dave reckons I'd be a great fit to train listeners at Peterborough Prison, what with my troubled past and everything, although, of course, he didn't allude to that last bit. He didn't have to because when I first applied to join the Samaritans as a volunteer, they conducted all kinds of police and criminal background checks on me. Luckily, they still accepted me because I was upfront about my past. I might not have done actual time but I've been arrested more times than I care to remember, as DS Mills can attest.

Now that it's Lexy's turn to talk, I feel bad for not paying more attention to her when I'm meant to be practising active listening, but in reality, I'm simply nodding along and pretending to be engaged because I'm wondering if I should challenge Leah about the paternity test. After all, if she can lie once, she can lie again. Wayne is not a fool, though. He would have insisted on seeing the results for himself. The doubt that had crept into my thoughts vanishes like a sudden lifting of brain fog. *Saffy is not mine.* And the sooner I figure out how to deal with that, the better. Even though it's killing me.

'Time for a break perhaps, a cup of tea and a biscuit?' Dave suggests, scraping back his chair. He's read the room well because by this point, we're all fidgeting in our seats and gasping for a brew. Or a roll-up, in my case.

'I don't suppose you have a lighter or a box of matches on you?' I ask Holly who has remained seated at the table even though the others have drifted away. Dave is over by the kettle, already munching on a crumbling Digestive while Ajay and Lexy have disappeared for a comfort break. I pat my pockets, hoping to discover a forgotten lighter, as Holly watches me intently from under her dark eyelashes. Everything about her is reassuringly brown. Not a dark root or a bleached hair in sight.

'I don't smoke,' she says cuttingly. 'And nor should you.'

To say I'm surprised is an understatement. The majority of people would have avoided giving an opinion and instead merely shrugged and muttered, "No, sorry." Clearly, she's not like *most people*. I'm not sure if I should be irritated or impressed. I go with the latter, for now, acknowledging that, 'I know I shouldn't, but you've got to have something in life.' Though it's a weak argument, it's worked in the past.

She raises an eyebrow at that before asking, 'Is it the most important thing in your life then?'

The frown is back on my face as I retake my seat next to her, sliding my pouch of tobacco back into my pocket as if it were a dirty secret.

'I'm not saying that,' I stammer, propping myself up on my elbows. But when I detect a strong odour of sweat coming from my armpits, I place them back down by my sides. And keep them there.

'What *are* you saying?'

She's intense. And I haven't seen her be like that with the others. Only me.

'Are you trying to tell me you don't have any bad habits?' I aim at playful, because if I'm honest I'm still unsure how to take her.

'Just the one,' she replies with a secretive half-smile.

'And that is?' I prompt, suddenly wanting to know everything about her.

'You first,' she interrupts, holding up a forceful palm that seems to mean business. 'I want to know what is more important to you than smoking.'

'That's easy, my girls,' I shrug.

'How many daughters do you have?'

Awkwardly I mumble, 'Two,' because my throat feels as dry as sand from the pain of leaving Saffy out of that number. After clearing my throat, I say, 'Daisy is nine, and Alice seven.'

'How lovely.'

'You?'

'Chance would be a fine thing,' she sighs, shaking her head and pointing to the angry looking scarlet birthmark on her face.

'You shouldn't put yourself down like that,' I protest hotly, feeling like I would strike anyone who did.

'No?' She arches a cynical eyebrow — I'm pleased to see they are natural and not tattooed or pencilled on — before abruptly flicking her long hair back over her shoulder to reveal the full extent of her disfigurement. Her eyes never leave my face and sensing that I am being tested, I hold her gaze.

I don't answer for a moment, and when I do, she rewards me with the most heartbreaking of smiles. I tell her firmly, 'No.' But inside I'm screaming the same word at myself, *no . . . no . . . no. Not now.* Not after I just made a commitment to myself about relationships and women. Because something — both spiritual and physical — just happened between us, and right now I feel as if I've stepped off the top floor of the city centre multi-storey car park and am falling. *And yet* . . . curiously, I no longer want that roll-up.

'You,' she teases playfully, tossing her head to one side.

Confused, I ask, 'What about me?'

'You're my next bad habit,' she laughs.

Her laughter is contagious so I laugh too. Correction, *she's* contagious. And just like that. It's done. And I'm not sure if I should laugh or cry.

207

CHAPTER 49: THE GRANDMOTHER

Daisy and Alice are standing dejectedly outside the church, while Rosalind Knowles tries to console them, octopus arms draped around their shoulders. At the same time, it appears like she's trying to prevent them from coming to me and I'm affronted. But her gaze keeps drifting over at me and darting away again as if she can't bring herself to look at me. I wonder what I am supposed to have done because those who have spilled out of the cool confines of the church are likewise staring at me in shock. Surely, I can't be punished or shunned, for simply nodding off in church, can I?

A surge of panic crawls over me as I start to realise what I'm guilty of, and I feel a stab of disappointment in myself. I've let my granddaughters down. Badly!

Just as I'm about to apologise to them, I'm startled to hear a familiar voice behind me exclaim haughtily, 'How dare you call me a whore.'

I turn to see where it is coming from, only to find Georgina Bell's nutty-brown eyes drilling into mine. My heart rate quickens but I'm not yet ready to back down. *Did I really call the woman a whore in front of the entire congregation as we were making our way out of the church?* A part of me wants to laugh aloud at that and give myself a celebratory slap on the back. It's not like she doesn't deserve it, after having an affair with Yvonne Castle's husband and then accusing me of, well, God knows what.

Georgina shoots daggers at me as if trying to set me on fire. I lower my eyes and pause for a beat, before growling, 'If the cap fits.'

'You're a fine one to talk,' Georgina snaps, cocking her handbag as if it were a machine gun while adding scornfully, 'Let's face it, you're not as innocent as you make yourself out to be.'

I prod the woman's scrawny chest with my finger and demand, 'What are you doing here anyway? How come you're following me?'

Georgina smooths her already blunt-edged hair with manicured fingers and huffs, 'You left me with no choice since you wouldn't return my calls.'

'You never were one to take a hint,' I snap, aware that nobody has moved and that everyone is watching us with bated breath. As I take in the villagers' bewildered expressions, I imagine they'll be asking themselves, "What happened to that nice little old lady we all thought we knew?" My stomach churns over when I glance at Daisy and Alice because their worried faces tell me more than words ever could.

As I sense that everything I have worked for is slipping away from me, out of reach, blood pulses in my ears, and fury takes hold. Nothing can prevent me from yelling, 'It's obvious you can't tell when you're not wanted because Charles couldn't stand you either. Whenever you phoned the house, he would get me to answer and tell you he wasn't in so he wouldn't have to speak to you. He also used to make fun of you behind your back and say that you ought to come with a warning label.' I know this, not because I was there in person, but because Yvonne Castle told me all about it. As she did everything else.

With a fierce hiss, Georgina comes back with, 'You're lying.'

At that I burst out laughing. 'Pot calling the kettle, don't you think?'

Pushing her lined, powdery face into mine, Georgina threatens, 'If you are who you say you are, which I very much doubt, then wait till I tell everyone what you've done.'

'And what *am* I supposed to have done, Georgina?' I scoff, but I back away from the overwhelming scent of lavender and lily of the valley that emanates from her. The stench somehow reminds me of death.

There is a lethal edge to her voice as she warns, 'I know that Charles's death was no accident and that you were the one who killed him.'

'Ladies, that's quite enough entertainment for one morning,' Rev Fleming interrupts with a birdlike flutter of her robes, but her beady eyes are gentle as they land on me. She then runs a predatory gaze over Georgina, before urging, 'May I remind you that Mrs Castle has not long suffered a bereavement and is not herself at the moment.'

When Rev Fleming places a compassionate hand on my arm, I'm touched by her concern. As she leads me over to Daisy and Alice, who are waiting by the church doors, I feel grubby with guilt.

Rather than being upset with me for my unforgivable outburst in church, as I had expected, everyone, including Rosalind Knowles and her petulant daughter, appears to feel sorry for me. Which is worse? I'm not sure. For once, though, I actually feel like I belong among the Reverend's flock. It's a pleasant if rare sensation. However, me being me, I can't resist casting a victorious sidelong peek at Georgina's lowered head and hunched shoulders. She didn't achieve her spiteful wish today as nobody took what she said seriously. Why would they? Accusing Yvonne Castle of harming her beloved husband is, to put it bluntly, ridiculous. That woman wouldn't have hurt a fly, as I can very much vouch for.

When I feel a small palm slide into mine, my heart melts as I look down at my eldest granddaughter's pale, freckled face. Daisy begs, 'Come on, Granny, let's get you home so you can take your tablets,' and gives my hand an extra squeeze of protection. The darling.

'Yes,' Alice agrees, bouncing up to greet me. She grabs my free hand and jiggles it like a firework on a stick. I've never met anyone quite like her. She's unable to remain motionless for even a minute.

Unlike her sister, who I fear is in danger of becoming someone else's carer (i.e. mine) — which is the last thing Daisy needs after years of looking after her mother — Alice seems oblivious to the severity of my meltdown.

She proves this by clucking innocently, 'We don't want you having another of your funny turns, do we?'

Is that what they call murder these days? I ask myself ironically, leaning heavily on the children as we crunch our way through the gravel . . . all eyes on us.

CHAPTER 50: THE FATHER

I'm not going to lie or pretend I'm not embarrassed by it, but I'm clearly the kind of guy who can't get by without a woman in my life. Strangely, I'm okay with that, given that I'm determined to take things slow with Holly. For now, we're just dating casually and seeing how things go. We have an unspoken rule that she doesn't come to my house, and I don't go to hers. She seems to understand that my girls come first and is aware of the tough time I've been through recently, including the death of Scarlet, losing custody of the kids, receiving the bombshell about Saffy, not to mention the fight with Wayne, the arrest and the killing of the old man. I may not have told her about that last part. I'm not a complete muppet.

Whenever I receive a call or text from Holly, I find myself grinning like a lovestruck fool. She's never off her phone and loves to send expressive emojis. We Facetime at least a dozen times a day and have decided to get together for a coffee one evening after training this week. I can't wait.

I'm cracking on with the decorating at 7 The Green in the meantime, and I've only got the kitchen left to finish. Lucky attempts to help by sticking an inquisitive nose into the paint tin and ends up dripping it all over the floor. I'm forced to bathe him after that and he doesn't like that one little bit. After shaking off the excess water, I end up almost as wet as he is so I wipe him dry with an old towel while he covers me with wet kisses. After a good brushing, he looks toothpaste-white and posh for once. Could he be a pedigree after all? The kind of dog Leah always dreamed about. If that's the case, the joke's on her. I think about Saffy all the time; wondering if she's missing me and how she's doing. It's going to be hard to break the news to Daisy and Alice that their baby half-sister isn't related to them after all, or that they won't get to see her again.

On that depressing thought, I snap a photo of Lucky and send it to Holly with a message, "Just bathed the dog. What sort of breed do you think he is?" She replies instantly, unlike Leah who would often take hours to respond, if at all, "A Bichon Frise" is her response.

"Is that a good thing?" I type.

"Yes of course. He's very cute and probably cost a grand at least. You should get him groomed professionally though if you can afford it."

I already know I can't afford it, so I don't bother to ask how much it would cost — especially since I have to trim my own hair with the kitchen scissors to avoid paying the barbershop's twelve quid, not to mention stumping up for a tip. Don't get me started on today's tipping trend!

I go back to painting the kitchen. As soft as I am for thinking so, the paint tin claims that the colour on the walls is sage, a pale green that resembles Holly's eyes. I turn my thoughts back to my girls, anticipating that they'll get the shock of their lives when they see the house. It looks completely different. Light. Bright. Fresh. Clean. Like a proper home. I've spent all week getting it ready and have barely slept.

I take a short break from painting to look about appreciatively while sucking on a mint that is meant to be a substitute for the tobacco I've decided to give up, with Holly's help. She also helped me pick out the new cups, plates, and kitchen accessories in charity shops. The cream blind was on sale from

Dunelm and I only paid a tenner for it. The neutral fake-tiled lino floor in the kitchen, I laid myself. It was a first for me and I've never sworn so much in my life. To match the pale blue walls in the living room, I painted all of the ugly orange-pine furniture cottage cream. The deep pile living room carpet was an offcut I dug out of somebody's skip . . . with their permission, I might add. There's also a newer second-hand mattress on the bed in Scarlet's room. Knowing their mother passed away on the old one, I couldn't expect anyone to sleep on it again.

I'm proud of all my efforts, if I do say so myself, and I've had a blast doing it. Most of the time, the radio has kept me company, and I'm not ashamed to admit that I've occasionally dad-danced around the living room while wearing only my pants to the sounds of classic nineties music. It's helped to divert my attention away from my problems, particularly the loss of my baby daughter. And at the end of the day, I still have the evening training sessions with Holly and the Samaritans to look forward to. I wonder whether things might finally be looking up for me.

I meant it when I promised Holly I would give mindfulness and meditation a go, as she's big into that. Although it's never been my thing before, I'm open-minded enough to consider it. Never mind the likes of Gary Pearce who would no doubt take the piss out of me for it. At thirty-two, I feel like I'm finally getting to know myself. 'Will the real Vince Spencer please stand up?' I chuckle to myself. Holly is also into appreciation, and I can tell you that it has taught me a few things. Because of her, I've learned to be thankful for what I have rather than what I lack.

I'm no born-again Christian but I give thanks every day for my new job. So what if it's unpaid? And as for Holly? Well, if it's meant to be, it'll happen. That's my new philosophy. We can't deny the spark that exists between us, but there's no urgency to progress things as we've both experienced severe hurt in the past. Pressure is the last thing either of us wants.

When the girls finally get to meet her, I hope they'll take to her. And I pray to God Alice won't spend the entire time gaping at Holly's birthmark. If anyone's likely to, it's my youngest daughter.

Holly isn't like any other woman I've been in a relationship with before — not that we are officially together — I remind myself. She speaks her mind, doesn't play games, and doesn't appear to possess a manipulative bone in her body either. Although she may not be as physically attractive as, say, Leah or Scarlet, it somehow makes my attraction to her stronger.

I'm startled out of my daydream when Holly sends me another text. "Is your mind still on tomorrow?"

Since she's spot on, I marvel at how someone I've not long met can know me so well. Aside from Saffy, the one thing playing on my mind is, as Holly suggested, tomorrow morning when the solicitor's letter challenging for custody of my daughters is to be mailed to Mrs Castle.

If only I could be a fly on the wall when that happens.

215

CHAPTER 51: THE GRANDMOTHER

Wisteria Cottage has another visitor. This time, however, it's the unremarkable mouse of the social worker with her blunt fringe and bored eyes, not Georgina bloody Bell, thank goodness for small mercies. And all because of the solicitor's letter that landed on my doormat two days ago with a nasty clatter informing me that the girl's father was seeking custody. I can tell you that rage kept me company for a while after that — *how can someone like him even afford a solicitor* — but hoping the threat of losing Daisy and Alice would simply go away if I ignored its contents, I hadn't let on to them. In hindsight, I should have known better, since Vince must have told Daisy during one of their private conversations on the "secret" mobile phone that I am not supposed to know about.

Daisy and I have been walking on eggshells around each other ever since the letter arrived. Neither of us wants to bring up the topic because it would mean me having to ask her what *she* wanted to happen, and she would then have to give me her answer. Have I done enough to win the child over or will she leave me the first chance she gets in favour of that man . . . her father, who is a complete waste of space? If only she could see that for herself. And if only I hadn't occasionally lost my patience with the girls or had those "funny turns" as Alice likes to call my temper tantrums. Maybe then, I would have more confidence in Daisy's decision. I don't deceive myself into thinking that Alice has any say in this. She will do what her sister tells her.

With a heavy heart, I carry the loaded tray of tea, cake, and biscuits into the living room where the social worker has been talking privately to the girls. "Would you mind leaving us alone for a short while, Mrs Castle, so Daisy, Alice and I can talk openly?" she'd dared to ask after being in the house less than ten minutes. I'd wanted to object as leaving the girls alone to talk "openly" was the last thing I wanted, *who knew what they might tell her*, but in the end, I had to concede and make myself scarce. When I pressed my ear up against the door to listen in, I could only make out the girls' odd, quietly muttered "Yes" or "No" stilted responses to the social worker's questions, so I'm no wiser as to their preferred choice. *Me or him.*

But with some of my typical steely resolution, I remind myself that it's not just about what the girls want. Who is in a better position to raise them will ultimately be determined by the courts. Surely, I have to prevail against someone like Vince Spencer, a former drug addict and thief. I mean, I'm Yvonne Castle after all. A respectable, churchgoing widow who has never been in any sort of trouble in her life, *at least as far as anybody knows*. Let's not forget all my charitable efforts and sense of community spirit. I'm certain that the family courts will take all of this into consideration.

I try to appear calm and relaxed as I enter the living room, but the moment I walk in, the conversation comes to an abrupt halt. I set the cups and teapot down on the coffee table, and the social worker is the only person who looks me in the eye. While Alice seems unusually thoughtful, albeit a little bewildered, Daisy pulls at the rough skin around her fingertips and stares morosely at her lap. I've seen her dad do the same thing. It's a nervous habit they both share. The doll has once again made an appearance. It seems to be present whenever things are going badly for Daisy, another reason why I'd like to send it to landfill.

Wearing a phoney smile, I enquire brightly, 'Who would like a slice of Victoria sponge and a cup of tea?'

'Yes please,' the social worker and Alice pipe up simultaneously as if nothing were wrong in the world.

'Daisy?' I ask, risking a glance in her direction.

There is a pause, after which she mumbles, 'No thank you, Granny,' then gets up, and disappears from the room, like a sad, fleeting shadow.

'I suppose that tells me everything I need to know,' I sigh, giving the social worker a look while I hand her a trembling cup of tea.

The social worker confidently chirrups, 'If only it were that simple,' as if she were an expert on children — something I very much doubt. I've never liked the woman. Wears far too much make-up for my liking. As for her awful, cheap-smelling perfume! Ugh. To be completely honest, though, I don't like that many people. With the exception of Daisy and Alice, of course, and even then . . . there are days when I could throttle *them*. Sometimes I start to question if I'm cut out to be a grandmother.

Before I can say another word, Alice jumps in with, 'We both want to live with our dad but we also want to stay with you, Granny.' A dimple appears on her left cheek as she whines, 'Can't you just share us?'

'Out of the mouths of babes,' the social worker observes, allowing her long brown hair to fall forwards on her wide shoulders. I think she's told me her name half a dozen times, but I keep forgetting it. I hold her responsible for this, for being so flipping forgettable.

Cradling my cup and saucer in my hand, I watch mesmerised as Alice helps herself to a thick slice of cake. I feel an urge to cry when she comes out with, 'Daisy is worried about you being on your own, and I am too.'

I murmur distractedly, 'Well, that's very sweet of her and you too, Alice, for thinking of me.' Then turning to the social worker, I ask bluntly, 'So what happens next?'

The social worker leans forward in her seat and gives a slight shake of her head, warning me, I think, that we shouldn't discuss it in front of the children. *Yet that's exactly what she had done.* Nor has she shared with me what was said. I am their grandmother to all intents and purposes and I have a right to know. Itching to find out, I say to Alice, 'Why don't you take a slice up to Daisy? I'm sure she'd love some really.'

'Okay, Granny,' she shrugs as she leaps to her feet and swallows the last of her cake before grabbing another slice and leaving the room. A picture flashes into my head of Alice devouring that extra piece of cake before she even makes it upstairs.

My eyes grow cold and my jaw tightens as I insist on knowing, 'Do you think he's got a chance of getting them back?'

'A chance, yes, but given his background, I think it's unlikely.'

I breathe a sigh of relief as I realise that fear has been causing the skin on my face and hands to perspire. Crossing myself devoutly and squeezing my eyes tightly shut, I mutter, 'Thank God for that.' Then, I question, *is it too much?* Have I gone too far? And when I see the woman's eyebrows rise, feigning astonishment, I warn myself not to overdo it.

'I'm confident the children are in the right place with you, Mrs Castle,' she affirms, with a quick sip of her scalding hot tea, as though she's in a hurry to finish it and get out of the door.

'Thank you. That means a lot,' I remark meekly. However, I'm secretly thinking how dare Vince believe he has a chance of stealing my darling grandchildren from me? It doesn't enter my head at this point to consider that my resentment towards him has become unjustified and toxic.

The social worker tuts. 'With his track record I'm fairly certain he won't get custody. Assuming,' she frowns and pauses to put her cup and saucer back on the table, before pursing her lips and continuing in a withering tone that causes me to break out in a cold sweat, 'that you have told us everything about *your* past and there are no surprises.'

CHAPTER 52: THE FATHER

Sitting across from each other in the Paul Pry pub on Lincoln Road, not far from the Samaritan's office, I'm acutely aware of the middle-aged couple at the adjacent table, who seem to be whispering about Holly and constantly glancing over at her. I clench my teeth and glare at them until finally, they look away. Just as well, because if it had continued any longer, I might have ended up dragging the husband outside for a scrap.

With a sympathetic stroke of my arm, Holly tells me, 'It's okay I'm used to it.'

'Well, I'm not. And it's bloody rude,' I say loudly so the couple, who are quickly downing their drinks and getting ready to leave, can hear. As soon as they're gone, I feel myself relax. Letting out a long exhale, I ask 'So, Holly, tell me about your childhood. You must be bored to death by now hearing me rattle on about my girls.'

With a comforting smile, she admits, 'On the contrary. I could listen to you rattle on about your girls all day.'

'You must be a sucker for punishment after working with kids all day.'

Fixing her lively gaze on me, she purrs, 'I love children and ever since I was a little girl I always wanted a family of my own.'

'It could still happen,' I tell her, knocking back some of my pint of Guinness and wiping the foamy moustache from my mouth.

Holly nervously blinks several times before saying, 'I guess this is as good a time as any to tell you that I can't have children.'

I frown. 'Are you serious?'

She nods regretfully. 'Does that change anything between you and me?'

This time, when I reach out a consoling hand, I'm surprised to find her arm is hard and muscular as though she works out. Don't ask me why, but I imagined she would feel a lot softer. Deciding that doesn't or shouldn't matter, I reassure her, 'No, of course not, but it's you I feel sorry for. You'd have been a fantastic mother.'

'Thanks.' She attempts a grin, but her eyes are sparkling with unshed tears. Biting on her lip, she continues, 'I suppose, knowing I couldn't have any myself, that's why I wanted to work with children.'

I cough nervously into my hand because let's face it, I'm a bit out of my depth here. But I tell myself it's all good practice for becoming a Samaritan volunteer, and for getting to know her better, so I venture hesitantly, 'How did you find out you weren't able to have kids?'

As if on autopilot she answers, 'In my late twenties I underwent a hysterectomy.'

I flinch and mutter, 'That's tough.'

'It was,' she confides, gazing away from me for a moment, before returning her gaze to mine. 'The doctors didn't want to do it, but the pain and bleeding from the fibroids meant they didn't have a choice.'

Being a dad of three, no, *two* children, I know a little something about periods and childbirth, but fibroids are new to me, so I ask, as politely as possible, "What are fibroids exactly?"

Without hesitating, she wades in with, 'Sometimes they're called uterine myomas but basically, they're non-cancerous growths that can be as small as a pea or as big as a melon. Unfortunately, in my case—'

She leaves the rest of her sentence unsaid, but I get it. Hers were obviously massive and so they removed her whole fucking womb when she was still only in her twenties.

Shifting awkwardly in my seat, I can only think of one thing to say, 'Fuck.'

'Tell me about it.' She grimaces, giving me a one-shoul-dered shrug.

I change the subject in case she's feeling uncomfortable. 'How come you decided to be a teaching assistant instead of a teacher?'

She bursts out laughing. 'Talk about a dramatic change of subject.' Then pausing to reflect, she swirls her Diet Coke around in her glass before confessing, 'I was told my face might frighten the children.'

'Jesus Christ,' I mutter, folding my hands into fists.

She chuckles. 'That was years ago now and thankfully attitudes have changed since then, hence I'm now considered employable.'

'How do you manage to stay so upbeat?' I marvel, impressed by her all over again.

She shrugs again. 'Like I said, you get used to it.'

She's wearing dark jeans and a plain navy top tonight, and her hair is pulled back in a messy bun, fringe resting on her eyes. As I've observed previously, she is such a natural girl. Anyone else would have tried to cover up a birthmark like that with cosmetics, but she doesn't give a shit what people think of her. Good on her, I say, because I reckon the world would be a better place if we all had more of what she has. Balls, that is . . .

'So, tell me about your childhood?'

Her voice is a little monotonous as she responds, 'There's not much to tell. I had an uneventful only-child upbringing in an ordinary house on an ordinary street with two very normal parents who are both still alive and very much still married. If you want boring, that's me.'

'That is boring,' I chuckle, fixing her with a gleam in my eye. 'But then again excitement and chaos can be overrated. I should know.'

'Do tell.' She wriggles forward in her seat and clasps her hands together in anticipation of hearing some juicy gossip.

I lift one eyebrow in a playful gesture. 'Another time, maybe.'

'That's no fun,' she groans.

I was thinking of Leah and Scarlet when I made that statement, but I don't want to ruin the date by discussing past relationships, so I say instead, 'Let's just say I've had my fill of both and I like the idea of having stability in my life for once.'

'Stability I can do.' She laughs once more, displaying a nice enough set of teeth. Like everything else about her, they're just average-looking. And once again, I get that funny feeling I have when I'm with her . . . a sense of being safe, which is ridiculous really, given that I'm the bloke and she's the woman. It should be the other way around. Not that I'm a misogynist!

'I like the way you laugh.' The words are out of my mouth before I can stop them, and I start to blush as a result. Daft sod that I am.

'Thank you, Vince. I like your laugh too,' she agrees, nodding her head.

It's a standard response and one I would have expected her to come out with. I'm starting to think it's her predictability that I find so attractive. She's nothing like Leah or Scarlet, and that makes her perfect in my eyes.

CHAPTER 53: THE GRANDMOTHER

'Perfect,' I say, smacking my lips together while gazing at my reflection in the hall mirror. I pinch some colour into my sunken cheeks before adding an extra splash of rose lipstick. Today I'm wearing a flowery summer dress, which is rare for me, but I want to look the part as we're attending our first book club meeting this evening. I've been told there will be nibbles and wine for members afterwards. I see this as an opportunity to redeem myself with the village women who may or may not have witnessed my embarrassing "turn" at church on Sunday. In addition, I get to demonstrate to Daisy and Alice, who will be accompanying me, just how frail and dependent I am on them. That shouldn't be too hard, in my opinion.

The mouthwatering smell of vanilla and raspberry wafts through the air, reminding me that I must take the mini pavlovas I made earlier out of the oven and the melting fruit off the hob in a short while. As I turn to go and check on them, I catch sight of Daisy walking down the stairs, frowning.

'Daisy, is everything okay?' I enquire, trying my best to smile more, care more, and be more . . . that damned Yvonne Castle is a hard act to follow.

'It looks like Alice has been in my bedroom again and has been going through my stuff,' Daisy complains, folding her arms and sighing.

'Oh dear, has something gone missing?' I ask in the most innocent manner that I can. We both know it's her mobile phone that has disappeared, and that she's not meant to have one in the first place, so she can't accuse me of anything. *What a dilemma for the child*, I think smugly, knowing it's safely locked up in my office. That'll put a stop to her having secretive conversations with her father. Perhaps even more distressing for her is the fact that her creepy doll has gone missing too. I swore I'd get my hands on it at some point and now I have. Its glassy eyes stare right through you, giving me shivers.

Daisy concedes with a shrug, 'I don't know. I'm not sure.'

'Well, why don't you go and ask her?' I suggest.

'I've already done that but she won't admit anything,' she scowls.

'I guess that's younger sisters for you. But do let me know if I can help with anything or if you need me to speak with Alice. I know that it can be hard sometimes being the eldest child.'

'Do you?' Daisy probes, seeming genuinely interested.

'Do I what?'

'How do you know what it's like being the eldest when you told us you were an only child, like Mum?'

'You're right, I don't,' I sigh, feeling my age, because it's difficult to keep up with the younger ones . . . and the lies I've told. Daisy is a lot sharper than I was at her age. However, because I was raised in a large family with seven other siblings, we were more worried about squabbling over food than reading. They were hard times that I'll never forget. You never quite get over being poor. Poverty leaves its mark, like trauma.

'Why don't you talk about her anymore?'

My head snaps up at the accusing tune and I'm filled with a sense of unease as I ask, 'Who, dear?'

'Mum,' Daisy mumbles, with an exasperated sigh. 'You used to talk about her all the time when we first came to live with you.'

The lie comes easily to me. 'I think I forget to talk about her out loud because I'm thinking about her all the time in my head.'

'That's how I feel,' Daisy exclaims, her eyes wide with amazement.

'Well, you and I are much more alike than you think.' I smother a chuckle.

She nods, but her expression becomes worried when I put a palm to my frigid old heart and grimace.

Taking in a deep breath, she asks, 'Are you okay, Granny?'

'Just a twinge.' I wince as though I'm in a lot of pain, but then I try to comfort her by adding, 'Don't you worry about me, love. Neither your mother nor me would want that.'

In a frightened voice, she asks, 'Are you sure?'

Waving her away, I mumble stoically, 'Of course, deary . . .'

'Do you need to sit down? Shall I get you some water?' she persists.

The sound of the landline telephone ringing causes both of us to glance at the living room door. I speculate that it might be Vince Spencer since he is unable to reach his daughter on the missing mobile phone, and so I point out, 'That might be your dad. Do you want to get it?'

Daisy appears conflicted as her eyes flicker longingly from me to the living room door where the phone can be heard ringing insistently, then back again. She lets out a long sigh and replies, 'No, I'm fine.'

My face creases into a grin when I realise that she doesn't want to leave me alone in case I suffer a heartache or a stroke — words I've been dropping into casual conversation a lot lately. *What can I say? I'm a wicked sinner and I'm going to hell.*

'You haven't forgotten about book club at seven, have you?' I remind her, changing the subject.

She excitedly exclaims, 'I can't wait! I've read seventy pages already even though the book is meant for adults, not nine-year-olds.'

I gush, 'Wow, that's amazing. I'm barely on page three. But then again, you're a much quicker reader than I am.'

'It's an awesome read,' she rambles, beaming.

'Why don't you go and read some more? See if you can make it to a hundred pages?'

I can tell she's tempted because she gnaws at her cheek, considering it, before posing the question, 'Are you sure you'll be okay on your own?'

I turn away from her, faking sadness, while remarking bravely, 'I've lived on my own before and I dare say I can do so again, if I have to . . .' It's all an act of course, but she doesn't know that. 'Now off you go. And don't dally,' I insist more forcibly, shooing her away with a quivering hand.

She scurries back upstairs then, throwing me one last troubled look over her shoulder before finally disappearing. As I head for the kitchen, I mumble grumpily to myself, 'The author of that book, *Where the Crawdads Sing*, can fuck right off.'

When I enter the kitchen and see that it is thick with smoke, my mood decidedly gets worse. At the same time, a scorching smell fills my nostrils.

'Oh no, the pavlovas,' I mutter angrily as I bat at the smoke and curse under my breath, 'Buggering, bloody bollocks.'

CHAPTER 54: THE FATHER

'I'm here and I'm listening,' I murmur sympathetically into the phone. After weeks of training, it's my first live call from a member of the public and my body is rigid with nerves. Every time I glance at Dave, who is sitting next to me supervising, he nods his encouragement as if to say, "You're doing a good job, keep going."

'Tell me more,' I respond to the silence, as I've been trained to do.

The distraught male caller replies, 'I've told you my name but you haven't told me yours.' I recognise the hesitancy and fear in his voice because I have experienced it so often myself. Men need friendship and intimacy as much as women but in general, they struggle to talk openly seeing it as a weakness. I've found that the reverse is true. It's a strength.

I tell him, 'It's Vince,' having previously decided to go by my real name rather than a fictitious one, as some volunteers do to protect their anonymity. This feels more authentic to me, not that I'm criticising others.

Sensing his reluctance to open up, I urge, 'So, Richard, what's been happening in your life?'

'I got made redundant last week and I'm in the middle of a messy and expensive divorce. Plus, my ex won't let me see the kids.'

It's a lot to process, and naturally, I feel for the poor sod. What man wouldn't? "Been there, done that and got the T-shirt, mate. Women, huh!" I want to commiserate, but that would be unprofessional, so I don't. Thanks to Holly's coaching on positive mindset, I am constantly reminded that there are those who are truly worse off than me. And Richard is one of them. Ten minutes later, after Richard has told me that he feels "A hundred times better for being listened to" I hang up the phone feeling on top of the world. My eyes well up with tears, soppy sod, as I realise that I have finally achieved my goal of helping someone. I may even have made a difference in their life. Dave beams and offers me a friendly high five when he notices how emotional I am. 'Well done, lad.'

'Lad!' I chuckle, 'I haven't been called that in a very long time.'

And then, just as I'm about to take my well-earned break, I feel my mobile phone vibrate in my pocket. When I fish it out and realise that it's Yvonne Castle's number, I tense automatically. *What does the old bat want now?* 'Hello.'

'It's me.'

When Daisy's voice answers instead of Mrs Castle's I'm relieved, but I'm also instantly anxious.

'Hi, love. Is everything okay? How come you're not calling on the mobile?'

'I've lost it,' she mumbles unconvincingly.

'What do you mean you lost it?' I ask, becoming suspicious right away.

I can picture my daughter squirming uncomfortably as she whispers, 'It's gone from under my mattress.'

'The bitch!' I exclaim without thinking, since I can guess who has taken the phone. Daisy's silence, though, alerts me to the fact that I've gone too far. We are talking about her grandmother, after all.

I mumble apologetically, 'Sorry, sweetheart,' and then I question hesitantly, 'Do you think your Granny found your phone and took it?'

'Maybe, I don't know,' Daisy replies grudgingly.

I'm surprised by her answer because, up until a few weeks ago, Daisy would have been the first to call her granny out on the slightest transgression. Does this imply that she is becoming fonder of Yvonne Castle than I thought? I'm desperate to get my kids back in my life so I can be the best father I can be to them, but I don't want to make things harder for them than they already are. I'm just not cut out to be a part-time parent. I want to see Daisy and Alice every morning before they go to school, not just on Saturdays. I also want to be there to pick them up at the school gate, take them home and give them their tea as well as read them a story every night before bed. Not that they need me for that. They're better readers than me. *But once a dad* . . .

Giving in to the depressing thought that this may not happen, my shoulders slump and doubt takes over. But I try to inject a lightness into my voice as I ask, 'What are you up to today? Anything exciting?'

Daisy's voice is more animated now that I've steered the subject away from her missing phone even though she was the one to bring it up. 'We've got book club later.'

I feel myself smiling. 'Book club, huh? Very grown-up.'

There's a loud clatter in the background followed by muffled shouting. Panic sharpens my voice as I cut in, 'Are you okay? What's that noise?'

I feel a chill travel down my spine when Daisy mutters, 'It's just Granny.'

I grind out through clenched teeth, 'What is she up to?' I bite back the *now* that I want to attach to that sentence for Daisy's benefit, so I don't come across as bitter, even though that's exactly what I am where that woman is concerned. I'm betting the feeling is mutual.

Daisy sighs. 'She's throwing out the pavlovas she made.'

Bewildered, I ask, 'Why?'

'Because she burned them,' Daisy chastises as if I should know this.

'She sounds mad,' I point out carefully, so as not to come across as accusing and end up antagonising her further.

'Yep.'

My body goes limp with dread, and I swallow nervously before saying, 'Do you need me to come over?'

Another sigh, and then, 'It's okay. We're used to it by now.'

'You should never have to get used to something like that,' I snap. Now I'm a changed man, the hypocrite in me would prefer not to be reminded of the violent fights that Scarlet and I used to have in front of our children.

'She's not well, Dad,' Daisy tuts defensively.

I'm attacked by a stab of pain knowing that my precious oldest daughter, who has always been a daddy's girl, is siding with her grandmother. But I also hate to be the one to make her feel that she has to choose between us, so I back down and say, 'Yeah, maybe.'

Sounding all grown-up, and ever so slightly like her grandmother, Daisy scoffs dismissively, 'There's no maybe about it.'

'So, you don't think she's putting it on for your sake?' I dare to contradict her.

'DAD,' Daisy objects, drawing out my name in the longest sigh ever.

231

CHAPTER 55: THE GRANDMOTHER

I sit back with a weary sigh, earning me an elbow in the ribs from Daisy, as we're forced to listen to Rosalind Knowles's phoney middle-class reading of a passage from our assigned book club read. Even if she tried, the woman couldn't be any less entertaining. She's the worst choice of narrator, in my opinion, but then again, the Knowles's are among the most influential in our village. I have a sneaking suspicion that Alice is as bored as I am, it's all she can do to remain still, but Daisy appears enthralled. With my history, I should be fascinated by this sinister story of murder and intrigue, but instead, I find myself staring at my vein-knotted, sinewy arms, recalling a time when my flesh was creamy white, firm to the touch, and youthful.

I twist in my seat impatiently and begin to look around, earning myself another of Daisy's stern looks. The evening is beginning to grow dark but through the open window, I can still make out the silhouettes of two donkeys in a field across from the village hall. The scent of freshly cut grass is carried inside by a mild breeze.

Wrinkling my nose, I give Rosalind's daughter a hard stare because of the whale eye she's giving me. Insolent child. Satisfyingly, her features stretch taut at that. I had been looking forward to this evening, wanting to ingratiate myself with the village women, but in all honesty, it's not my cup of tea. I can't wait to leave.

Maybe on the way out, I'll accidentally-on-purpose misplace my walking stick and trip and fall, so that everybody rushes to assist me. I can picture them saying, "Oh, that poor dear woman, thank goodness she has her grandchildren to help care for her," which ought to appeal to Daisy's compassionate side. After that, no one will remember my angry outburst at church. I dislike exposing myself as weak and helpless, as it goes against the grain, yet it's a necessary evil if I want to be sure the children won't leave me. Time is running out for me to gain their full trust, which had been my original intention since only then, with my influence, would they be able to see their father for the man he is. If I have to rely on pity, so be it. I'm not too proud for that.

My mind drifts once again to Vincent Spencer. The thought of losing Daisy and Alice to him is unthinkable. I wouldn't be able to handle it. There's no telling what I might do. But now I know that the social worker — who I've nicknamed "Brown Mouse" like a Girl Guide — is on my side, I believe I have a strong chance of keeping custody of the girls. All I have to do on my end is keep my nose clean. And how difficult can that be?

Thank heavens and hallelujah, the reading is finished and it's time for some nibbles. Alice is out of her seat ahead of everyone else and is racing over to the canapé table like a playful young rabbit. Sausage rolls, vol-au-vents, crustless sandwiches and sweet pastries are all beautifully arranged, but my elegant mini raspberry pavlovas — as I had anticipated — are the real showstopper. Making a second batch was worth the effort.

'I'm so glad you could come,' Rosalind trills, heading in my direction.

She catches me as I'm about to swallow the last of my minuscule, unbuttered, low-calorie egg and cress sandwich. I'm forced to choke it down in an unladylike way before mumbling, 'It was worth it just to hear your excellent and highly atmospheric reading.'

Even though she blushes, she accepts my praise with an unassuming, 'Oh, not at all. I'm sure anyone could have done it better than me.'

I give a not-so-subtle nod of agreement, but it passes over her, as a rain cloud might, because such a jibe couldn't possibly be aimed at her.

'Daisy seems to be enjoying herself,' Rosalind observes, glancing around as though trying to locate my granddaughter. I get the impression that she is a favourite with Rosalind, because of their mutual passion for books. With a twinge of jealousy, I move away, leaving the younger woman open-mouthed, as though she was hoping we would talk more.

'These sausage rolls are yummy,' Alice mumbles beside me, brushing pastry crumbs from her dress. Verity, Rosalind's daughter, is close by. The two of them have become inseparable. When I envisioned Yvonne Castle's grandchildren moving in with me, I imagined a happy little bubble where it was just us three. Unfortunately, things haven't turned out that way, in which case, wouldn't it be cruel of the courts to remove Alice from her new school and the friends she has grown to love? Daisy, on the other hand, has not been persuaded to give the village school another shot. She can't be homeschooled forever though. For one thing, I lack the necessary training and experience. I also lack the patience . . . which is being tried right now, with Alice pawing continuously at my dress and pleading, 'Granny, please can we have one of your pavlovas?'

'All right then, but just one each.'

'Just one!' Alice sulkily complains, while gripping my hand and swinging it in hers, as if though we were connected by an invisible skipping rope. She does this all the time, and I find it incredibly irritating — for some reason, even more so today.

'We have to make sure there's enough to go around,' I remind her.

'I bet I can eat all these sausage rolls without being sick,' Alice boasts, as another beige sausage roll vanishes into her mouth.

'You could not,' Verity giggles.

'So, could. Just watch me,' Alice challenges, jutting out her chin.

Alice then grabs the entire tray of sausage rolls and starts to cram them into her mouth. 'See! I told you.'

'That's enough, Alice. Stop that,' I reprimand sternly.

Her face drops and she becomes even more whiney, I assume from tiredness, because it's almost nine o'clock and past her usual bedtime.

'It's not fair.' The little minx dares to stamp her foot at me. This behaviour is completely out of character for Alice and my hackles go up as I realise that she's showing off in front of Verity. I'm incensed that my granddaughter feels she has to impress the Knowles family.

Bristling, I lean in to hiss, 'Nobody likes a greedy gut, Alice.'

Her chin begins to wobble then, indicating that she is about to have one of her dramatic meltdowns, and before long, tears are streaming down her face. Crying I can handle, but what I can't tolerate is her incessant clawing at my hands and clothing. It gives me a claustrophobic feeling, like when my husband Ted used to pull at my nightclothes in bed expecting sex.

'I'm not fat, Granny. I'm not,' she practically yells.

'I never said you were fat, and please keep your voice down,' I hiss in indignation.

'You might not have said it, but that's what you meant,' Alice sobs loudly, and I can feel heads turning to stare at us.

Later, I will deeply regret allowing my impulses to get the better of me. But right now, when I'm at my wit's end, all I can think about is wrenching myself away from her and so I find myself screeching hysterically, 'Oh for God's sake, Alice, stop your pawing. I can't stand it.'

And I give Alice's hands a mild slap, undoing the promise I made to myself earlier to keep my nose clean. The sting of my flesh coming into contact with hers echoes throughout the room until everyone, including Daisy, is staring at me with shocked eyes.

CHAPTER 56: THE FATHER

'Dad, it was just a tap,' Daisy takes her head out of her book long enough to glare at me, sighing like a grumpy teenager.

'Just a tap,' I protest, wide-eyed, shifting Alice to both knees so that her weight is evenly distributed across my lap. She has been gaining weight lately, and I'm not sure if I should accept it and leave the kid alone or have a conversation with her about it. Making up my mind to speak to Holly about it later, I grumble, 'Not according to Alice.' In the car on the way here, both appeared unusually subdued, but I was able to eventually coax the truth out of Alice who hasn't stopped crying since I brought her back to 7 The Green. The day I had been hoping for, surprising the kids with their new-look home, was ruined the second we got in the door.

'She's making it out to be something more than it was *and* it happened days ago,' comes Daisy's response from the sofa.

'Your granny slapped your sister in front of a load of other people, I might add, and you're telling me Alice is making it up.'

Daisy's face reddens and it looks like she might burst into tears too. 'I never said that. I just don't want to get Granny in trouble,' she complains.

'She's already in trouble,' I mutter, shaking my head. Bile rises in my throat when I think about that woman putting her hands on my daughter. Just wait till I see her. I'll let her have it, for sure. *But wait*, that could go against me with the judge in my custody hearing next week. Better to pass on this information to my solicitor rather than tackle Mrs Castle directly.

Turning my attention back to a snivelling Alice I ask, 'You okay now, princess?'

She nods sadly through her tears. 'Can I go and play with Lucky now?'

'Sure you can.' It breaks my heart to see my daughter in such distress. My own eyes sting as I watch her walk away, head down, shoulders slumped, dragging her feet.

My phone vibrates in my pocket. I take it out and read a message from Holly. I must have a stupid lovestruck grin on my face because when I glance up, Daisy's eyes are burning into mine.

'Who is that?' she demands.

'Just a friend.' I wince, putting the phone back in my pocket.

'Just a friend?' Daisy parrots sarcastically, giving up the pretence of reading her book and sitting up straight. 'A man or a woman friend?'

'Does it matter?' I shrug, but I won't lie, my face is bright red. I wasn't prepared for an interrogation from Daisy this soon, but she's like a police sniffer dog when it comes to my love life.

'I think so,' she murmurs, sounding considerably older than she actually is, more like a jealous girlfriend. Like Leah, in fact.

'Her name's Holly,' I clumsily admit, lurching to my feet as my daughter's accusing stare makes me feel like a liar. If this is how being cross-examined in court feels, I'm going to shit myself next week.

'Holly,' Daisy sneers as if she's already decided not to like my so-called *friend*.

'It's not like that,' I trail off because *it is like that* and Daisy is aware of that. She knows me too well. So, I say instead, 'You'll like her when you meet her. She's—'

She shoots me a critical look before declaring icily, 'I doubt that and besides, I don't want to meet any more of your girlfriends, Dad.'

'Okay,' I sigh, stumped, and shuffle awkwardly while glancing down at my trainers. When my phone pings in my pocket again, I let out an even bigger sigh, realising I should have put it on silent.

Daisy, the warrior, is on her feet now. 'You promised that you were going to put us first from now on. That there would be no more girlfriends and that we were your top priority.'

'I am. I do,' I argue lamely. I'm full of shame right now. It sits heavily in my gut like an all-you-can-eat buffet. 'And she isn't strictly my girlfriend,' I end feebly. This is also a lie because things between Holly and I have moved on far more quickly than either of us anticipated.

In a dangerously quiet voice, Daisy insists on knowing, 'Has she been here, to this house? Mum's home?'

Silence is my only option if I don't want to tell another lie, so I stay shtum. And I stick my hands in my pockets, giving off a guilty vibe. Our rule of not visiting each other's houses came to an end weeks ago.

'She has, hasn't she? Oh my God, I bet she's been in Mum's bed too.'

"I ain't saying nada", as the saying goes, but I manage to give myself away with an impish grin because it feels like I'm being accused of cheating all over again. By my daughter, this time.

'You can't be alone for one minute, can you? And you know what happens when you get a girlfriend,' Daisy fumes, folding her arms and narrowing her eyes.

I make the fatal mistake of asking, 'What?' and I realise at the same time that I'm behaving like a child to her adult. Didn't I make a promise to myself that I wouldn't let this happen again? Daisy needs to be allowed to have a childhood without having to take care of the adults around her.

'You become useless, that's what. And you know how to pick them, don't you, Dad? Because look what happened with your last girlfriend. She hated us and because of her, *because of you*—' Spittle flies from Daisy's mouth and she takes a moment to wipe it away, before cutting out my heart by saying, 'We had to go and live at Granny's. And at least she wanted us, which is more than you can say.'

With that, having said her piece, which I suspect has been a long time in coming — not that I blame her — she bursts into childlike tears.

I extend my hand to comfort her, but she deliberately dodges me. My voice breaks a little as I attempt to placate her. 'Don't be like that,' I beg.

'Like what?' Daisy yells, throwing both hands up in the air in surrender, before storming outside to join her sister. I shudder at the disappointment I saw in her eyes. I will never forget that look; it made me realise how unworthy I am of my kids. But is it enough to make me give up Holly? Would that be the right thing to do? Daisy's right. About so many things. I *am* useless. Isn't that what Leah always used to call me?

'Useless, that's what I am,' I mutter furiously to myself, as I dump pens, Post-it notes, business cards, a stapler and other odds and sods onto my desk from a drawer. 'It's got to be in here somewhere.' I sigh in frustration and massage my temples. *Think, darn it.* But no matter how hard I search, I get the feeling that Daisy's phone is lost forever, along with the missing birth and death certificates. Not mine, I might add. I've locked up any proof that Nancy Tyrrell ever existed in my filing cabinet. Who knows when she might come in handy again? Daisy could easily have discovered the key to my study, hidden in the fire grate, and let herself in once she deduced that I was the one who took her phone from under her mattress. But why would a child be interested in old records? It doesn't make sense.

The only other people who have been in the house recently are Georgina Bell and the social worker, not forgetting Vincent Spencer, who waited downstairs at the girls' insistence one day when he arrived early to pick them up while they were still getting ready upstairs. Is it possible that without my knowing he secretly crept upstairs and went through my personal belongings? But how would he know where the key was? Or had Geogina sneaked upstairs on the pretence of wanting to use the bathroom to enter my study? Although "Brown Mouse" has spent more time in the house than anybody else, what could she gain from going through my things? Unless it was to learn more about my background as she mentioned when she was last here. Of course, the other possibility is that having pretended to suffer from frailty and memory loss, I am now being punished for it by exhibiting the early stages of dementia.

If the girls' father hears of this, he could use it against me, saying I'm unfit to care for two young children. But I will not overlook the fact that he was previously a suspect in Scarlet's murder, and if necessary, I will make it my mission to remind the courts of this. Let's just say that if he wants to play dirty, two can play that game. Alice has probably already told him about the very mild smack I gave her on Wednesday. Not that I haven't apologised repeatedly for it, but since then, things haven't been the same between us. She is wary of me now.

Over coffee, I told the social worker about the incident to protect myself, in case it was blown out of proportion. These days, she comes to visit me frequently, and not just to see the girls. Personally, I believe she is lonely and in need of companionship. Or perhaps it's the other way around? In all honesty, I can't decide. Either way, she has befriended me, and I intend to use this to my advantage. If the social worker involved in my custody case is on my side, I can't be all bad.

"Mrs Castle, you are allowed to discipline the children under your care, provided it is deemed reasonable," she'd explained to me over a Hobnob.

"Try telling that to Alice," I'd huffed, pouring her another coffee.

But her counsel also came with a caveat, "However, there are strict guidelines laid down in Section 58 of the Children Act 2004."

Thinking that she sounded like a human dictionary, I'd laughed, "Well, that bit of advice was about as useful as a chocolate teapot." I was relieved to discover that, despite being down in the dumps, I was still on form.

I'm distracted from my thoughts when I hear the back gate slamming shut, followed by raised voices fluttering up from the garden below. It's another sweltering day so the Velux windows are open. The sound of quarrelling can mean only one thing. The girls are back.

'It's all your fault,' I hear Daisy screech.

Alice comes back with an equally outraged, 'You're the one who has been in a bad mood all day.'

'Because of *you*.'

I feel the tightness in my shoulders release, and as I turn away from the window and move towards the door, I find myself grinning. I'm glad they're home, quarrel or no quarrel. Without them, the house is silent and empty. A piercing scream breaks the silence. *What on earth . . .*

I don't know how I scramble downstairs so fast without breaking a leg, but Alice's sobs and Daisy's screams propel me all the way. If I didn't know better, I'd think somebody was being murdered. Perhaps the children are fighting for real this time. I've caught them at it once before, remember?

When I finally stumble outdoors into the garden, I'm met with the two terrified children clutching desperately to each other. Their startled expressions are fixed on a corner of the garden that's hidden from my view.

'What is it?' I gasp, feeling my own jaw drop.

Daisy stammers, 'The . . . the doll,' pointing as she keeps one mothering arm around her blubbering smaller sister, who has now averted her gaze from whatever it was they were staring at.

My heart is thundering in my chest as I ask uncertainly, 'What doll?'

'It's Daisy's poor doll,' Alice sobs, lowering her head and avoiding eye contact with me.

'Don't be daft,' I murmur, sucking in my breath. 'It can't be.'

'It is,' Daisy yells, continuing to point.

I investigate, and when I find that a corner of the garden has been dug up, likely by a fox, and that the doll's undressed body has been partially exposed, I'm no longer surprised by the girls' reactions. Her plastic eyes have been dug out and her long hair hacked off. Even worse, her head is partially severed and positioned horrifyingly backwards, giving the impression that she is looking over his shoulder. Talk about creepy.

'Girls, get inside,' I bark.

But instead of running inside the house, as one might have expected, Daisy changes into a self-styled Amazon Prime detective and begins questioning me non-stop. Questions that I'm sure won't go away any time soon. Questions that I'm unable to . . . and refuse to answer.

'Why has it turned up here?' Daisy accuses, and then, 'You did this, didn't you? You stole my doll and buried her in the garden, thinking nobody would ever find it. And now, because of you, my sister is going to have nightmares for the rest of her life.'

I want to tell her, childishly, to "Join the club," but I don't. Instead, I ignore her, spin on my heel, enter the shed, and retrieve a shovel that bears dried-on bloodstains I'd rather not be reminded of.

243

CHAPTER 58: THE FATHER

As I glimpse my reflection in the mirror, I realise that blood is smeared down one side of my face. Grabbing a handful of cheap, scratchy toilet roll from one of the foul-smelling toilet cubicles, I rub at the shaving nicks on my chin until they disappear, wishing I could too. Along with the dirty bastard who walked out just now without washing his hands. I detest that. Gives all of us blokes a bad name in my opinion. Call it my only superpower if you like, but I pride myself on always putting the toilet seat down when I'm finished with it. Not that it earned me any brownie points with Leah, who I sometimes think pissed standing up like any ball-breaking man.

Scratching absentmindedly at my crotch — *another bloke thing* — I notice that there are dark rings under my eyes. It's gut-wrenching having to admit that I look old and haggard at thirty-two. But is it any wonder when two sleepless and guilt-ridden eyes are staring back at me? I've never felt more of a villain than I do tonight, knowing I'm going to be breaking up with Holly and that she doesn't deserve it. She hasn't done anything wrong, after all. I'm entirely to blame. For everything. I never should have got involved with her in the first place. I see that now.

I let out a sigh of exasperation when my phone rings. I switch it on to silent. That's the fifth time Daisy has tried to call me from her grandmother's number in as many minutes. No doubt to give me a hard time again, otherwise she wouldn't be trying to get in touch so soon after I dropped her off at Mrs Castle's house. *First things first.* I have to have the difficult conversation with Holly before I return Daisy's call. That way, I can report back that I am now single again and can keep my promise to prioritise my daughters. As I should have done all along.

The faces of my two children come unbidden to mind. One is angry and accusing. The other is disappointed and sad. So, I ignore the wave of fear that feels as if it has been injected into my veins by the largest syringe in the world and brace my shoulders as if about to step into a boxing ring with bully-boy Pearce. The door to the pub toilet creaks as I ease it open and my eyes shiftily hit the floor when I see Holly waiting patiently for me at the table she now calls "ours".

I walk, reluctantly, past a scruffy row of beer-drinking, teeth-gnashing, football fans kitted out in their favourite team colours, all eyes fixed on the enormous TV screen, where grown men in shorts are exploding with rage over a referee's unpopular decision. Focusing on my own dilemma, I feel heat travel up my neck as I sit down next to Holly. As if she did it on purpose, she's looking really nice tonight, beautiful in fact. Her hair falls loosely around her shoulders, and when her eyes meet mine, they sparkle with admiration. I stifle a groan, realising that I don't deserve it.

'I thought you were never coming back and that you had escaped out of the toilet window.' She chuckles and takes a sip of her Diet Coke.

Two things strike me at the same time. First, she has no idea how close to the truth she is, and, second, the fact that she abstains from alcohol. She's completely teetotal, which is unheard of in my part of the world.

'I wouldn't do that to you,' I mumble, trying my best to sound sincere, when inside I'm actually thinking, *I so bloody would* . . . anything is preferable to having to end a relationship. Yet, I went ahead and broke Scarlet's heart when I left her for Leah. That shows how much of an arsehole I was. But I've changed since then. I'm a softie at heart.

'I know you wouldn't.' She throws me an approving wink, before adding, 'You're not like other men,' which makes me feel ten times worse.

I roll my shoulders back and look up, as though appealing for God to intervene, before stammering, 'Holly, I . . .' and end up coughing nervously into my hand. I've stumbled at the first hurdle, unable to conjure up a single word of the rehearsed-in-my-head adult conversation I intended to have with her. Instead, I simply sit there looking like a complete fool, white-faced and helpless, as a look of confusion flashes across Holly's face.

Luckily, Holly is switched on enough for the two of us because she asks with a slight tremor, 'Is there anything wrong, Vince?'

My voice breaks a little as I admit, 'There's something important I want to say, but, oh God, I'm just so nervous I can't get my words out.'

Flashing me a sympathetic smile, she gives a laugh. 'I've seen you naked, so I can assure you there is nothing for you to be nervous about.'

Feeling it's expected, I fake a laugh and then clamp my mouth shut for fear of saying the wrong thing. Hurting her is the last thing I want to do. She's such a sweetheart. But is she *the one*? Because if that were the case, would I really be contemplating breaking up with her? Even if that was what my daughter wanted me to do?

When she says with a playful smirk, 'Shall I put you out of your misery?' I feel hopeful. Don't ask me why.

'Please do,' I groan, wanting so much to be rescued.

'I think I know what you're trying to say to me,' she confides.

'You do?' I ask, incredulous.

Is she truly that kind, that she's going to make this easy for me and let me off the hook? Finish with me before I do her. Or maybe, agree mutually to call it quits. A small, egotistical part of me is offended that she doesn't think I'm worth fighting for. A bit of a bummer, actually.

Her words make my heart flip over when she announces with a big cheesy grin, 'The answer is . . . yes.'

Thrown, I pause to gulp at a mouthful of air as if it were my last, and sensing in my gut that something isn't right, I question hoarsely, 'What do you mean, yes?'

With an excitable shuffle, Holly exclaims, 'Of course I'll marry you, Vince. I knew you were the one for me the instant I laid eyes on you.'

Oh God, what have I done?

CHAPTER 59: THE GRANDMOTHER

'Oh God, what have I done?' I ask myself for the hundredth time today when my mobile phone rings and I recognise the number. Ever since the children came back from their father's yesterday afternoon and discovered the mutilated doll in the garden, this is the call I have been dreading. Daisy hasn't spoken to me all day and Alice just snivels and looks away whenever I glance at her. Daisy seems intent on keeping her younger sibling away from me, as though I would deliberately hurt her. As if I would ever harm my precious girls in any way. In the next breath though, I'm cursing them as I take the call since it's clear to me, they've been in communication with their father.

'Hello,' I say overbrightly, nervously smacking my lips together. On the other end, the social worker's tone is uncharacteristically abrupt—

'Mrs Castle?' Brown Mouse queries frostily. As if it could be anybody else! The stupid woman. Wasn't she the one to dial my number?

'Yes, dear,' I answer meekly, dabbing a small trickle of perspiration from my forehead. I can feel the dampness spreading to my underarms and the small of my back.

My body tenses when she tells me, 'There's been a change of plan.'

My head is filled with the worst-case scenario . . . that of losing the children. *Please, God. Not that.* Yesterday, I tried so hard to win them over, but to no avail. Daisy wouldn't listen to any of my wildly imaginative explanations, like the doll being stolen by Verity Knowles to spite us and then strategically placing it in the garden to ensure that we found it. She quite rightly accused me of lying, asserting that it was impossible for a child Verity's age to get away with something like that by herself. I went too far by suggesting she had an accomplice in her mother. At that moment, I realised that, for once, I wouldn't be able to talk my way out of this. Defeated by a nine-year-old, I turned to bribery and offers of extra special treats, even a new phone, but it all fell on deaf ears. They had made up their minds to hate me and there was nothing I could do about it.

In the words of my late husband Ted, "It's all gone tits up." However, once an abuser, always an abuser, and he had no idea how fortunate he was that despite his repeated appeals and claims that he was an old man and no longer a menace to society, he was never granted the parole he so desperately sought and ended up dying in prison, which was no more than he deserved. But in the unlikely event that he was ever released, I had planned on ending his life sentence for him. He had it coming after what he put me through. Life should mean life in my book.

'Are you still there, Mrs Castle?'

No. I'm reliving the past, I want to tell her. Instead, I heave a sigh. 'Yes,' I play dumb, stalling for time.

'The girls have told their father that they now wish to live with him.'

I gaze out of the kitchen window. A lone white cloud, which I feel represents me, drifts over the vast expanse of cornflower blue.

'Did they say why?' I ask, with a catch in my throat.

A pause down the line, before the social worker haltingly states, 'They did as a matter of fact. They said that you often lose your patience and snap at them.'

With a hint of irritation in my voice I reply, 'Yes, well, they do rather question everything I say, Daisy in particular, which is why I told her that she had all the charm of a wet sock—'

'Mrs Castle,' she interrupts, sounding shocked. 'This is not something to be taken lightly. It is a serious matter.'

The woman is no fun. But she's right. This is no laughing matter. My heart is so frantic I can feel it banging in my chest, giving me acid reflux.

'There was also the incident of the smack,' she cautions. As if I need reminding!

'You said that I was allowed to discipline them,' I vehemently protest, blood pulsing in my ears.

'It all adds up,' she sighs.

I angrily point out, 'I thought you said it wasn't up to the girls.'

'That's correct, but their wishes will, of course, be taken into consideration.' She clears her throat. 'I will also be presenting my recommendation to the court.'

Feeling on safer ground now, because the woman has always supported me — *did she not say as much herself? Did she not refer to me as a friend?* — I ask more confidently, 'What *are* your recommendations?' Then, in an attempt to ingratiate myself with her, I try to remember her first name. But it's no good. It's gone from my memory as usual. Was it Mabel? Paula, perhaps? Or Hilda? Nope. None of those. Darn it. You could knock me down with a feather when she comes out with—

'I personally feel they will be better placed with their father—'

It's my turn to interrupt now, crying, 'You can't do this to me! When nobody else wanted them, I took them in.'

'And we're very grateful for that, Mrs Castle, but, as you can appreciate, Vincent Spencer is their father.'

Standing there marooned, alone in the world and without any friends or family, I wonder if this is how the real Yvonne Castle felt when her beloved Charles passed away, and her daughter abandoned her? If so, that could explain why she was so desperate to befriend me. More fool her.

Whatsherface reassures in a smarmy manner, 'I'm sure the girls' father will be amenable to you seeing them at some point in the future, after things are settled next week at court.' Then, as if enjoying herself, she adds doubtfully, 'If that's what the girls want,' insinuating that it's unlikely. I must be getting old because I seriously misjudged this woman, who isn't anywhere near as nice as I imagined her to be. Who is though?

'I wouldn't bet on it,' I bark, hating the thought that "that man" has won. People who advise against taking things personally are the biggest hypocrites because, of course, one should. *They are* personal. And everyone knows that.

'I'm sorry things haven't worked out the way you anticipated, but based upon what he's said, it sounds like he sincerely cares about those children.'

Naturally, I find fault with everything she says. First of all, she doesn't sound sorry. Not one bit. Furthermore, the man in question has a history of domestic abuse and has been accused of it more times than he has had hot dinners. In addition, he is a known thief, was once addicted to drugs, and is a liar and a cheat. What else can I say? The more I consider that someone like him could be picked over me, the more enraged I become. I think that's one insult too many. The last straw, so to speak.

'That's not what you said before,' I exclaim fiercely, wanting to poke her eye out with a pencil. No strike that, a spoon.

'In the end, the court will decide.' She tries to make me feel better as if there was still hope, but when she goes on to say, cuttingly I might add, 'But I think it's only fair to warn you that the girls have said they don't feel safe with you.'

251

CHAPTER 60: THE FATHER

Who would have thought that I would end up getting engaged, having woken up yesterday morning intending to break things off with Holly? And now I'm here, outside a jewellery shop of all places, helping my new fiancé choose a ring, when my focus should be on my two young daughters.

When I finally got to speak to Daisy last night and she told me that she and her sister had changed their mind and wanted to move in with me, I sensed she was withholding something. I was so made up over their decision though, that I decided it didn't matter. So I rang social services and told them that the girls were struggling to cope with their ageing grandmother, who was likely suffering from early dementia. Quite how they will react to finding out they have a new stepmother is another matter.

Rather than waiting until I can afford it, Holly has offered to pay for the ring herself. I'm trying to be a modern man about it, but I can tell you it bothers me. My humiliation has reached new heights now that my girlfriend is having to pay for her own engagement ring. I'm so broke. And, let's not forget, useless. Even though I might be all of the things Mrs Castle tells my daughters I am . . . a thief, a drop-out, and a former druggie, not to mention a killer if you factor in the unintentional running over of the paedophile, I'm still a big softie. Pathetic, I know.

When Holly mistook my pathetic attempt to break up with her for a marriage proposal, she was so ecstatic that I felt compelled to go along with it. Loser, right? But how could I have dumped her and destroyed all her dreams when she was crying tears of joy? Fuck knows it's not like she hasn't been through enough in life. I wasn't going to add to her trauma by making her feel unloved, unattractive or not good enough. But what the fuck am I going to tell the girls? More precisely, Daisy? Shit. That's one introduction I'm dreading. It gives me ball ache just thinking about it.

If I'm being completely honest, I guess I'm hoping that everything will magically fall into place. Who knows, maybe Holly will go off me once she realises what a useless twat I am. It's not like I have much to offer a woman like her, who has a job. Her own house. A decent car. Everything that I don't. For now, I'll just play along and hope for the best. I've already told Holly that I'm hoping the girls will be allowed to move in with me next week after the court case is over and I have also warned her that we won't be able to tell them about the engagement straight away. She understands that we'll have to take things slowly so we don't overwhelm the girls. She's great like that. It helps that she's a teaching assistant and works with kids.

'This is the one,' Holly exclaims excitedly, pointing to a ring in the shop window.

I'm forced into smiling because I'm unable to resist her enthusiasm any longer. 'We're not even inside the shop yet,' I mansplain.

'I know that,' she replies, biting her lip and narrowing her eyes — two entirely unfamiliar actions for Holly.

Now that we're engaged, I figure she won't be on her best behaviour all the time. Isn't that how it is with most, if not all, women? A man can be shot for having such thoughts so

I keep them to myself and grumble instead. 'Have you seen the price of it?'

'I think I'm worth twice as much,' she jokes. And then, with a smile and a softened gaze, my Holly is back.

'You are indeed, but it'll take me forever to pay back five hundred quid.'

She slips her arm through mine and murmurs sweetly, 'I've told you that you don't have to.'

'I know. But that wouldn't be right. I'm the man.'

'My man.' She snuggles into me and sighs contentedly into my ear, convincing me that everything will turn out fine. It has to.

'Vince!'

Startled, my head snaps up and spins around to find the source of that familiar voice. A shudder rips through me and every hair on my body stands on end when I see Leah marching towards us with deadened eyes and a spiteful curled lip. Her hands are gripped tightly around the handle of Saffy's buggy, displaying white knuckles. This tells me everything!

As soon as she's close enough, she lets rip with, 'Don't tell me you're getting engaged. Already!'

'Leah.' I nod curtly as I peer into the buggy in the hopes of catching a smile from Saffy, but my little one is fast asleep. Tears form in my eyes as I am overcome with an intense feeling of longing to hold her. Blinking them away, I return my attention to the two women glaring at me.

'This is Holly,' I announce with a cough of an apology. 'Holly, Leah.'

The ex-girlfriend and the new fiancée look each other up and down. When Leah opens her mouth again, she is scathing. 'Somebody downgraded.'

I can't quite decide what makes me more angry: seeing Holly lower her head in shame over the insult or trying to hide her birthmark.

'Don't be a bitch, Leah,' I warn.

254

Furious, she snorts, 'Bitch, huh? That's what you call me after nearly two years together.'

Leah has a ball of gum in the side of her cheek as usual, and her lips are pursed with anger. She goes on, unstoppable in her rage, 'Two years I might add in which you never once proposed to me or bought me a ring.'

Holly's head bounces on her shoulders. 'You didn't deserve it after the lies you told about the baby, making Vince think she was his,' she scowls.

While I'm grateful to Holly for coming to my rescue, *I didn't know she had it in her*, Leah does have a point, and I can understand why she's so pissed off. Deliberately ignoring Holly's attack, Leah waves her own diamond ring in our faces, yelling 'I'm fucking glad Saffy's not yours. At least Wayne put a ring on my finger once he found out he was the dad.'

I shoot her a fierce warning look, and I'm deliberately being sarcastic when I tell her, 'That's not all he gave you though, is it Leah? You had a black eye the last time I saw you.'

Her face pales at that. Like the idiot I am, I feel my heart soften. Surely to God, I can't still have feelings for her? Rather than having a go at her, I want to wrap my arms around her and reassure her that everything is going to be all right and that I will always be there for her and Saffy. But I can't do that here, in front of Holly. Whatever would she think? Instead of taking offence or defending Wayne, Leah surprises me by storming off, quipping over her shoulder, 'Useless fucking arsehole.'

CHAPTER 61: THE GRANDMOTHER

There is a note pinned to the windscreen wiper of my car. The third one this week. I give it a hard stare before ripping it off and quickly reading it. "You are not who you say you are," it claims, just like the other ones did. The paper has a distinct old-lady smell about it. You don't have to be Albert Einstein to figure out who put it there. Georgina bloody Bell, of course. Honestly, she's like the sneaky character in a zombie movie who's been bitten but is trying to keep it quiet.

Daisy has followed me around to my side of the car out of curiosity. At least she's talking to me again, now that I have promised them the surprise of their lives. A shock, more like, when they find out what it is. And also because I have reluctantly accepted their decision to live with their father, having informed them that I won't be putting any objections in their way. The trust of the innocent is the liar's most useful tool, as the saying goes, as neither Daisy nor Alice can be hundred per cent certain that I had anything to do with the doll's demise. This doesn't mean I'm completely off the hook though or that I won't be taking my revenge. Nobody rejects Nancy Tyrrell that way and gets away with it.

Beneath the simpering smiles, I am mad as hell with the children. After all I've done for them, who can blame me? I am aware that they will never forgive me for what I am about to do, but given that I have already lost them, and thanks to that awful Vince Spencer, I have nothing to lose. Once the girls move in with him, I don't think for a second that I will be permitted to have a relationship with them.

Daisy asks, pointing to the note in my hand, 'What's that?'

'Nothing,' I mutter and slide the note into my pocket.

'Who is it from?'

'Nobody.' I shoot her down with a stern look, and she rolls her eyes before piling into the back of the car next to her belted-in sister.

Half an hour later, we're in a posh hair salon in Stamford, where the girls are behaving shyly in front of the staff, all of whom seem like Victoria Secret models. Exquisite gold mirrors adorn the walls and glass chandeliers dangle from the ceilings. The blood-red chaises longues are made from plush velvet. The place reminds me of an old-fashioned whorehouse, not that I've ever been in one. I'm not even sure they still exist.

'Why are we here?' Daisy whispers in my ear, so as not to be overheard by the young blonde female hairdresser. She is less confident in social situations with strangers than Alice. As if to demonstrate this, Alice is now seated and is being fussed over by a different hairdresser.

'It's my special goodbye treat,' I assure Daisy, grinning indulgently at the hairdresser who is armed with a cape and is waiting to slip it onto Daisy's shoulders.

'But I don't want my hair cut,' Daisy objects, anxiously smoothing down her waist-long hair, as if terrified of losing even an inch of it.

'It's just a trim. To tidy you up ready for moving in with your father.'

She frowns, looking doubtful, but she nonetheless follows the stylist over to a chair beside her sister. As she takes

257

a seat, her gaze meets mine in the mirror, and I give her an encouraging nod of approval.

The owner has been observing us covertly all this while, and I quietly take her to one side before whispering, 'As I told you on the phone, they're both riddled with head lice and we can't get on top of it.'

'But are you sure you want it *all* cut off?' she asks in disbelief.

I nod determinedly. 'Yes. Every last inch.'

With a heavy sigh, she continues, 'I know what young girls are like about their hair. It's their pride and joy.'

Exactly, is what I'm thinking, but in an attempt to shut her up, I make a compassionate face. I'm also thinking she should mind her own bloody business.

'And they don't know—'

'Oh God, no, if they did, they'd howl the place down.'

An hour later, as predicted, both girls are sobbing uncontrollably in the back seat — my, time flies when you're having fun. With their matching pixie haircuts, I couldn't help pointing out how different they looked as we were getting back in the car. Like street urchins. When I see Daisy tug angrily at her shorn hair, I almost feel sorry for her. The worst part is that neither can escape what they look like when the other is in front of them.

Daisy cries angrily, 'We don't even have head lice,' and she kicks the back of my chair so forcefully that I feel a tremor run up my spine.

'It was Verity's mum who pointed them out to me. She said she could see the lice crawling about in your hair. That's why you weren't allowed to go to their house on Friday to play, Alice,' I lie, unable to resist the dig.

Alice lets out a louder cry at that. Tears are streaming down her plump cheeks, turning her face all blotchy. The poor love.

'You did this to get back at us!' Daisy launches another attack, this time thumping the back of my seat, right behind my head. *That's my girl.*

'It's just hair, Daisy, it will grow back,' I sigh, as if everyone expects too much of me, rather than the other way around. 'I had no choice but to ask them to cut it all off. You wouldn't want people to know you're infested with lice, would you? Children have been bullied for far less.'

Daisy seems to take that piece of advice to heart. 'But you could have warned us,' she pouts. 'And now I look like my doll.'

That makes me grin, but I'm careful to hide it. Instead, I murmur sympathetically, 'I'm sorry, Daisy. I only did what I thought was best.'

'It's okay, Granny,' Alice pipes up, and the sweetness of that child moves me so much, that I have to shift in my seat and turn to look at her.

'I happen to think you both look really lovely,' I tell them with, what is for me, a sincere smile. But when real fear suddenly appears in their eyes, and they start yelling and begging me to turn around, I panic.

But turn around, I do. Just in time to avoid getting struck by the car hurtling towards us. 'How in the world did I end up on the wrong side of the road?' I let out a scream as I yank the wheel to the left and return us to the right lane. I imagine all of our hearts are thundering in our chests as we begin to calm down once we realise that we are safe.

'Sorry, girls,' I mumble sheepishly.

I receive no response. No surprise there, given that I just about nearly killed everyone, but Daisy sits up and pays attention when the car takes a turn she wasn't anticipating.

'Where are we going?' she quizzes, like the amateur detective she is.

I shake my head, sighing, 'Questions. Questions. Always questions.'

When the realisation dawns on her, her voice becomes panicked as she exclaims, 'Why are we going to The Green?'

I take a chance and risk another glance over my shoulder, wanting to see her face when I say, 'I'm taking you home, just like you wanted.'

After that, both girls fall silent, although I imagine they'll be exchanging wary looks and wondering what the heck is going on. Neither of them speaks again until we arrive at number7, exit the car and are outside the back door.

'How are we meant to get in when Dad's not here,' Daisy frets, biting her lower lip. 'We don't have a key.'

I wink mischievously at her, and then shatter the glass in the door with the steel end of my walking stick. Both girls gasp in horror when it splinters everywhere. Daisy, in particular, will recall the night her mother was murdered, when somebody else used a similar technique to break the glass.

CHAPTER 62: THE FATHER

When an unknown number calls my mobile, I'm at Holly's house, in Holly's bed, celebrating our spontaneous engagement. I raise a finger to my lips to warn Holly not to say anything before I respond. With a shrug, she sits up in bed and spins around the diamond ring on her finger, grinning. Should we ever actually get married, I imagine she'll be the kind of woman who gets super excited about every detail. The flowers. The buffet. And, of course, the dress, which I imagine will be a plain affair.

'Hello?' I enquire.

'Dad, it's me, Daisy.'

I immediately cover my genitals with a pillow, as if my daughter were in the room with me and take a deep breath.

'Hi, Daisy. What's up?' It's my standard response.

I'm distracted though because Holly has snaked one arm around my chest and is playfully tweaking my nipples, something I usually like. But when a distraught, tearful voice whimpers, 'You have to come and get us.' I jolt upright and thrust Holly off, earning me a look of concern.

'Get you? Where from?' I ramble, hating that I smell of sex when I'm talking to my nine-year-old who sounds absolutely terrified.

'We're at home,' she replies, but her voice keeps fading in and out as if someone else was putting the phone between Daisy's ear and theirs so they can hear what I'm saying. But that's daft, since if that were the case, they would just put me on loudspeaker . . . Unless they don't know how to. Somebody elderly, maybe. Like their grandmother.

My feet skid across the floor as I leap out of bed. 'Is your grandmother there with you?'

Daisy mumbles a very telling, 'Uh huh,' but she sounds distracted and there's a background whispering sound that suggests somebody is telling her what to say.

I tug on my pants and shorts, ignoring Holly, whose eyes are on stalks, as she tracks my speeded-up movements around the room. I say into the phone, 'Is she telling you what to say, love?'

Once more, Daisy repeats in a timid voice, 'Uh huh.'

What is that old bitch up to now? I think, while speaking in as normal a voice as possible, to avoid frightening Daisy any more than she already is, 'That's okay, love. You don't have to say any more. I'm coming to get you.'

Now that she is out of bed, Holly is also getting dressed and mouthing "I'll come with you" at me, but I dismiss her with a shake of my head and a wave of my hand. *What is she thinking?* I don't need this, right now.

'How long will you be?' Daisy asks, her voice wavering.

Clenching my jaw, I mutter, 'Just as long as it takes me to drive to your granny's house,' because the fear in her voice is making me feel physically sick. Once again, I feel useless. Helpless even, since I'm not there when she needs me. What good is a dad if he can't keep his kids safe?

'We're not at Granny's house,' Daisy whispers.

I reply, a little taken aback, 'But you said you were at home.'

'Yes, *our* home. Mum's home. At The Green.'

Firmly, I tell her, 'In that case, I'll be there in ten minutes,' and end the call. I turn to face Holly and say with a catch in my voice, 'I've got to go.'

'I gathered that,' Holly exclaims. There is a deep burning question in her gaze but she doesn't voice her concerns. Instead, she throws me her car keys and says, 'Take mine, you'll get there quicker.'

I respond numbly, 'Thanks,' and blow her a kiss before slipping my trainers on and sprinting down the stairs while struggling to breathe and feeling like I'm drowning. I know my daughter, and I could tell by the sound of her voice that something was seriously wrong. Throwing myself into the driver's seat of Holly's two-year-old dark grey Nissan Qashqai I rack my brain as to what could have gone wrong. Now that Daisy and Alice have decided they wish to live with me, and not their grandmother, has Mrs Castle finally lost her mind? Is she really that vindictive? Would she do them harm? Despite how I feel about her, I've always credited her with having the girls' best interests at heart but now I'm not so sure.

My whole body is rigid with fear as I try to start the car. It takes me a couple of attempts because I'm not used to driving an automatic or anything as new as this — Holly does well on a teaching assistant's salary, *new house, smart car* — but I get there in the end, and I'm soon out of the driveway and tearing down Sugar Way before making a left into Oundle Road. Like Holly's newly constructed two-bedroomed terraced home, the car is spotless. There are no personal items on show, just like at her house. Not a single lipstick, water bottle or packet of mints are to be found. We might joke about her "non-cluttered until she met me" way of living, but it seems strange that she doesn't have a single photograph of any of her family or friends in her house. But that's just me. And what do I know?

From what I can gather, Holly has a good relationship with her parents and sees them every Sunday without fail. I'm surprised she hasn't invited me to meet them yet, what with us now being officially engaged. But why am I wasting time thinking about Holly when I have more important things to concentrate on? Like, are my daughters in danger and, if so, should I call the police? Or is that a bit extreme? Let's face it,

I don't have a clue what's really going on, only that Mrs Castle has taken her granddaughters to my house without my permission. How did they even get in? On top of that, I get a call from my daughter who sounds scared and begs me to come and get her. Would the police think me crazy for wasting their time?

Fuck them, they've wasted enough of my time over the years, and on that depressing thought, I fish my phone out of my pocket and bark, 'Google, dial 999,' being sure to keep one eye on the road in front of me.

While I wait to get put through, I put my foot down and accelerate, travelling faster and faster, as the car trawls past blurry images of shops and houses. When I enter the Dogsthorpe area of town, I'm shivering with fear and adrenalin, wondering what awaits me at 7 The Green.

CHAPTER 63: THE GRANDMOTHER

'I won't let you hurt my sister,' Daisy growls as she moves to stand guard in front of Alice, who has retreated into a corner of the room. We're in Scarlet's old room. The door is securely shut, the curtains are drawn, and the interior is dark with imaginary shadowy figures hiding in every corner. The room is also filled with Scarlet's scent — white musk, coffee beans and springtime fabric softener — which keeps her alive in all our minds.

'Who said anything about hurting anyone?' I object harshly, collapsing heavily onto the bed and motioning for Alice to join me. Daisy, however, puts an arm out in front of Alice and prevents her sister from obeying.

I bite my tongue until I taste blood, yet when I wearily ask, 'When are you going to stop fighting me, Daisy?' my voice sounds emotionless.

Daisy looks right through me and remains stubbornly silent. A feeling of unease persists between the two of us, but she tenses up and frowns the moment I reach over to get a pillow off the bed. It bears the same significance whether or not it is the one that was used to take Scarlet's last breath. I plump it up and let my hands sink into its velvety smoothness, whispering softly under my breath, 'You've obviously seen this before.'

That gets me an arched eyebrow but no response. But I am aware that my words must stab at her small heart. 'Does it mean anything to you?'

With tears flooding her eyes, Daisy gulps and backs away, retreating into an even darker corner, while murmuring, 'No.'

Taking advantage of her distress, I move quicker than any bird of prey and grasp Alice's hand, pulling her onto the bed with me. She doesn't resist, simply keeps sobbing. Irritation courses through me and I'm tempted to tell her to dry her tears and be a big girl, but now isn't the right time for a lecture on how to conduct oneself.

'Tell me more about that night and what happened when you found your mother,' I demand of Daisy. Her eyes widen with alarm. But her cold accusing glare comes back to rest on me when I aim my walking stick at her, as if it were a weapon of mass destruction. *Jab. Jab. Jab.*

When the steel end of the stick comes into contact with her clasped fingers, making a loud knuckle-cracking sound, she gives a startled shake of her head before muttering angrily, 'I hate you. I wish you weren't my grandmother.'

'Well, in that case, think of me as your very own fairy-tale godmother because the truth is we are not related at all,' I tell her delightedly, cackling like the old witch that I am.

With a sharp intake of breath, she sharply retorts, 'What do you mean? Are you saying that Mum was adopted?'

'No,' I reply bluntly as I absentmindedly stroke Alice's head, which is now resting against my chest, in an attempt to soothe her. 'I'm saying that I never knew your mother.'

Wide-eyed in disbelief, Daisy stutters, 'What? You've gone mad. Lost your mind,' and she draws a crazy circle close to her ear, before hissing, 'Alice, get away from her. She's dangerous.'

I pin a terrified Alice to my side without once glancing at her as she wriggles to escape my grasp. Despite the gammy leg, I am strong for my age, and Alice is going nowhere. Her frantic movements remind me of a rabbit caught in a trap, squirming to get free and prepared to bite off its limb to survive. But why am I wasting time on Alice when I only have eyes for Daisy? I know that a real grandmother wouldn't have favourites, but Daisy has always been mine.

Scowling, Daisy threatens, 'If you do anything to hurt my sister, I'll—'

'You'll do what? Hurt me?' I chuckle sarcastically, and then point out, 'Don't worry, Daisy. I know exactly what you're capable of.'

She clenches her teeth and juts out a furious jaw, warning, 'Let her go.'

I reply scathingly, shaking my head, 'Alice doesn't matter. She never did. It's you that I find fascinating. I have from the start. In fact, from the very moment I first laid eyes on you.'

Confusion flashes across Daisy's face. Every inch of her skin appears to crawl with uncertainty. She looks so innocent, so pallid, and so helpless as she stands there. But then I remember that I'm dealing with Daisy Spencer, who has just as many dark secrets as I have. So, I ask in a purposefully enigmatic tone, 'And do you remember when that was?'

Brow furrowed, as if she's having trouble understanding, she says, 'I have no idea what you're talking about.'

'Oh, but I think you do, darling child. You see, it was right here in this very room. Do you not remember?'

Alice whimpers, looking at her sister with the most appealing Bambi-sized eyes, 'What is she talking about, Daisy?'

Daisy's enraged gaze flickers between her sister and me, and it contains more than a trace of guilt when she murmurs, 'I don't know, Alice. I told you she was mad.'

'That's it, continue lying all the way to the finish. I wouldn't expect anything else from you. Bravo,' I exclaim jovially, as if I were proudly watching her perform in a school play.

At that, Daisy determinedly crosses her arms over her chest, gives me a cold, serial killer-style stare, and retreats into stubborn silence once more.

'We are so alike, you and I,' I utter, with something like awe.

Daisy's fiercely intent gaze comes back to rest on me as she snaps, 'I'm nothing like you.'

I chuckle softly. 'But you're wrong there, dearie, because, well, didn't we both get away with murder?'

CHAPTER 64: THE FATHER

Shattered glass crunches under my feet as I enter the house through the broken back door, a horrible reminder of the night Scarlet died. The house is in darkness and the unnatural silence of it causes every hair on my body to stand on end. *Where is everyone and what has that woman done with my children?* Hearing the faint creak of a floorboard somewhere above me, I head upstairs, dread behind every step. Even though I always leave the door to Scarlet's bedroom open, it's closed now. Detecting a snivelling sound on the other side of the door, I thrust it open. It takes a moment for my eyes to adjust and to make out the shapes of the figures in the room, so I flip a switch and flood the room with light.

When I see Alice being held in a vice-like grip in Yvonne Castle's arms, my heart feels as if it will explode in my chest. Then, my gaze flits to Daisy, who, now that she's seen me, starts to tentatively edge towards me. I'm shocked by their appearance. Their beautiful long hair is shorn off. I can guess who is responsible for this because there's no way either of my daughters would have agreed to this. Another thing to make my blood boil.

As soon as Daisy's out of reach of her grandmother's grasping, clawlike hands, she runs to my side and clings to me, trembling from head to toe.

I growl menacingly at the old woman sitting on the bed and demand, 'What the fuck is going on?'

Mrs Castle's voice tinkles with laughter as she replies, 'You tell me,' but her expression stiffens as she barks, 'Haven't you worked it out yet?'

Daisy interrupts by blubbering, 'She's not really our grandmother,' sounding as though she's finding it hard to believe what she's saying.

When I ask wide-eyed, 'What do you mean she's not really your grandmother?' I feel sweat form on my forehead and trickle down my neck.

Daisy, who has taken to hiding behind me, pipes up, 'She's never even seen Mum.' It's no wonder my daughter is scared. The look on Mrs Castle's face terrifies even me and I'm a grown man. It is cold, vacant and inhuman. In a different century, she'd have been burned alive for being a witch.

'I never said that,' Mrs Castle protests, pulling a disapproving face. 'If you don't listen more and stop jumping to conclusions, you'll never make a good detective.'

Daisy moans, 'But you said . . .'

With a faint smile on her lips, Mrs Castle cuts her off. 'I said that I wasn't her mother. I never claimed that I'd never seen her before.'

'What did you do to our real grandmother?' Daisy asks, her eyes burning with hatred and looking very much like her mother right now, I can't help thinking.

'That's the crucial question, isn't it?' Mrs Castle sniggers, but a moment later she's grimacing and shoving Alice off her lap as if her leg had gone numb or something. Alice looks wistfully at me, which makes my heart melt, but her grandmother signals her to stay where she is. 'You would have loved Yvonne Castle, Daisy,' she sighs regretfully. 'She was such a lovely lady and my best friend. It's unfortunate that we had to part ways.'

I stammer, swallowing anxiously, 'Are you suggesting that you did something to her?'

'If by "did" you mean "unalive her", as you young ones call it, then the answer is yes,' Mrs Castle responds callously.

I look at Daisy. Her shocked expression mirrors mine. I'm about to challenge Mrs Castle on this but she continues to talk over me, in the same monotonous voice, declaring, 'She was sad and lonely and didn't want to go on living, which was really your parents' fault, Daisy, because of the way they treated her. Poor thing.'

'Just you wait a minute,' I splutter in what is for me a commanding tone, but I must hit a nerve because the next minute she's yelling—

'Don't you dare try and take charge of this situation or me!' Spittle sprays from her mouth onto the pillow in her lap, sending a shiver up my spine, because I remember what another one just like it was once used for. 'I went through years of that with my husband, Ted, who pretended to be a good man right up until our honeymoon ended and then turned into a controlling, abusive, bastard.' Pausing to let out a long exhale, she continues, 'You men are all the same.'

'Not all men,' I object weakly, wondering whether to take this personally but also feeling obligated to defend my gender even though I know she's right and that the majority don't deserve it.

'So you stole Mrs Castle's identity and then got rid of her,' I surmise out loud, realising that I don't have all the answers yet, hence my next question. 'But what have Scarlet and the girls got to do with any of this?'

With a vile chuckle, she arches a cynical eyebrow and tauntingly asks Daisy, 'Do you want to tell him, or shall I?'

'Tell me what?' I press, and as I take a step towards the bed, she stops me by raising her stick in the air as if about to bring it down on my head.

Daisy puts a restraining hand on my arm, and murmurs, 'Dad, don't, please.' I'm not sure if she does this to prevent me from moving or speaking. She seems to already know what her grandmother will tell me.

'Do you recall your mother making a telephone call the night she died?' Mrs Castle ignores me once more, acting as though I don't exist, and speaks exclusively to Daisy, who is staring at her fixedly and unmoving. This reminds me how she used to act whenever we caught her sleepwalking. Of course, she was younger then, but the recollection still makes me shiver.

When Alice's fearful eyes find mine, begging me to save her, I exclaim, 'That was you on the phone, wasn't it? You were the one who scared Scarlet that night and threatened her.'

With a playful smirk, Mrs Castle scoffs, 'You got there at last. Despite my best efforts to persuade her differently, she recognised right away that I wasn't her mother. She could tell by my voice, even after a ten-year absence.' In a mournful, self-pitying voice, she pleads with Daisy. 'I couldn't let her ruin what I had, what I'd worked for all those years. I wasn't going to lose everything after all my hard work.'

Filled with justifiable rage, I confront her. 'None of it was yours in the first place. You stole it. You're nothing more than a common criminal.'

'Not like you I'm not!' she fiercely exclaims and puts a hand to her temple as though in agony. 'I'm something of a mastermind, actually, cleverer than the police or anybody else. Nobody suspected me. Not once.'

'All that will change when I tell them what really happened . . . what you did,' I sneer, unable to bring myself to look her in the eye. Several thoughts race through my mind at the same time. What an evil woman she is. And to think she's been looking after my children all this time.

Mrs Castle looks at Daisy sharply before stating, 'He won't do that though, will he, Daisy?'

'Too right I will and what's more, I'll see you in jail for this.' I figure that if she believes I won't report her to the police, then she's either truly psychotic or she thinks me more of an idiot than I actually am. In addition to killing Scarlet — or so it appears — she also murdered the girls' actual grandmother. Something that I'm unable to get my brain around right now. But something else is going on here that I'm not yet aware of, judging by the terrified expression on Daisy's face.

'You're absolutely right, Vince.' Mrs Castle nods conspiratorially and lowers her voice as though she were in a five-star hotel timidly asking for directions to the ladies' powder room. 'I did come here that night to kill Scarlet, to shut her up . . .' She licks her lips like she's about to devour a delicious French pastry, before glaring at Daisy.

After a long, premeditated pause, during which she never once takes her eyes off my firstborn daughter, she eventually says, 'But when I got here, it was too late. Somebody had already beaten me to it.'

CHAPTER 65: THE GRANDMOTHER

'Stop it. Stop talking. I don't want to hear any more!' Daisy lets out a piercing, blood-curdling scream, clasping her hands to her ears and moaning, as if in agony. Everyone turns to stare at her, open-mouthed. Even Alice has stopped crying and is gazing at her sister in alarm.

Vince reaches out a quivering hand to Daisy, obviously wanting to comfort her, but she resists and wrenches herself away from him before hanging her head in defeat. The sound of her whimpering almost breaks my heart.

With a worried fatherly expression on his face, which restores my heart to ice, Vince asks, 'Daisy, what is it? What don't you want to hear?'

His look of confusion will cheer me up for many an hour in the future. I've never hated any man quite as much as him. Except Ted, maybe. Oh, and Mr Burgess, my neighbour, who hasn't complained to me once from across our shared fence since I took him the meat pie — which may or may not have contained an excessive quantity of heart-slowing medication. The last I heard he'd been carted off in an ambulance and I very kindly told the paramedics that I'd water his prize roses for him. Shame on him for threatening to report me to social services for yelling at the children. I mean, who doesn't shout at their family? It's perfectly normal, and even healthy in my opinion. But back to Daisy's father . . .

'I can help you out with that, Vince,' I tell him with authority.

'Don't, Granny, please,' Daisy pleads.

'Oh, *Granny* is it, now that you want something from me,' I tut. 'Don't worry, Daisy. Your secret is safe with me.'

Vince immediately jumps in with a smug, sure-of-himself. 'Secret? What secret? My kids don't keep any secrets from me.'

I swear, I wouldn't have retaliated if he hadn't made that last assertion or used the word *my* in such a possessive manner as if he were excluding me from *my* grandchildren as I've come to think of them. Still, there's no point crying over spilt milk, because I couldn't help but taunt him with, 'I didn't kill Scarlet, did I, Daisy?'

Her head snaps up then and her eyes bore into mine. I hesitate, as if debating whether to continue, before ordering her to, 'Tell him.'

'Tell me what?' Vince prompts his daughter. But Daisy is looking at me. Not him. When she finally speaks, the words are dragged out of her and cloaked with sadness and regret.

'I did it. I killed Mum,' she sighs, collapsing her shoulders and dabbing at a tear that has landed on her cheek. Others soon follow. 'It was me who held the pillow over her face until she stopped breathing.'

She does look at her father now. It's not a pleasant sight. The lines around his face have deepened, similar to the grooves in my car's spare tyre. He groans in agony, his body rigid with shock, and falls to his knees on the floor. When he finally fixes his heartbroken gaze on Daisy he grinds out through clenched teeth, 'No. Tell me it isn't true.'

Then he's back on his feet again and pulling Daisy into his arms, tight enough to force the air out of her lungs, much in the same way as his ex-wife and her mother died, as they sob on each other's shoulders. I feel an unexpected pang of jealousy as I watch them, and I'm left thinking, *Well this won't get the baby a new dress.* But then something unexpected occurs to me since I get the impression that this is all an act. Vince Spencer may have just realised his worst fear, but I have a sneaking suspicion that he knew all along. And one thing I don't take kindly to is being outwitted.

I narrow my eyes and coldly say to him, 'You knew, didn't you?'

He whips around to face me, and I see a glint of anger in his eyes that is aimed at me rather than Daisy. However, he is the first to look away after our eyes unintentionally lock. Before he can respond, a traumatised Daisy comes out with, 'I was so tired and all I wanted to do was go to bed so I could read my book, but she . . . Mum . . . kept calling out to me, wanting me to do things for her. She was swearing and being horrible. It was late. I just wanted her to stop. I didn't mean to,' she implores her father before stuttering wide-eyed, 'I didn't want to hurt her, but right then I hated her more than I loved her. So, I picked up the pillow—'

In the silence that follows, which is broken only by the sound of a distant police siren getting closer and closer all the time, we all stare transfixed at the pillow on my lap. When I jut out my chin, take a big breath and remind her, 'You see, Daisy, we are alike after all,' her gaze hits the floor in shame and I flinch at that, before continuing with a lump in my throat. 'You might not be my flesh and blood but I have loved you like my own since that night when I crept up those stairs and saw you standing there.'

'It was you I saw,' she gasps, only now realising it, I think. 'I thought I was having night terrors again.' She turns to face her father, who is chewing on his lip and frowning. 'Like I used to when I was little, when I would wake up to find an old lady sitting on my bed. I thought that's what I saw that night because the next thing I knew you were gone, and so I went back to bed, but then you came Dad and I wasn't scared anymore.'

With a bitter laugh, I give a stunned-looking Vince a hard stare and rejoice, 'So, you see, I'll get to keep my house and you'll have your daughters and you will allow me weekly access to my granddaughters.'

'That's never going to happen.'

Curling my lip, my eyes disappear into slits as I glare at him. 'Get used to it, Vincent. There's nothing you can do about it.'

'Bitch,' he manages between clenched teeth, then goes over to the window and peers out, letting a sliver of flashing light push through a gap in the curtains. 'The police are here. I called them,' he declares icily.

A knot of anxiety gathers in my chest, but my voice is calm as I concede graciously 'Very well, I'll go quietly but I won't talk, Daisy, I can promise you that. Your father will explain that this is all a misunderstanding, a family quarrel and nothing more. That way not one of us will have to go to prison.'

277

CHAPTER 66: THE FATHER

Rather than going quietly, as she had promised to do, my former mother-in-law is squawking like a parrot with ruffled feathers as she is hoisted to her feet and told to, 'Put your hands behind your back,' by one of the uniformed policemen who charged up the stairs just now. The other officer, a young man named PC Carter, claims to know Mrs Castle and seems surprised to see her in violation of the law, that is, being arrested.

'Tell them, Vince, that I haven't done anything wrong,' Mrs Castle rages, indignation fuelling her voice as she is hand-cuffed. Alice is clinging to my side, snivelling and hiding her head in the creases of my trouser leg now that she is not under that bitch's control. She glares at Daisy and slaps her sister's hands away when she tries to comfort her. The prospect of Mrs Castle telling the police what Daisy has done paralyses me with fear, so I force myself to man up and nervously say, 'She's right. She hasn't done anything wrong. It was all a mis-understanding, wasn't it girls?'

As sweat dampens my T-shirt, I offer my daughters a reassuring smile, praying that they'll play along, but Alice gasps in horror at the lie and shoots me a filthy look, while Daisy squirms guiltily.

'Is that right?' The arresting officer comments dryly, looking doubtful.

I risk a glance at Mrs Castle then, and I notice that her expression is one of anticipation. Reading between the lines, I can tell she wants me to *get on with it*. So, I do, although not very well, stammering, 'I'd completely forgotten that I'd asked my,' I almost gag at the word, '*Mother-in-law* to bring the children over or that they didn't have a key on them.'

The same officer scowls. 'Did you also give her permission to break in?'

'No,' I reply feebly, stalling for more time. Then, after taking a deep breath I let the lie out slowly, telling him, 'But she said she thought she could hear someone inside, like before, when her daughter—' I finish lamely, unable to go on, but luckily PC Carter helps me out. I get the impression that he wants it to be true as much as I do.

'So, believing that Scarlet's attacker had come back, she broke the glass in the door?'

'That seems unlikely with two small children in tow,' the arresting officer objects cynically. 'I mean, why would she risk them being attacked?'

'Yeah, well, we never know how we're going to act in an emergency until it happens,' I reply, pinching my nose in frustration, because this nightmare is refusing to end and I'm all out of luck at this point. Until—

'It doesn't really matter because that isn't the reason she's being arrested.'

'It isn't?' I gasp, mouth agape.

'It was merely a coincidence that you reported her; we already had a warrant out for her arrest,' PC Carter explains, shaking his head in disbelief. It appears to be personal with him. As if she'd let him down in some way.

At that, Mrs Castle's head bounces up and her eyes sparkle with what appears to be hatred as she exclaims, 'What am I meant to have done now?' in a deeply offended tone before letting out a furious sigh.

'All in good time.' The policeman handles her more gently now that her hands are bound. When he turns her around to face us, I drop my eyes and scuff my shoe against the floor. Daisy stares ahead with an empty look on her face.

With a cold tone, Mrs Castle threatens, 'I have a right to know why I am being arrested, young man.'

The officer clasps his eyes shut for a moment, as if counting to ten, before reciting formally, 'Yvonne Castle, I am arresting you on suspicion of the murder of Charles Castle. You do not have to say anything but it may harm your defence if you do not mention when questioned something that you later rely on in court. Anything you do say may be given in evidence.'

She throws the officer a poisonous look as she bristles with annoyance, then bursts into hysterical laughter, scoffing, 'I've never heard anything quite so ridiculous in my life. Uncuff me this moment or you'll regret it.'

'I'm afraid we can't do that.'

My mind is whirring into action and I'm experiencing a rush of excitement. If what she is being accused of is true, does this imply that my Daisy is off the hook? But only while Mrs Castle remains silent, I realise. But even if she did implicate Daisy, would anyone believe her, though, if she's found guilty of killing Charles Castle?

As she's led out of the room, she continues to complain and curse aloud. I hold her eyes for a second, and she gives me a nod, before casting a glance at Daisy with something like warmth. That's when I realise that she's promising not to say anything about Daisy. I get it then, what tonight was about: this was Mrs Castle's last desperate attempt to remain in the girls' lives by blackmailing us. We will definitely have nightmares for the rest of our lives about whether or not we can trust her to remain silent. But I'm forgetting Alice, who is also in on the secret. But my youngest is a kind, gentle girl who can easily be tricked into believing that her grandmother is a liar and her beloved sister isn't a killer living in our midst.

Warm, sweaty fingers link through mine as we listen to the policemen's boots thudding down the stairs, followed by Mrs Castle objecting to everything. I look down at the fingers that held the pillow over her mother's face and close my eyes, resisting the urge to tear my hand away.

'We're safe now, Dad,' Daisy whispers.

But are we really? And is Alice? I think to myself in silence.

'Dad?' she prompts, nudging me with a sharp elbow.

This time, her voice startles me out of my reverie and my bleary, bloodshot eyes crack open. When I glance at her, I'm horrified to discover that there are no worry lines etched across her face and that she has turned on her smile, like a light, and is gazing imploringly at me with angel's eyes. Could Yvonne Castle have been right? Was there any truth to her statement when she claimed that she and Daisy were alike?

CHAPTER 67: THE GRANDMOTHER

As I'm led from the holding cell up the stone steps to the numerous chambers off a long corridor with barred windows, I imagine that I can hear the sound of a spade scraping on hard, unforgiving earth. In my mind, the gravedigger has hard, calloused hands, devoid of feeling. Rather like me. The fact that the police have squandered time excavating Charles Castle's grave instead of digging up Yvonne Castle's remains from beneath the compost heap in my allotment seems abhorrent to me. As you sow, so shall you reap, as the proverb goes.

The judge we have today is said to be among the best. And a quite amiable sympathetic sort at that. But since I am smarter than everyone I know, I am not searching for any of those things, which are beneath me. Haven't I got away with murder? That's already one life sentence without even trying to prosecute me for Charles Castle's death, which I had been tricked into believing was from natural causes. I was shocked to learn that this was not the case. I was even more shocked when they exhumed his body and evidence of foul play was discovered, and illicit drugs were found in his blood. That meant that innocent, gullible and sweet woman Yvonne Castle was as much of an imposter and a liar as I was. I'm paying the price now that I know she killed her husband, but no one will believe me when I tell them the truth — that I never even met the man and that, as I've often boasted, I've covered my tracks perfectly, leaving behind no trace of my former life. My secret file, which I kept secured in my locked office, has inexplicably disappeared containing any proof that Nancy Tyrell ever existed. Even if I could provide evidence to support my claims, I would still face charges of killing Yvonne. I can't seem to win either way.

The courtroom is not at all how I imagined. It's nothing like any of the TV courtroom dramas I've watched. There are no gloomy lighting fixtures, lustrous timber panelling or shorthand typists dressed in tweed and sporting cat-eye prescription spectacles. Instead, the room is well-lit and has a modern scent, like polish and floor cleaner. The only person dressed in black robes and a scratchy horsehair wig is the dusty, antiquated judge, who seems to expect a round of applause for simply entering a room. Like everyone else, I get to my feet, but I can't help but notice that he looks as if he recently celebrated his 100th birthday.

He observes me with interest, but my attention is on the two women standing at the back of the room, whispering among themselves. Georgina bloody Bell, who I've been informed is a prime witness, and my social worker. At first, I'm surprised that she's here, as she can offer nothing to either strengthen or weaken my case, but then I console myself thinking that she must be here out of friendship to support me. What other reason could there be? However, the two of them seem too pally for my liking, as if they already know each other. But that can't be right, can it?

Anger courses through my veins when Georgina is called to give evidence. As she climbs the steps to the witness box, her heels tap the floor in a lively rhythm. Once there, she's asked by a clerk if she wishes to affirm or swear and she regally chooses the latter. She then places a hand on the Bible and swears to tell the truth, so help me God, and I'm thinking chance will be a fine thing. I can't help but worry if the judge, who is speaking to her in a soft and kind manner and asking her to confirm her identity, will treat me with the same decency. When the female prosecutor, who looks like she's still in full-time education asks her, 'Mrs Bell, could you please identify the woman standing in the dock?' I feel my back arch.

Georgina says in a trembling Marilyn Monroe voice that reverberates throughout the room, 'Her name is Yvonne Castle.'

'And when did you first meet Yvonne Castle?'

'Oh, it must be about thirty years ago now when I went to work at the same school as her husband, who I knew from before.' With a sneer in my direction she goes on, 'Charles and I were old university friends, you see, and Yvonne was always rather jealous of our close friendship.'

I angrily correct her, 'Thirty-two years ago,' which earns me a severe look from the judge. 'And he couldn't stand you, by all accounts.'

'Mrs Castle, please do not interrupt or speak until asked to do so.'

'Sorry, Your Honour.' I bob as if performing a curtsey, then add as an afterthought, 'But, as I've said many times before, I'm not Yvonne Castle, and therefore I could not have killed the man known as Charles Castle.' From inside the dock, I cling onto the wooden plinth in front of me until my knuckles turn white. I'm unable to resist shouting over the judge's renewed demands for my silence, 'Ask Georgina. She'll tell you. She knew straight away when she first saw me that I wasn't Yvonne Castle.'

This creates an unwanted buzz in the public gallery as journalists frantically whip out their notebooks to scribble things down.

'Silence, please,' The judge commands, looking for all the world as if he'd like to throw something at me. This time I do as I'm told and remain silent. The prosecutor looks mildly amused and then questions Georgina again. 'How sure are you that the woman in the dock is Yvonne Castle?'

She glances over her shoulder at the social worker, her rouged face creased into an arrogant sneer, then she trills, 'I recalled telling my daughter at the time that I immediately recognised Yvonne Castle when I came across her again and would have known her anywhere.'

'Wait, what? Your daughter was my social worker!' I gasp, before demanding, 'How is that possible or even legal?' My eyes find the boring brown blob in the centre row and she dares to smile at me.

'You did this,' I cry, stabbing a finger at her, but she doesn't even flinch. Enraged, I continue, ignoring the judge's repetitive pleas for "order", saying, 'You stole my papers when you were in my house and the two of you were in on this together somehow.' My jaw tightens and my throat constricts as I turn to confront Georgina again and yell, 'You lying bitch. I didn't kill Charles Castle and you know it, because I'm not Yvonne Castle. My name is Nancy Tyrell. Why won't anyone believe me?'

CHAPTER 68: THE FATHER

Now that I'm here, inside prison walls, a place I've always feared I would end up, I find I can manage my claustrophobia. I'm on the male wing of HM Peterborough, which is a mixed prison that houses both male and female inmates. A senior prison officer is escorting me through a maze of corridors as we make our way to one of the classrooms. As we go along what's known as Main Street, a large area that accesses exercise yards, education departments, workshops and various outreach facilities, we pass prisoners playing table tennis and pool. I am then ushered into a well-lit room with circular tables and blue upholstered chairs.

As a man gets up to greet me, I quip, 'Well, well, well, if it isn't my old pal Gary Pearce,' and give him a high five.

'Vince, how are you?' He grins, seeming happy to see me.

'I can't complain,' I shrug nonchalantly, dropping onto the chair next to him and waiting for him to sit back down.

'Looking good in your civvies.' He winks playfully at me.

'I always feel guilty walking in here wearing proper clothes,' I confess.

'How are things at home?' he asks.

'Good,' I nod even though "fair" would be a more accurate description.

'And your kids, how are they?'

If he notices my face darken, he doesn't say so. Rather, he shifts the conversation, asking, 'Have you still got your dog? I miss mine like mad.'

'Yep, we've still got Lucky,' I confirm, lowering my voice to enquire, 'So, how did your first one-to-one go?'

'Oh man, I was shitting myself at first, but then, when I got into it and focused my mind on just helping him, it got better and he opened up about what he was going through in here.'

'That's fantastic, Gary. I'm dead chuffed for you.'

'Thanks, but what you said is true. Even just by listening, I felt like I was making a difference. And with five more years left in here, I have the power to affect a lot more lives.'

I was chosen as a candidate to work with prison convicts, providing them with the tools they needed to help other prisoners, just as my mentor Dave had foretold all those weeks ago. One of the first new volunteers to sign up was Gary, who'd been sent down for attempted burglary (he was a notoriously slow getaway driver). It's odd how life can change direction when you're least expecting it. Two months ago, I bet Gary would never have imagined himself as a Samaritan. And I never thought I'd be in paid work so soon either. Although it's only part-time, it's better than nothing.

I'm still thinking about Gary and wondering what happened to his dog as I drive home. I'm also kicking myself for not asking him about it. Butch, I think its name was. I hope it wasn't destroyed for being an illegal breed.

I pull up outside 7 The Green and when I see Holly's car parked outside, I feel my heart flip. What the fuck is she doing here?

She and I have an agreement that I will introduce her to the kids when I know they can handle it. She has supported my decision so far, even though it limits our time together. So, what's changed, I wonder? I park and get out of the car, feeling my face pucker into a deep frown. My pulse quickens as I race

287

up the path, go around the back and let myself in. It's only been a few months since Yvonne Castle brought our world crashing down on us. The girls are nowhere near ready for this next step.

I hear Holly talking nervously about this and that before I even see her. She pauses when I go into the living room, but as soon as I notice my daughters' terrified expressions, my focus quickly shifts to them.

Now that I'm in a tight spot, I decide to get the introduction over with fast, so I announce in a forced cheerful tone, 'Girls, this is my friend Holly.'

'He means fiancée,' Holly gushes, flashing her diamond ring in Daisy and Alice's faces. When they turn their horrified, sickly white faces towards me, I cringe inside. *Liar*, the look on Daisy's face implies.

'What is it? You two look as if you've seen a ghost,' I make a joke, but it backfires when I realise that they are staring at Holly as though they already know her. I find this confusing as it can't be true. So, I ask, 'Do you know each other or something?'

Daisy, who sounds like she's on the verge of tears, says, 'She is, *was* our social worker,' and my heart twists in my chest.

'That's right!' Holly exclaims, bounding over to the girls to add, 'And I helped your daddy get you back.'

My lip twitches in annoyance and my patience starts to fray, as I stammer helplessly, 'Holly, I don't understand.'

'What's there to understand?' She shrugs, pouting her lips, which I see are painted a dark shade of red. She's also wearing a lot more make-up than she usually does. With a triumphant gleam in her eye, she continues, 'Yvonne Castle isn't the only person capable of befriending someone in order to get what she wants.'

My voice goes hard as I reply, 'So, who are you really, Holly, if you're not a teaching assistant? And is that even your actual name?'

'Of course it is,' she sniggers as if she has done nothing wrong. I assume from this that she is suffering from a mental illness, which she has deviously been concealing from me up until this point. I wonder, is she dangerous?

She suddenly blurts out, 'I'm Georgina Bell's daughter and Charles Castle was my real father,' which puts me on high alert.

I'm still reeling from this bombshell when she shoots me a withering look. 'That woman got everything she deserved for murdering my father. When I found out that Daisy and Alice were in Mrs Castle's care I made sure I was assigned as their social worker so I could get to meet her. My mother only wanted justice for Charles but I was determined to take my revenge because if it weren't for Mrs Castle, my real dad would still be alive. He'd been in love with my mum for years, you see, ever since their university days, but when that bitch Mrs Castle finally got wind of their long-term affair she put a stop to it the only way she knew how, by killing him. I know that my mum thinks she is an imposter who stole the real Yvonne Castle's identity, but I don't buy that.'

'You and your mother set her up, knowing that she might not be who she said she was,' I retort fiercely.

Flinching at my tone, she lowers her eyes and sulkily remarks, 'She deserved to have her granddaughters taken away from her so she could see how it felt to lose someone you love. Besides, it was worth it to get your daughters back for you.'

'I'll be the judge of that,' I warn, my voice tense as I watch her squirm under my enraged glare.

'Suit yourself,' she sneers. Her behaviour is becoming increasingly unpredictable, and I am now certain that she poses a risk to herself as well as my family. I have to keep them safe, so I paste a phoney smile on my face in an effort to hide my anger long enough, I hope, to get Holly out of the house. Naturally, I'll make sure she receives all the help she needs. I won't just abandon her.

Daisy glances at me reproachfully and gives a small shake of her head as if to warn me against doing anything stupid. But Holly catches the look and glowers at me as if I don't deserve her trust. Sensing that it would be best to keep her talking, I point out conversationally, 'That means you lied, not only to your employer and the police but to me too. Our meeting at the Samaritans wasn't coincidental at all, was it?'

She rolls her eyes in mock despair, then tilts her head to one side and smiles, though I can't help but notice that it doesn't reach her eyes, which are quite dead. My heart thuds harder in my ribcage when she says, 'I told you I would do anything to have a family of my own. And now I have one.'

THE END

ACKNOWLEDGEMENTS

I was in the process of writing another book (to come later) when this idea came to me, and I knew then that I would be abandoning my current work and starting on this one. The opportunity to write about a reasonably well-off widow living alone with her cat in an idyllic rural village setting in contrast to the other main character who is a petty criminal, a former drug addict and a suspected murderer living on one of the most deprived social housing estates in the UK, was impossible to resist.

For those of you who adore cats, as I do (who doesn't?), I hope I didn't keep you on tenterhooks for too long waiting to find out Hero's fate. The cat in the description is my very own Hero, who now has a baby brother named Halo, and I wouldn't let anything bad — not even imaginary — happen to either of them.

Yvonne Castle and Vince Spencer are not as they first appear and I for one really enjoyed taking Vince's character on a journey and seeing him develop into what I hope is a likeable character. A loveable rogue, if you like, who will do anything for his children, whereas Mrs Castle's character arc is quite the opposite, shall we say. And quite the surprise!

This book is dedicated to the memory of Rikki Neave. His story is not mine to tell, but when his tragic tale first surfaced in the 1990s it deeply affected me. Like many parents living in close proximity at that time, I followed his case and hoped for the best. In other words, that somebody was keeping him safe. Unfortunately for Rikki, this was not the case.

Once again, I've set this book in and around my hometown of Stamford, and the pretty village of Ryhall is the next one along from me and I know it well. On publication day, I left copies of *The Grandmother* in and around the village for residents to find, as a gesture of goodwill for setting my book there. Please note that The Green and the Nene Fields estate are fictious places in Peterborough, and any descriptions of the locations and references to high crime rates are entirely my own.

As always, I would like to say a massive thank you to everyone at Joffe Books for all their hard work in getting this story ready for publication. They have been an absolute pleasure to work with. Go Team Joffe. As always, special thanks go to Kate Lyall Grant, Joffe's publishing director.

If you are not from the UK, please excuse the English spelling. Oopsy daisy, it's just the way we do things across the pond. Apologies also for any swearing but this is down to the characters and has nothing to do with me. Lol. The same goes for any blaspheming.

Now for the best bit where I get to thank my lovely readers for all their support, especially all the bloggers and reviewers. You know who you are!

Your loyalty and friendship mean everything. As do your reviews. ☺

THE JOFFE BOOKS STORY

We began in 2014 when Jasper agreed to publish his mum's much-rejected romance novel and it became a bestseller.

Since then we've grown into the largest independent publisher in the UK. We're extremely proud to publish some of the very best writers in the world, including Joy Ellis, Faith Martin, Caro Ramsay, Helen Forrester, Simon Brett and Robert Goddard. Everyone at Joffe Books loves reading and we never forget that it all begins with the magic of an author telling a story.

We are proud to publish talented first-time authors, as well as established writers whose books we love introducing to a new generation of readers.

We won Trade Publisher of the Year at the Independent Publishing Awards in 2023. We have been shortlisted for Independent Publisher of the Year at the British Book Awards for the last four years, and were shortlisted for the Diversity and Inclusivity Award at the 2022 Independent Publishing Awards. In 2023 we were shortlisted for Publisher of the Year at the RNA Industry Awards.

We built this company with your help, and we love to hear from you, so please email us about absolutely anything bookish at feedback@joffebooks.com

If you want to receive free books every Friday and hear about all our new releases, join our mailing list: www.joffebooks.com/contact

And when you tell your friends about us, just remember: it's pronounced Joffe as in coffee or toffee!